P9-DHH-047

14 DAYS NOT RENEWABLE

Please Don't Lose the Date Card

CONCORD
FREE PUBLIC LIBRARY

Concord, Massachusetts

Last Ditch

Leo Waterman Mysteries by **G.M. Ford**
from Avon Books

WHO IN HELL IS WANDA FUCA?
CAST IN STONE
THE BUM'S RUSH
SLOW BURN

Last Ditch

a leo waterman mystery

G.M. FORD

AVON TWILIGHT

This is a work of fiction. Names, characters, places and incidents either are the product of the author's imagination or are used fictitiously. Any resemblance to actual events, locales, organizations, or persons, living or dead, is entirely coincidental and beyond the intent of either the author or the publisher.

AVON BOOKS, INC.
1350 Avenue of the Americas
New York, New York 10019

Copyright © 1999 by G. M. Ford
Interior design by Kellan Peck
ISBN: 0-380-97557-2

All rights reserved, which includes the right to reproduce this book or portions thereof in any form whatsoever except as provided by the U.S. Copyright Law. For information address Avon Books, Inc.

Library of Congress Cataloging in Publication Data:

Ford, G. M. (Gerald M.)
   Last ditch : a Leo Waterman mystery / by G.M. Ford.—1st ed.
      p.   cm.
   I. Title.
PS3556.06978L37   1999   98-39880
813'.54—dc21   CIP

First Avon Twilight Printing: March 1999

AVON TWILIGHT TRADEMARK REG. U.S. PAT. OFF. AND IN OTHER COUNTRIES, MARCA REGISTRADA, HECHO EN U.S.A.

Printed in the U.S.A.

FIRST EDITION

QPM   10 9 8 7 6 5 4 3 2 1

www.avonbooks.com/twilight

To my beloved Son,
Jedediah Castiglione Ford

Last Ditch

1

THE PROSECUTOR LOOKED LIKE HOSS CARTWRIGHT.

"Mr. Waterman . . ." she continued. ". . . in your capacity as a licensed private investigator, did you have occasion to be employed by anyone present in this courtroom today?"

"Yes, I did."

The assistant DA's name was Paula Stillman. Before this morning, I'd never heard of her. For the past ten days, the papers had been quoting reliable sources, all of whom whispered that Mel Turpin, the DA himself, was going to step in and take the reins. On the surface, it made sense. After all, what could be better? A state supreme court justice on trial for murder. Not only that, but the case was a slam dunk. Big-time moral high ground. *Más* photo ops. It was money, baby. Money.

Mel Turpin knew better, and so did I. It didn't matter that the case against the judge was a grounder. What mattered were the pictures. And the pictures were going to get real ugly. The evening news anchors were going to put on their Mr. Serious faces and warn their viewers about the graphic nature of the photographs they were about to see and suggest that children and the faint of heart might want to leave the room.

What politicians like Turpin and my old man understood was that the average citizen had a short and very selective memory. Two weeks after the trial was over, all the voting public would remember were the pictures they'd seen on the tube. Exactly who had done what to whom and why would get downright fuzzy for most of them. Mel Turpin was smart enough to make damn sure that his cherubic countenance was not among those ill-recalled images. That's precisely what assistant DAs like Paula Stillman were for. Photo fodder.

"Could you please point out that person," Stillman said.

The defense attorney jumped to his feet. "Your Honor," he said in a world-weary voice, "the defense is prepared to stipulate that the defendant . . ."

Dan Hennessey was the best legal help money could buy. On those few occasions when I'd seen him in action, he was all controlled confidence and meticulous motions. He always seemed to have a little something extra in his sock that the opposition wasn't expecting. It wasn't surprising. He had the best help money could buy. The way I heard it, even a junior partnership in Hennessey, Howell and Kidd was worth a cool million a year. If you were ambitious enough and good enough, clerking for Dan Hennessey was the next logical step after Stanford Law Review. I'd never before seen him desperate.

"Excuse me. Excuse me, Your Honor," Stillman interrupted. "Once again, Your Honor, if Mr. Hennessey doesn't mind, I'd like to try my own case here."

Judge Bobbie Downs had a reputation for quick and dirty jurisprudence and for making a fair number of procedural mistakes. I figured Hennessey had danced in his office when he heard she'd been assigned. That was before the defendant decided to lend a hand on his own case. Downs waved the gavel at the defense table, indicating that Hennessey should slide his charcoal-gray Armani back into his seat and then turned to me.

"Mr. Waterman."

I pointed at Judge Douglas J. Brennan, who was seated next

to Hennessey at the defense table. "He's right there next to defense counsel," I said.

Stillman spoke directly to the judge. "Your Honor, please let the record show that Mr. Waterman identified the defendant Douglas J. Brennan."

"So noted," she said.

Brennan sat there like a bird of prey. His fierce eyes hooded, looking downward toward his piously folded fingers, allowing the mane of white hair and the square chin to command the room on their own. I felt like Adam in that painting from the Sistine Chapel. Except, in this picture, God wasn't pointing back my way.

"And what was it that Mr. Brennan wanted you to do?"

Hennessey started to rise, but Judge Downs waved him back down.

"He wanted me to find his housekeeper. A woman named Felicia Mendoza."

"Did he tell you why he wanted Miss Mendoza found?"

"He said she'd stolen a number of things from his house. Jewelry. Mementos. Things with sentimental value was how he put it."

"And did Judge Brennan give you any indication as to why he wished to employ a private detective in this matter, rather than . . . say taking the more traditional path of simply calling the police?"

"Your Honor, Ms. Stillman is leading the witness," Hennessey complained. "If she wants to—"

All it got him was a frown and another gavel wave.

"He said he didn't want to make a big deal of it. He said the stuff wasn't of great monetary value, and he didn't want to make trouble for the woman. He said she didn't speak much English, and he didn't want to scare her. The judge said he thought he could convince her to return his belongings, so he just wanted me to find her for him."

"And did you do so?"

"I found her," I said.

Hennessey was on his feet again. "May we approach the

bench, Your Honor?" You had to admire a guy who thought of himself as plural. She waved him forward. Stillman followed along. They formed a tight muttering knot around the judge. My name and the word "prejudicial" were being bandied about. Damn right I was prejudicial. Prejudicial as hell.

I FOUND HER sleeping on the floor in a Catholic women's shelter down in Tacoma. They didn't want to let me in, but since I'd tracked her that far, and had made it plain that I wasn't going away, they figured they didn't have much to lose by letting us chat. Two very large women stood by her side and glared at me while we talked. She was maybe five foot two, with a big pair of liquid brown eyes taking up most of her round face. Her English was just fine, which was more than could be said about the rest of her. The right side of her face was blistered and the color of an eggplant. The insides of both her arms were pitted with burn marks, old and new, and from what she showed me of her shoulders and the backs of her legs, it was obvious that she'd been systematically beaten for years. Seems the judge, while on a judicial junket to Central America about six years before, had more or less bought her from a Guatemalan orphanage. Four hundred bucks and the promise of American citizenship. She was twelve at the time. Being twelve and not speaking a word of English, she had to watch a lot of daytime television before she picked up enough of the language to become absolutely certain that the judge's little sexual idiosyncrasies were neither a standard part of the American courting ritual nor a painful prerequisite to U.S. citizenship. She'd run away for the first time three weeks ago. The judge had tracked her down at the bus station and used a steam iron on the side of her face. She'd hired an attorney. Said she learned about lawyers watching *"Anoder World."*

I gave her my card and the hundred and seventy bucks I had in my pocket. I spent the thirty-minute drive back to Seattle analyzing my options and trying to keep my lunch down. In retrospect, I did a hell of a lot better job with the lunch than I did with the options.

Stillman went on. "So then, Mr. Waterman . . ." She gazed back over her shoulder at the defense table. ". . . before we were interrupted, you indicated that you were successful in your search for Miss Mendoza, is that correct?"

"Yes," I said.

"In what condition did you find Miss Mendoza?"

I told her. Hennessey objected three times during my recitation. Once complaining that my entire conversation with Felicia Mendoza was hearsay, once to decry my lack of medical credentials and a third time to object to the jury being allowed to see the postmortem photos of Felicia Mendoza's horribly crosshatched back, buttocks and upper thighs. He went O for three. Trolling for grounds for appeal, I figured. Make the judge rule on as many matters as possible. Hope she'll screw up something important. When your client, two weeks before he goes on trial for murder, gets caught trying to off one of the key prosecution witnesses, you are then forced to cast upon the waters the very straws at which you may later be forced to grasp.

"What did you do next, Mr. Waterman?"

I SLID THE CHECK, face-down, across the table.

"I'm returning your retainer and your advance for expenses," I said. "Twenty-four hundred dollars."

The judge pulled the crisp white napkin from his lap and dabbed at the corners of his mouth. He looked down at the check as if I'd pushed a turd over next to his elbow.

"It can't be *that* hard to find one little wetback," he said.

If he'd said something else, I most likely would have let it go. I'd have said something noncommittal, made my excuses and headed up the road. Yeah, sure. And if Mama Cass had shared that ham sandwich with Karen Carpenter, they'd both be alive today.

I leaned over the table, putting my face close to his.

"Maybe it escaped your notice, Judge, but slavery, sexual and otherwise, went out of fashion quite a while back."

He never batted an eye.

"Oh, dear," he teased. "Moral indignation? How quaint."

I held his gaze. "Listen to me, Judge. I've never rolled over on a client in my life. I've gone to jail for refusing to divulge." I held up a finger. "But you know, in your case, just this once, I might be willing to make an exception."

He made a dismissive noise with his lips. "I was like a father to that girl," he mocked.

I ignored him. "The only reason I'm not going to the authorities is because Miss Mendoza is going to do it for me."

"I *am* the authorities, you moron."

I stood up and pitched my napkin into my plate.

"God help us all, then."

"Your father would be terribly disappointed in you," he said.

"I don't think so."

He used his napkin to polish the rim of his water glass.

"And to think I came to you because—"

I cut him off. "You came to me because you thought you could trade on your relationship with my old man. That's why you came to me. That and because you couldn't take a chance on a big agency. They'd drop a dime on you in a New York minute. You figured you'd find somebody who needed the money."

"Exactly," he said. "And that is precisely why no set of spurious allegations from an illiterate—and, I might add, illegal—alien and a low-rent private dick can possibly cause me even the slightest bit of concern."

My fist itched to wipe the smug look off his face.

"You know, Judge," I said instead, "my old man was a great believer in the notion that timing was everything. And you know what? I think your timing on this thing is lousy. As a matter of fact, I don't think it could be worse if you tried. Domestic violence is the crime of the month. Right now a guy will do more time for belting his old lady than he would for holding up a Seven-Eleven."

He seemed to be paying attention, so I pressed on. "You read the papers. You know what I'm talking about. Presidential advisors. City councilmen. Actors. Athletes. You want to screw up your life forever, you just kick in your ex's front door." I shook my head. "We're awash in post-O.J. rage here, Judge." I gave him my best smile. "Hold onto your shorts, Your Honor, because unless I'm mistaken, the illiterate—and, I might add, illegal—Miss Mendoza is about to rock your little world." He didn't exactly faint, but the shit-eating smirk was sure gone. If he said anything to my back, I didn't hear it.

"And during this meeting with Mr. Brennan, am I to understand that you did *not* divulge Miss Mendoza's whereabouts."

"No, I didn't."

"And why was that? Hadn't the judge retained you to provide him with that very piece of information?"

"The judge didn't need a private detective," I said. "He needed a pimp."

"Your Honor," Hennessey bellowed. Even while springing to his feet in protest, he still managed to button the single button on his suit coat. Muscle memory, I figured.

Hennessey ranted; Stillman did her best to appear appalled; Judge Downs had my answer stricken from the record and gave me the gavel shaking of a lifetime. As for me . . . I tried to look chastened.

NINE DAYS after I gave the judge his money back, at seven-thirty on a Saturday morning, I groped for the ringing phone, knocked it over onto the floor where it ricocheted off the oak planks and disappeared under the bed. I had to find the cord and drag the whole thing up over the covers like a stubborn puppy. I heard a dial tone, but the damn thing was still ringing. Rebecca elbowed me hard in the other ear.

"It's the doorbell," she moaned.

Even in my dream state, there was no doubt about what I was looking at through the crack in the door. Two cops. Detectives. Not local. Detective Gregory Balderama and Detective Sergeant Vince Wales. Tacoma PD. Balderama was younger. Under forty with a thick head of carefully coiffed black hair. He stood on the porch, shifting his weight from foot to foot. Wales was old school. Wrinkled. Fifty or so. No more than five years from a pension. Once we agreed on who we all were, he thrust a photograph under my nose.

"You know this person, Waterman?"

It was a woman. Maybe forty years old with a thick neck and dirty blonde hair. A head shot. In this case, a shot of a head that had been shot in the head. Twice. Once just under the right eye and once, it looked like, in the right ear. A symmetrical pool of dark liquid fanned out around her wide face like a pagan headdress.

"I don't think so," I said.

Balderama stepped forward with another picture.

"What about this one?"

It looked to be a hundred pounds of raw beef liver in a blue dress. I pushed his arm away and turned my head.

"Jesus Christ," I complained. "What the hell was that?"

"Whatever it was, was carrying your business card," he said. He pulled a plastic bag from his coat pocket. Sure enough, one of my cards rested on the bottom of the bag.

I pointed at the photo. "Lemme see that," I said.

I held it by the edges, as if something might get on my hands. It was hard to tell that it had ever been human. The skull had been pounded flat. The arms were splayed at impossible angles and the shinbone on the left leg was visible in two places.

"Jesus Christ," I said again.

Sergeant Wales filled me in. The deceased were found in the basement of an abandoned building in downtown Tacoma. The first woman had been shot three times. Two in the head. One in the upper right chest. The second woman had been beaten to death. The ME thought baseball bats. From the imbedded fragments taken from the body, at least two separate bats. One steel, one aluminum. The ME said even her toes had been pulverized.

"No ID on either of them?"

"Just your card, Waterman."

I shrugged. "Wish I could help."

Balderama took over. "The medical examiner says she was Hispanic. Probably South American. Somewhere between eighteen and twenty-five. A hundred ten pounds. No vaccination marks. Maybe an illegal alien . . ." He stopped when the photograph slipped from my hand and floated to the ground.

"Come in," I said, when I could speak again. "Give me a few minutes to get dressed."

An hour later, Rebecca came padding through the living room in her bare feet, following the smell of coffee back toward the kitchen. As Wales and Balderama stood and mumbled introductions, Duvall picked the pictures up from the coffee table. Wales tried to stop her, but it was too late.

"Small caliber. Probably a twenty-two," she said. "The ear wound was point-blank. Classic wise guy pattern."

She winced slightly at the second photo. "Cripes," she said. "Somebody use the poor thing for a piñata, or what?"

Her exit left the cops openmouthed. I gave 'em a break.

"She's a pathologist for the county ME," I said.

When they could breathe again, we got back to work.

From what Wales and Balderama told me later, they went from my house right to the shelter. The other woman's name was Jill Clark. She was a volunteer. A couple of days later, when the *Seattle Times* ran a different picture of her, I realized that she was one of the women who'd been in the room while I interviewed Felicia Mendoza.

The two women had gone to a movie together. The seven o'clock showing of *My Best Friend's Wedding* at the Uptown Cinema. A sixteen-year-old usher named Shantiqua Harris remembered seeing the women leave together at the end of the show. Shantiqua had noticed how protective Jill Clark seemed to be of the smaller woman and had wondered if they were lesbians. That was the last time either woman was seen alive. Two kids looking for a lost kitty found the bodies.

Wales and Balderama interviewed the rest of the shelter staff and the doctor who had examined her. They interviewed both Felicia Mendoza's priest and her attorney. Then they consulted their direct superior, took three deep breaths, said three Hail Marys and requested a Murder One warrant for Washington State Supreme Court justice Douglas J. Brennan.

Local legal wisdom made the case against the judge to be pretty much a dead heat. A mountain of circumstantial evidence and hearsay, all pointing at His Honor, but nothing to connect the judge directly to the murders. When the judge hired Dan Hennessey, most legal pundits figured he had better than a fifty-fifty chance of walking. Apparently, however, the judge was not similarly convinced.

Stillman finished up for me. "And after telling the police your story, the rest, as they say, was history. Is that correct, Mr. Waterman?"

"Yes, it is," I said. "Until . . ."

"Until what, Mr. Waterman?"

"Until about six weeks ago, when one of my . . ." I groped for a word. ". . . contacts told me that somebody had a contract out on my life."

"And you believed this person?"

"Absolutely."

FRANKIE ORTIZ sitting at my backyard patio table drinking iced cappuccino with Rebecca was the equivalent of Charlie Manson sipping tea in the Rose Garden with Hillary Clinton. Frankie was a little guy. No more than five-six or so. I'd always thought he looked like the old-time bandleader Cab Calloway. Thick, processed hair combed straight back. A bold, wide mouth accented by a pencil-thin mustache which clung precisely to the outline of his prominent upper lip. He had a penchant for light-colored suits and two-tone shoes. Frankie worked for Tim Flood.

Tim Flood and my father had started out together working for Dave Beck and the Teamsters. At the time, their official title had been "labor organizers." Revisionist history now labeled them as thugs, but neither of them minded. My father had parlayed his local notoriety into eleven terms on the Seattle City Council. He'd run for mayor four times, suffering a narrow defeat on each occasion. Tim Flood had gone on to become Seattle's homegrown version of organized crime. Tim Flood had his fingers in every pie. My old man had his relatives in every city and county department. The way I figured it, six of one, half a dozen of the other.

Rebecca was beaming. "Oh, Leo . . . Mr. Ortiz tells the most outrageous stories," she said. "I can't believe it."

"I'll bet," I said.

I figured Frankie was probably skipping the one about how he'd shot Sal Abbruzio in the spine for skimming the numbers take. And you sure wouldn't want to tell the one about cutting off Nicky Knight's fingers in the back booth at Vito's. Especially not the part about Big Hazel freshening their drinks between fingers. Not before dark anyway.

"Frankie," I said, and offered my hand. He took it.

I dragged a chair over next to Rebecca and put a hand on her knee. She crossed her legs and gave my hand a pat.

Frankie took a sip of his cappuccino. "You know, the kid's gonna graduate this June," he said. "June eighth."

The kid was Tim's granddaughter Caroline Nobel. A few years back, I'd gotten her out of a nasty situation involving some dangerous tree huggers who thought they could save the planet by blowing things up.

"Gonna be a schoolteacher," he said.

"Great."

"I think it's what's keepin' the old man alive. He ain't been outta the house in years, but he says we're goin' to the ceremony. His doctors are shittin' bricks. Say it'll kill him."

"How is the old man? He still lucid?"

Frankie smiled. "Depends on who he's talkin to. Caroline comes around, they have a hell of a time, laughin' and carryin' on. His doctors try to talk to him, all of a sudden he thinks he's friggin' Cleopatra.''

Another four minutes of mindless small talk and Rebecca finally picked up the vibe. Frankie was old school. Nothing personal, but Frankie Ortiz didn't do business in front of women. She shot me a pitying look and got to her feet. "If you gentlemen will excuse me, I best go inside before I get the vapors.''

Frankie rose and shook her hand in thanks. He stayed on his feet until she closed the French doors behind her and then sat back down.

"Nice girl, Leo. You're a lucky guy.''

"Thanks, Frankie. You just stop by to shoot the breeze, or did you have something a little more substantial you wanted to discuss?''

I think he was surprised at how polite I was. Usually he likes to dance around a bit, at which point I usually get impatient and impolite, and then the whole thing goes to shit. Today he got right to it.

"Got a call from a guy we know in Vegas," he said. "A *macher*." He said it right, with the back-of-the-throat noise. "You know what a *macher* is, Leo?''

A *macher* was a maker. A big shot. A guy who could make things happen. I knew the breed well. My old man had been a *macher*.

"Yeah, I know what it means," I said.

"So the guy says to me, he says, 'Hey Frankie, didn't you tell me about some private dickhead guy named Waterson or something who helped you and Tim out that one time wid the kid?' ''

Frankie looked up at me to see if I was paying attention. I was.

"So I says to him, 'Yeah, that's right, why?' And he says, there's a couple of dweezels been losing big lately out at the south end of the strip, tellin' the workin' girls the dough they're pissin' away is no problem 'cause there's more where that came from. Say they're headed up north to pop a Seattle private dick named Waterville or some such shit. My friend says he thought maybe we'd like to know. From what he hears, these bozos been tellin the honeys that they crewed for this same party a while back. He asks me if we know anything about what's goin' on." Frankie made a face. "And I ask him, 'Hey . . . what the fuck are you callin' us for? The friggin' newspaper knows more about the shit goin' on around here these days than Tim and I do; we're strictly legit. Only staff Tim's got anymore are the nurses in charge of wiping his wrinkled ass, for Christ sake. We're not exactly still in business, if you know what I'm talkin about.' " He sounded almost wistful. Almost.

"You trust this Vegas guy?" I asked.

He tilted his head and pursed his lips. "I don't trust anybody, Leo," he said. "But I was you, I'd watch my ass."

"And that, of course, explains why you were wearing a bulletproof vest," Paula Stillman prodded. It was a smart move. Most citizens don't jog in a Kevlar vest or carry a nine-millimeter automatic, with two extra clips taped to their chests. Tends to chafe. Stillman knew she could count on the defense to bring it up, so she did it herself. Hennessey would sure as hell try to show that my state of paranoia was somehow responsible for the gunplay rather than the two professional shooters the judge had hired to put me out of my misery.

ABOUT TWO MINUTES after Frankie said his good-byes, I'd called the cops. Balderama and Wales had sympathized and offered twenty-four-hour police protection, but I knew what that meant. Two weeks down the road, they'd need the manpower for something else, offer us the services of a retired school crossing guard, and we'd be right back where we started. Rebecca and I talked it over and decided that we weren't going to let anybody bring our lives to a grinding halt. The way we figured it, if we stopped our lives, the judge won. The way I figured it, if I let scumbags like the judge run me around, I might as well find a new line of work. Like selling Amway maybe.

I settled for the loan of a Kevlar vest and took what I considered to be prudent steps to protect us. We had a first-class alarm system installed in the house. Rebecca and I now locked our cars in the garage every night, instead of leaving them strewn about the driveway. She was carpooling to work with Judy Benet. I made it a point to meet new clients in busy public places in broad daylight. We consoled ourselves by telling each other that these precautions were appropriate for the late nineties and what's more, long overdue. Neither of us believed it for a minute, but for some reason, neither of us was willing to abandon the illusion, either. Go figure.

While I normally only carried a weapon when it seemed likely I might need one, these days I didn't go to the john without considering the question of how many rounds I was carrying. The judge's trial began in a couple of weeks. I figured that once I testified, the threat was over. At least, I hoped so. Despite our best efforts, the strain was wearing us down. Without consciously willing it so, lately, more often than not, we found ourselves staying at home, watching the boob tube in darkened rooms. I spent the nights lying awake listening to Rebecca toss and turn and trying to remember what programs we'd watched.

My sleep patterns had been a mess ever since Frankie's little visit. I'd taken to dawn runs around Greenlake as a way to work off some of the stress. I hated running, but what the hell, I was up.

It's a little under three miles around the lake. When I was a kid, I'd run around and around until I lost interest. Back then, it was more of a swamp than a lake. These days, they pump it full of reservoir water to keep it pretty, and if I manage to jog around it once without pulling a muscle or projectile vomiting it makes my whole day.

I always start and end at the south end of the lake by the Mussert Shell House. It's a dark little glen with an attached parking lot and the only part of the lake that doesn't directly front a city street. I figured if I started and ended there, I could make all the noise I wanted and not bother anybody. After all, wouldn't want the sound of my puking and wheezing to keep anybody up. It never occurred to me that it was also an excellent choice for a kill zone.

I was walking in circles out at the end of a twenty-foot floating dock that juts out into the lake, trying to catch my breath and spitting into the water, when he walked by on the path, giving me a curt nod of the head before disappearing behind the Shell House.

He should have gone shopping at Eddie Bauer first. Or maybe REI. Gotten himself a nice earth-tone Gor-Tex shell, some chinos, a pair of waterproof wafflestompers and a FREE TIBET button. If he'd blended in better, he and his partner would have ended up back in Vegas with the hookers, and I, in all probability, would have ended up dead. As it was, he stuck out like a barnacle in a béarnaise sauce.

About forty years old and twenty pounds overweight, he'd greased his hair into an old-fashioned pompadour with a sharp part on my side. Bob's Big Boy. Not only was he wearing the last leisure suit in America, but the poster boy for polyester was also carrying a four-foot floral arrangement wrapped in newspaper. Flowers for his girlfriend. Long-stemmed. Real long. At five-fifteen on a Tuesday morning. Every hair on my body suddenly stood on end.

The fact that they were here at this time of the morning meant they'd been casing me for a couple of days and knew my habits. The fact that I hadn't spotted them meant I was getting old and sloppy.

I reached behind me and tried to bring the automatic out from under the back of the vest, but I was sweaty and everything was stuck to me. Before I got my hand to the gun, he came roaring back around the corner of the building, sprinting down the asphalt ramp toward the landward end of the dock, spewing flowers in his wake. A pair of blue steel nostrils the size of my fists now protruded from the front of the flapping newspaper. He was no more than twenty-five feet from me when he let fly with the sawed-off shotgun, emptying both barrels. Double ought buck shells contain what amounts to four thirty-two-caliber projectiles, coming at something like a thousand miles an hour. Three of them hit me directly in the Kevlar vest. The fourth, although I didn't know it until later, entered the soft flesh of my left arm just above the elbow. At the time, I was too busy to notice. The last image I had was of him, still in full stride, cracking the gun and reaching into his pocket for more shells.

The impact blew me completely off the end of the dock, sending me down into the dark water, where my primal urge to breach and breathe was instantly overcome by the certainty that if I so much as poked my head above the surface, he'd blow it clean off.

I groped around in front of me in the murky water and found one of the concrete-filled drums which had been sunk in the lake to hold the dock in place. The ribbed metal was cold and slick with algae. I wrapped both arms around the barrel and pulled myself to the bottom of the lake. The water was about six feet deep and teeth-chattering cold. I'd been out of breath from running, and whatever air I had in my lungs had been driven out by the impact of the slugs. I'd only been down about ten seconds, but shotgun or no shotgun, I had to breathe.

With the last of my strength, I pulled myself past the submerged barrel, pushed hard off its surface with my feet and came up under the dock. I held my nose and mouth with my hand, forcing myself not to sputter or gasp. I eased my lungs full and looked up. Through the cracks between the boards, I could see the outline of his feet silhouetted against the gray morning sky. He had no reason to be careful; he'd seen the slugs hit me full in the chest. He was standing out at the end, waiting for me to float up so he could pump another load into me.

As I moved his way, I pulled the nine-millimeter from the small of my back and thumbed off the safety. I moved slowly, walking on the bottom, making sure I didn't create ripples. I got right between his feet, put the muzzle of the gun tight against the treated boards, checked the angle to make sure it was perpendicular and pulled the trigger three times. He hit the deck like he'd been dropped out of a helicopter.

I swallowed some more air, dipped my head under the water and pulled myself out from under the dock. He lay with his face no more than a foot from mine, rocking in agony and moaning, his eyes screwed shut, both hands clutching his groin. I was so close that when I shot him in the forehead, I saw hair fly from the back of his head.

I didn't have time to dwell on it. The sound of squealing tires jerked my head toward the parking lot. His partner had probably been watching my car, in case I changed my morning routine. The sound of two weapons had brought him running.

I heard him shout. "Lamar, you okay?" He waited a minute and then tried again. "Lamar, come on, answer me, boy."

I stood shivering in the chin-deep water using the now-departed Lamar as a shield. The partner poked his head around the corner of the building and then quickly pulled it back. He was blond and younger.

"Lamar, can you hear me?" he shouted.

I reached under the front of the vest and tore off one of the extra clips which I'd taped to my chest. I put it on the dock next to Lamar's nose. A small stream of blood rolled down the side of the dock and into the water beside me. In the distance, a siren was winding our way. Somebody had called the cops. I mouthed a silent prayer.

I'll give the kid credit for loyalty or maybe some sort of overdeveloped sense of male bonding. Even with an approaching siren whooping in his ears, he wasn't about to leave his buddy. He came out from the building in a combat stance. Moving quickly, waving a square black Uzi from side to side, spinning as he searched for a target.

He spotted the body. "Oh, shit, Lamar," he cried.

He never saw me. When he looked to the right, I bobbed up out of the water, steadied both hands on the edge of the dock and shot him in the chest. He staggered backward and then sat down on the pavement with his legs spread out before him like a child at play. The Uzi slipped from his fingers, ratcheting off several rounds as it hit the pavement, and then suddenly everything went quiet. I was still standing in the water, shaking uncontrollably when the cops arrived and pried the automatic from my stiff fingers.

Stillman again spoke directly to Judge Downs.

"Your Honor, please let the record show that Mr. Waterman's assailants have since been positively identified as Lamar B. Highsmith of Winnemucca, Nevada, and Johnny Dale Smits Jr. of Hayden Lake, Idaho. Mr. Highsmith was pronounced dead at the scene, the victim of multiple gunshot wounds. Mr. Smits will be appearing as a witness for the prosecution later in these proceedings."

"So noted," she said.

They said I missed his heart by an inch, but if I were to judge, I'd say I must have nicked it. Faced with the death penalty for aggravated murder, Johnny Dale Smits rolled over like a trained seal. Once he started talking, they couldn't shut him up. In return for life without possibility of parole, he confessed to everything but the Lindbergh kidnapping. The grand jury had been particularly interested in the part of his story about how the judge had insisted that Felicia Mendoza must not be shot, how he wanted what he called "that little greaser" to suffer big-time before she died. I heard that one of the grand jurors fainted during Smits' vivid depiction of the crime, and that a veteran court stenographer had to be excused.

A week later, a scant forty-five minutes after Judge Downs issued her final instructions, the jury delivered a verdict of aggravated murder in the first degree, with a recommendation for the death penalty.

On my way down the courthouse steps after the verdict, Rebecca clung to my good arm with both hands. About halfway down, Tracy Tanaka of KOMO TV-9 shoved a microphone in front of my face. "How do you feel about the verdict, Mr. Waterman?" she asked.

I answered without thinking. "I feel lighter," I said. "Much lighter."

Tracy made a disgusted face and sprinted up the steps toward Dan Hennessey. Rebecca hugged my arm tighter.

2

First I tried the Zoo, but Terry, the bartender, said they hadn't been in for the better part of a week. "End of the month," he explained with a wink. "This time of year, they probably gone to the beach."

Terry's phrase "gone to the beach" was absolute testimony to the flexibility of language. In polite society, the notion of having gone to the beach conjures the heady aroma of tanning unguents and salt air, the images of colorful umbrellas and graceful children cavorting o'er sparkling sand. In this case, however, the phrase "gone to the beach" meant the Boys, having swilled the last of their monthly stipends, were temporarily broke and sleeping down on the waterfront in Myrtle Edwards Park. A monthly pilgrimage which provided not only a scenic marine environ suitable to the season, but front-row panhandling access to the swarms of cash-heavy tourists who strolled the area during the daylight hours.

Harold Green, Ralph Batista and George Paris had once been local people of some repute. They were the remnants of another age, the last mortal remains of my old man's grass-roots political machine and my most tangible connection to a famous father who, to me, had become little more than the collection of tall tales which his life had engendered.

Whenever I can, I like to find them a little work. Relatively sober, they make great surveillance operatives. They can hang around a building forever and nobody notices them. They're invisible. Mr. and Ms. Clean White America have systematically trained their optic nerves to exclude the poor and the homeless. So untidy, you know.

I used to wonder about this selective vision. At first, I went along with the traditional wisdom which said that the sight of society's dregs simply hit too close to home, for most people. That the destitute merely provided a grim and unwanted reminder of the tenuous nature of our own purchase on middle-class life. "There but for fortune go I" and all that. Lately, I think maybe it goes a bit deeper.

I've come to believe that these vagrants unwittingly stumble into the minefield of our deepest unacknowledged fears. You know the ones. The voice that wonders just how long you're going to be able to keep fooling all of the people all of the time. The insistent whisper that questions if you really deserve all the blessings you have and knows, with absolute certainty, that the answer is an unequivocal *no fucking way*.

I've come to see that the problem is not one of caring or kindness, but rather of self-preservation. We can't help ourselves. We keep our distance. We quicken our steps, square our shoulders and put on that thousand-yard stare. Forced close to them, we hold our collective breaths as if it were possible for the filament vapors of fear and failure to crawl down our throats and come to rest in our lungs like tumors. We don't mean it. We're not unkind or uncaring. It's just that terrible, lingering doubt that forces us to live our lives in constant fear, as if to consider the hopelessness of *their* plight for even an instant would surely weaken us, leaving us forever more susceptible to fortune, to disease, to folly.

My timing was perfect. I rolled the Fiat into the Vine Street parking lot just as the sun winked for the last time and then disappeared behind the Olympics. The distant mountains stood like jagged jack-o'-lantern teeth, fearsome and uneven in the orange mouth of the sunset. Thin needles of airborne foam prickled my cheeks as I locked the car and started across the parking lot. Ahead in the distance, the white concrete silos of the Pier Eight-six Grain Terminal surrendered to the dark northern sky. On my left, an insistent wind ruffled the surface of Elliott Bay, sliding on the muscular blue water, horizon to horizon, steadily toward the black boulders of shore. I turned up my collar and was about to duck my head into the wind when I saw them.

George, Harold, Ralph and Nearly Normal Norman lounged about the leeward side of a mossy hillock at the near end of the park, passing a trio of bag-shrouded bottles among them. Ralph's shopping cart rested atop the crest like a modern-art monument to dubious acquisition.

George was the only one facing my way, but he was either too involved or too shitfaced to notice my approach. Probably both. He'd been a banker once and a serious mover and shaker in the Downtown Businessmen's Association. He'd been on the street for the better part of twenty-five years but, remarkably, didn't look much worse for the wear. His sharp features and slicked-back white hair gave him the look of a defrocked boxing announcer. He pulled a bagged bottle from Ralph's hand and raised it to his lips.

Ralph Batista had once been a high-ranking official with the Port of Seattle and had mustered the longshoreman vote for my old man. Like the others, his unquenchable taste for the grape had eventually drowned whatever life he'd had, leaving him adrift among the flotsam and jetsam of the streets with an ever-present smile and paucity of functioning brain cells. Ralph had attained nirvana through numbness.

The wind carried his voice to me.

"If Bo Derek married Don Ho, she'd be Bo Ho."

Harold Green choked a couple of ounces of whatever he was drinking out through his nose and then wiped his face with his sleeve

"Bo Ho," he sputtered. "That's good. Bo Ho."

Harold had sold men's shoes at the Bon Marché and had been a minor functionary in the Retailers Union. He used to be taller. Each passing year carved another couple of pounds from his gaunt frame, further emphasizing his baseball-sized

Adam's apple and cab-door ears. He was beginning to look like Mr. Potato Head.

As I started across the grass toward them, Norman piped in.

"If Snoop Doggy Dogg married Winnie the Pooh, he'd be Snoop Doggy Dogg Pooh."

"Snoop what? Who the fuck is that?" George demanded.

"The rapper, man. You know. 'Gin and Juice.' "

George shook his head. "Rap is crap," he declared.

Norman rose from the ground, steadied himself for a moment and then began to shuffle from side to side. At six foot seven and drunk as a skunk, he moved with all the grace of a giraffe on Rollerblades. He sang. If that's what you called it.

Little or nothing was known of Nearly Normal Norman's background. When he first blew into town about five years ago, I'd inquired as to his family's state of origin and had, on successive attempts, been met with answers of Rhode Island, Indiana and Sri Lanka. In kinder, gentler times, Norman would have been wearing paper slippers and crocheting pot holders in a nice warm sanitarium somewhere. The miracles of Reaganomics had put him on the street.

Other than a nuclear thirst, what kept this particular group of guys together was their similar financial status. Normal had some sort of small trust fund that paid out by the month. The other three had managed to work long enough to have earned meager monthly stipends from their respective employers. Not a full pension, not enough to make it alone, but enough, when you added in the money I paid them, to collectively keep them in liquor and mostly out of the rain.

Norman waved his massive arms and continued gyrating wildly.

George blinked twice and pointed my way.

"Well, look what we got here," he slurred.

Ralph swiveled his head and then waited for his eyes to catch up.

"Leo," he shouted.

"Howdy, fellas," I said.

"Pull up some grass," said Harold.

George waved him off. "Gotta be careful with that kind of talk, Harry," he said. "Remember, Leo here used to smoke that wacky weed. Doan want him to relapse or nothin'."

Harold grinned. "I remember. Wasn't a Hostess Cupcake or a Ding Dong safe around the kid."

Norman had stopped dancing and was now patting his pockets.

"You wanna burn a bowl, Leo? I think I got some real good bud somewhere here on me."

I held up my hand. "No thanks, Normal. I've only got a second."

"Oh, yeah," George groused. "Mr. On Television got no time for the likes of us riffraff."

I sat down on the damp grass next to George and threw an arm around his bony shoulders. "On the contrary, my good man, spending some time with you riffraff is just what I had in mind."

"We seen you today . . . on the TV down at Steve's Broiler," Ralph said. "Ya really stuck it to the old judgy wudgy."

"They're gonna fry him," Harold offered.

"Not in our lifetimes," I said. "He'll die of old age before he exhausts his appeals. Either that or some guy he sentenced will punch his ticket for him and save the state the trouble."

"Your old man never liked him," George said suddenly. He took a short pull and then continued. "Always said Dougie was a prisoner of his dick. Wild Bill never had any respect for a guy couldn't control himself that way. Figured if a guy could be led around by his fly, he wasn't good for nothin' else." He took another pull, longer this time, and then thrust his bottle in my direction.

I took it. With these guys, the act of swillage had attained full-scale religious significance. To refuse was the worst sort of heresy. I knew the drill. As far as they were concerned, only teetotalers ranked lower on the evolutionary scale than sippers. I sniffed. Peach schnapps. It could be worse. I brought the bottle to my lips and took a full swallow. I let

the thick liquid slide down my throat and then passed the
bottle on to Ralph.

While we sat there on the grass playing musical bottles and
shooting the breeze about old times, Normal stood on the
side of the hill batting at himself like he was on fire. Having
determined that his weed was not in any of his outer gar-
ments, he was now working his way down through the six
or seven layers beneath. Clothes were beginning to pile up
around his ankles like molted skin. The wind carried the
smell of mothballs and body odor to my nostrils.

"Could you guys use a day's work?" I asked.

Normal stopped patting himself. Ralph set the bottle in
his lap.

"You got work for us?" he asked.

"No, he's taking a friggin' survey," George said.

I ignored him. "Yup. Fifty a day each. Free lunch. Free
beer. Maybe even a little schnapps when the job is done."

When the cheering subsided, I saw that Normal had found
what he was looking for and was now using his thumb to
tamp a small green bud down into the bowl of a wooden
pipe. Out over his shoulder the lighted green globe atop the
Seattle Post-Intelligencer building spun slowly. Big red letters.
IT'S IN THE PI. IT'S IN THE PI.

I got to my feet. Already, I could feel the schnapps in my
head. It was escape now or show up at home walking on my
knees, smelling like reefer. I no longer kid myself about just
having a few. I've never wanted a few of anything in my life.
With me, it's like the old song says: all or nothing at all. Time
to get the hell out of here.

"Pick you guys up right here at ten tomorrow morning,"
I said over my shoulder. Norman began rapping again.

*"Rollin' down the street, smokin' endo, sippin' on gin and juice.
'G's up, hoes down.'"*

3

WHOEVER SAID THAT AT EITHER END OF THE SOCIOECONOMIC SPEC-
trum there exists a leisure class was absolutely correct. It was
ten twenty-five when I pulled Rebecca's blue Explorer into
the driveway and turned off the ignition. The bitching started
immediately.

"What are we doin' here?" George demanded. "You forget
somethin' or what?"

"This is where we're working," I said.

In the rearview mirror, Harold looked confused. "What are
we gonna do here, Leo? We gonna guard the joint?"

"Yard work."

Big-time silence. Then George spoke.

"Yard work. Wadda ya mean we're gonna do yard work?"

"The pay's the same either way," I said.

"I thought we was doing detective work," said Ralph.

"Nope," I said, stepping out onto the asphalt. "Rebecca
and I figured this was a chance to do a few of the things
we've been talking about doing ever since we moved in.
Come on."

Nobody moved. Instead, they all looked to George. He sat
in the passenger seat with his arms folded across his chest,
slowly shaking his head. "Yard work," he said incredulously.
"Are you shittin' me?"

I walked around to his side and pulled open the door.

"Come on, man. Nothing too heavy. Just going to clean things up a bit and burn some trash." I spread my arms, palms upward. "Not a bad day. Not too hot, not too cold, not raining. Come on," I wheedled. "It'll be tons of fun."

George folded his arms higher and tighter and then turned his face away. "Just because we're bums don't mean we'll do yard work, for Chrissakes," he muttered. "We got standards, ya know."

"What if somebody found out?" Harold whined.

Before I could respond, Normal kicked open the rear door and stepped out. He left the door open as he bent over, took me by the shoulder and whispered in my ear.

"You say we could burn stuff?"

I didn't like the gleam in his eye. Not one bit. It reminded me of that Applewhite character. You remember, old Onion Head. The one who cut off his own balls and then talked his followers into offing themselves so's they could rendezvous with the big spaceship in the sky. That one. The look in that man's eyes is going to the grave with me. These days, anytime I find myself harboring retro-romantic notions regarding the intelligence of my fellow creatures, I just conjure up the image of his face and that faraway lunar look in his eyes, and then I immediately go out shopping for newer and better weapons.

"A small to medium fire," I amended.

He pulled me closer, crushing me in his vicelike grip.

"I get to tend it."

"Okay," I said tentatively, taking a mental inventory of all available smoke detectors, fire extinguishers and garden hoses. "We'll do it way in the back of the yard by the cliff."

The house where my parents had lived from the time I was seven was the only part of my trust fund which I was legally able to use prior to my forty-fifth birthday. Since my father's death in seventy-four, I'd always chosen to rent the place out rather than live in it rent-free. Call me sentimental, but a couple of grand a month for doing nothing had always

seemed preferable to rattling around in a twelve-room house
with a couple of ghosts who weren't talking to one another.

Earlier this year, however, circumstances had conspired to
force me to either putt or get off the green regarding my
relationship with Rebecca. And after a mere nineteen years
of dating, too. What's the world coming to? Everybody's in
such a hurry. Anyway, Rebecca and I talked it over and
reached an adult, collaborative decision that the most sensible
course of action would be to move into the newly renovated
family manse. Something about the twelve rooms with a
view, rent-free, attracted her.

"Okay," sighed George. "What the hell. We been to Rome;
we might as well see the Pope." He opened the door and
slipped out onto the pavement. "What's for lunch anyway? And
where's that cold beer you was runnin' your gums about?"

Norman grinned, reached into the backseat and lifted Harold out by the front of his coat.

Ralph stayed put. "Ain't been here in a long time," he said
to nobody in particular, running his eyes over the front of
the house.

"Let's go, Ralphie," Norman growled. "Time's a-wastin'."

Ralph didn't move. He sat there staring at the house in
silence.

"The hell I will," he said finally.

The idea of Ralph being anything but agreeable left everyone openmouthed with wonder. Everybody but Norman.
Norman wasn't about to take no for an answer. He bent at
the waist and leaned into the car, reaching out a big paw.

Quicker than I'd ever seem him move, Ralph popped open
the far door and hopped out, very nearly slamming the door
on Norman's hand. He leaned hard against the door, pointing
a grimy finger in my direction.

"You got no goddamn respect, Leo. You had any goddamn
respect you'd leave things the way they was, not be changin'
everything around all the time. Your folks wanted anything
different they'da changed it on their own, you hear me? You
got no goddamn respect."

I figured he meant all the changes to the house. After twenty years as a rental, the place had needed major work, so the trust had arranged for it to be completely renovated, from top to bottom. Inside and out. They'd gutted the place. The original house was a dimly lit place of heavy drapes and dark wood, a place where the silence was punctuated only occasionally by the sounds of clicking heels and closing doors. Now, everything inside was light and open spaces. Outside, the jungle of shrubs and vines which once totally covered the exterior of the house had been hacked into submission and the bricks sandblasted back to their original rust color.

Ralph started toward the street, shouting as he walked.

"Ain't nothing the same anymore. Can't nobody leave nothing alone." He stopped and shook a fist at me. If he'd had fangs, they'd have been bared. "You do your own god-damn yard work. You want everything different, you do it yourself. I ain't havin' no part of it."

He turned on his heel and headed for the street.

"Ralphie," George yelled. "Come on back here."

But it was no good. Ralph kept waving us off and walking until he rounded the corner on Terry and shuffled from view.

"How much did he drink last night?" I inquired.

"No more'n usual," said Harold.

"Maybe a little less," confirmed George. "Maybe that's it. Maybe he's parched. A man'll do weird shit if he's parched."

"Sure got a bug up his chimney," said Norman. "You want I should bring him back, Leo?"

"No," I said. "We'll leave the slave labor to Judge Brennan."

BY THE TIME we broke for lunch at one, we'd made serious progress on both the yard and the cooler. In the yard, the old cedar fence that ran along the cliff had been pulled down board by board, the rotting posts torn from the ground and added to the substantial blaze which Norman lovingly tended in the rear corner of the yard.

Harold yelled across the yard, "Leo, we need more suds."

I turned off the Weed Eater, smeared my sweaty brow with my bare forearm and strolled over to the cooler. All that remained was the sixer of Bud Light I'd told Rebecca not to buy.

"It's not empty," I called.

"Nothin' but Light shit."

"Well, have a Light. I'll get some more of the other out of the fridge as soon as I finish this section."

"I'll wait," he said.

I made a disgusted face. "What? One light beer's gonna kill you?"

From behind me, George piped in. "Light beer's like screwing in a canoe."

Normal nodded and grinned. I was supposed to bite, so I did.

"How's that?" I inquired.

"Fucking w-a-a-a-y too close to water," they said in unison.

They yukked it up, hooting and hollering as they stomped about.

"Let's break for lunch," I said and headed inside for beer.

The tray of cold cuts Rebecca got from Safeway was a big hit. What the catering manager had assured her would be ample for a party of eight disappeared, right down to the paper doily, in about twenty-five minutes.

George belched loudly into his fist and said, "Ralphie don't know what he's missin'. Poor bastard."

"He hates missin' a free meal," Harold agreed.

"A free anything," Norman added, tilting his head back and swallowing the last pickle slice whole, like a gull downing a herring.

"Sure had a burr under his saddle," I said.

George pounded on his sternum with the top of his fist.

"I think maybe it was just too much for him. You know, seein' the house lookin' all different, you know, with other people livin' in it and all."

"I'm not other people," I protested.

"You know what I mean. He and your old man were real tight, and you know Ralphie's the sentimental type."

"Really," I said. "I hadn't noticed."

George nodded solemnly. "Oh, yeah. Couple of weeks ago we snuck into that new theater up on Seventh and Pike, the one with all the screens." He pointed at Harold. "You ask Harry, halfway through *The English Patient* Ralphie boy was blubbering so hard we had to get the hell out of there before we got pinched."

"Snot-nose kid behind the candy counter wouldn't give us no more napkins," Harold added.

"What are we gonna burn next?" Normal asked, eyeing the redwood benches beneath us.

"That thing," I said.

I pointed to the right rear corner of the house, where the partially collapsed remains of a small greenhouse listed precariously to starboard. Right after my parents moved into the place, my mother had gotten into a screaming argument with the landscape contractor and decided that henceforth, landscapers be damned, she was going to propagate and plant her own shrubbery. The old man, as I recall, thought the idea ridiculous, but after a couple of weeks of listening to her gripe, he'd relented and called in a crew. I could still hear his voice as he spoke to the foreman. "What the hey," he'd said. "Who knows, maybe it'll keep her out of the house." The foreman had nodded knowingly.

Twelve years later, during my sophomore year at the University of Washington, she had a massive cerebral hemorrhage and died while repotting tuberous begonias. The doctor said she never knew what hit her. If the peaceful expression on her death face was any indication, I suspect he was correct in his assessment.

I never went in there again, and, to my knowledge, neither did my father. Instead, for months afterward, whenever I came by to see the old man, and he wasn't there, which, of course, was most of the time, I'd slip out into the backyard, kick up a few stones and pitch them at the squares of glass, shattering the individual panels one at a time, until the wooden frames stood open and empty, and the native sword fern and braken began to reclaim the littered ground around the railroad tie foundation. If the old man noticed, he never said a word to me.

Sometime back in the late eighties, while the place was rented, a freak windstorm tore a limb from the huge oak at the north end of the yard and dropped it onto the side of the little building, crushing half the roof and demolishing the whole south wall. Since then, it had stood as a ruin, a skeletal and deformed reminder of the impermanence of even the most artful joinery.

Despite its seemingly decrepit state, the remaining structure fought us every step of the way. After failing to push it over by hand, we attached ropes to the upper corners of the nearest remaining wall. George and Norman manned one rope, Harold and I the other. On the count of three we commenced our "dragging stones for the pharaoh" impression. All we lacked was a bald guy with a drum.

When I'd planned the job, I figured it wouldn't take much to pull the rest of it down. In my mind's eye, I'd imagined the moment when it came clattering to the ground and figured our biggest problem would be keeping out of the way as it fell. It didn't work out that way.

Instead of collapsing before the might of our combined muscle, the old frame seemed to dig in its heels, to grit its jagged glass teeth, as if somehow determined to resist us for all it was worth. It came down incrementally, inch by stubborn inch, groaning and popping as each handmade joint fought for its integrity, never giving in to gravity, forcing us to pull it all the way to the ground and then to jump up and down on it as it lay there. I think my mother would have liked that.

I issued each of the fellas a pair of leather work gloves and a hammer. It took an hour to break the sash into pieces and feed it to the fire and another hour of raking through the debris to fill the wheelbarrow nearly to the top with shards of broken glass and yellowed window putty.

By three-thirty, all that remained was the raised bed on which the greenhouse had once stood, a twelve-by-twenty-

foot altar edged by ancient railroad ties. We were leaning on
our rakes and resting on our laurels when Harold pointed to
the raised rectangle which had once been the floor of the
greenhouse. "How come nothin' grows in there, Leo? You'd
think with all the years it would have growed over like the
rest of this shit here."

" 'Cause it's not dirt," I said. "It's cedar sawdust. They
wanted to put in a concrete floor, but my mother insisted
they fill it up with cedar sawdust. She said it would be easier
on the legs and back and keep the bugs away besides."

"I remember," George said. "Ralphie got it for her from
that old shake mill down by where he worked on the docks.
A whole dump-truck load. Got it free, too. Your old man said
he'd be damned if he was gonna pay good money for sawdust. Said the next thing you knew, they'd be charging us
for bark."

Harold nudged me with the handle of his rake.

"Wasn't there some talk of schnapps?"

"Rebecca's bringing it." I checked my watch. Three-thirty.
"She should be along any minute now."

I thought I may have detected rumblings of mutiny among
the troops. I had a few more things I wanted to do, but they
were right. It was time to quit. They'd put in a better day's
work than I could have hoped for. A day of manual labor
and a couple of six-packs each had made them dangerous to
themselves and others. They'd had enough.

Except for Norman. "What are we gonna burn next?" he
wanted to know. I didn't like the way he was looking at the
rest of us, so I decided to humor him. I pointed to the
foundation.

"The railroad ties," I said. "I've got a little earthmover coming in tomorrow. One of those little Bobcat front-loaders. He's
going to spread the sawdust over the rest of the yard and
then turn the whole thing over so we can plant grass." I
reached up and clapped Norman on the shoulder. "Tell you
what, big guy, if you're still rip-roarin' and ready to go, why
don't you see if you can pry the ties off the sides."

"And then burn 'em?" he leered.

"Yeah," I said. "Then you can burn 'em."

He lit out across the yard just as the back door opened and Rebecca stepped out onto the patio. She'd been home long enough to change into a pair of stonewashed jeans and a gray Husky T-shirt that said WOOOF across the front in big purple letters. She came down the four brick steps and stood by my side. She surveyed the yard.

"Wow," she said. "You guys have been busy. The place looks great. It looks so much better back here with that eyesore gone."

Normal returned from the garage with a five-foot metal pry bar which he jammed into the sawdust directly behind the ties.

George and Harold wandered over to pay their respects. After the standard small talk, they began to shuffle nervously about until George finally took the lead. "Ah, Miss Duvall. You didn't by any chance . . . I mean, Leo said you was going to . . . I mean . . . he said that when you got here . . ."

Rebecca arched an eyebrow my way. I gave her the nod.

"It's on the kitchen counter, George," she said.

"Handy dandy," he said over his shoulder.

We watched them disappear into the house.

"Where's Ralph?" she asked.

"He seemed to think yard work was beneath his dignity. He got all pissed off and left."

"Ralph? Really?"

Before I could reply, a resounding crack split the air and the entire front wall of the foundation hit the ground with a thump. Norman grinned our way. Five feet of composted sawdust, deep brown, like devil's food cake, stood without support, perfect and molded. Actually more like marble cake, as a thin line of white ran about a third of the way down the center of the pile.

Norman scooped a tie up under each arm and headed back toward his beloved fire. "Howdy, Miss Duvall," he said on the way by.

I trotted along after him. "Put them on one at a time, Norman. We don't want the fire getting too big."

"We don't?" He sounded surprised.

Technically speaking, burning is illegal within the city limits. All afternoon, I'd been expecting a fire truck to show up. I didn't want to blow it now.

"No, we don't," I insisted. "One at a time."

When I turned back, Rebecca was over by the pile, down on one knee, picking at the sawdust with her finger. I moseyed over and stood next to her. She was using her manicured index finger to clear powdery debris out from around the white streak.

"Cedar sawdust," I said. She ignored me.

"Leo, go in the garage and get me one of those new paintbrushes we had left over from when we painted the trim in the study."

"What—" I started.

"Hurry," she said without looking up.

"What's the problem?"

"Will you just get the damn brush," she snapped.

When I returned, she quickly tore the plastic protector from the brown bristles and started to brush away the loose material along the length of the streak, carefully exposing what appeared to be a long mottled stone of a grayish hue, thinner at the center than at its somewhat bulbous ends.

Suddenly she got to her feet. Her face was flushed. She took a deep breath. "It's a femur," she said.

"A what?"

"The largest of the leg bones."

"From what?"

She put a hand on my shoulder. I could feel her trembling.

"No, Leo," she said. "You don't understand. The question is not from *what*. The question is from *who*."

"Who?"

She nodded. "It's human."

4

I SQUINTED MY EYES, SQUEEZING THE DISTANT DOTS OF LIGHT INTO a continuous river of yellow brilliance which flowed along the Interstate like luminous lava. Below the crowded highway, the same bright beams lived secondhand lives on the shimmering surface of Lake Union. Any illusion of tranquillity was short-lived, however, lasting only until a single-engined float plane taxied into view from the north, its red wing lights whirling, its long hollow feet gouging a cold reminder of darkness into the bright skin of the water.

Rebecca leaned over and kissed me on the ear.

"You okay?" she asked, rubbing the back of my neck.

I sighed. "This is embarrassing."

She patted me on the shoulder. "Believe me, Leo, I know what you mean," she said. "I had to call my own office to send a forensic team."

I threw an arm across her shoulders and pulled her close to me. We'd been sitting together on the back steps for a couple of hours, twiddling our thumbs, trying to keep out of harm's way.

It was three hours since I'd stuffed the Boys into a cab and sent them on their way, and the backyard looked like an archeological dig. Tommy Matsukawa led a team of three forensic technicians who, one trowel at a time, had removed the sawdust covering the skeleton, sifted the removed material through four successively finer screens and then checked what they had left with a metal detector.

They'd set up a small bank of halogen lights at either end of the dig and now, when it seemed like they must be just about down to the bones, they brought in a shop vac to suck up the last of the dust. I was feeling about as whiny as the sound of the electric motor.

It had been hard on Rebecca too, sitting there, not interfering, letting the people who worked for her do their jobs. To make matters worse, Jeff Byrne, the medical examiner himself, had showed up about a half an hour ago, given us a curt nod and now hovered about the line between the light and the darkness like a vampire. Around here, the ME is an elected official, just another politician. Jeff Byrne hadn't cut into a cadaver in twenty years, but he knew a potential photo op when he saw one. Tommy turned off the vacuum cleaner, and suddenly all was quiet. The machine rattled as he pushed it over toward Mary Kenny, who stood with her hands thrust deep in the pockets of her bright yellow medical examiner's jacket, transfixed, staring off into space.

"Go through this, will you, please, Mary," he said.

Mary rolled it over to the side and began to remove the bag from the machine, as the other two technicians set up a thirty-five-millimeter camera on a tripod and began taking pictures. I counted the flashes as they moved around the bones. Thirty-two flashes.

When they'd finished, Jeff Byrne wandered over into the light and stood next to Tommy, looking down. He was a taciturn man of about sixty with a full head of curly hair, once blond, now turned a sour yellow. He wore a spotless gray suit with a burgundy silk tie pulled down and a pair of cordovan loafers. I suspected he'd been on his way to dinner when he got the call. Together, they made a complete circle of the foundation, pausing for a long while at the north end of the skeleton, kneeling, pointing and whispering between themselves and then continuing on around, checking the bones from all angles. When they were back where they began, Tommy shaded his eyes from the harsh light and cried out like a carnival barker.

"Don't be shy, folks," he called. "Step right up and see the wonder of the ages, Queen Anne Man."

I stayed put. Rebecca nudged me with her elbow. She knew I didn't trust Tommy. "It's just bones," she said. Yeah, sure.

Nothing gave Tommy Matsukawa greater pleasure than grossing me out. He'd trained the clerical staff to buzz him whenever I'd stop by the ME's office to see Rebecca. Then he'd come trotting out of the pathology lab with some rancid piece of festering flesh to wave under my nose.

Rebecca grabbed my elbow and hauled me to my feet. "Come on," she whispered. Together, we walked down into the yard.

I don't know what I was expecting, but it wasn't what I saw. I guess I'd been hoping that the body had been that of some unfortunate tramp, drunk, fallen into a sawdust bin and unknowingly dumped with that long-ago load of cedar bark, something like that. But even an amateur like me could see that there was no way that had happened. These bones were laid out too perfectly for that. These bones hadn't been dumped; they'd been carefully buried.

I stood down by the feet as Rebecca slowly made her way around the skeleton. She started by pulling a small tape measure from her pocket and measuring the leg bone we'd first uncovered. She walked slowly, pausing again at the north end, pulling her glasses from her shirt pocket and peering myopically at the top of the skull for a long moment and then moving on, working her way around the edge until she was back by my side. She took ahold of my arm and whispered in my ear.

"A man," she said. "Six-two or -three. From the crowns on the lower teeth, probably quite affluent. Been in the ground at least twenty years, probably more. It's hard to tell because of what he's been buried in."

I sensed a hitch in her delivery. "Yeah," I prodded.

"The left hand is missing."

I could tell from her eyes that she had more to say.

"What else?"

She took a deep breath and put on her Miss Professional face.

"Gunshot wound to the back of the head."

"You can tell all that from walking around a pile of bones?"

She nodded. " 'Fraid so."

"She's the best," Tommy piped in.

She took me by the arm and led me over to the skeleton. She pointed down at the nearest leg. "You can tell from the length of the leg bone how tall a person was . . ." She waffled her free hand. "Within an inch or so," she said. We took two steps before she stopped again.

"The pelvis. It's a man. No question. Any first-year med student . . ." she began.

I was feeling numb by the time she pulled me up toward the head. She dropped her eyes to the skull and then looked over at Tommy.

"May I?" she said.

Tommy reached into the pocket of his jacket and produced a pair of rubber gloves. "Sure," he said. "Here." He passed her the gloves. "We're gonna tag and box it next anyway."

Rebecca took the gloves and worked them on with expert ease. I don't know why, but when she reached down for the skull, I turned my head away, as if I didn't want this gaunt stranger to see my face. When I looked back, Rebecca held the skull in both hands. She looked up and spoke to Tommy.

"You won't believe the condition of the bone," she said.

"Solid?" he asked.

She nodded. "Not a mark on it." She looked back at the rest of the bones. "Must have been the sawdust medium. No worms, no bugs, no boring insects. Nothing but microorganisms. It's perfect."

Tommy Matsukawa agreed. "If it was complete you could use it, as is, for a college lab skeleton. Amazing."

Byrne spoke for the first time since he'd arrived.

"I'm going to have to call SPD now," he said, pulling up his tie and smoothing the sides of his hair with his palms. I watched as he walked to the far end of the yard and pulled a cellular phone from the inside pocket of his suit coat.

Rebecca turned the bottom of the skull my way. There was no denying the jagged hole, three-quarters of an inch across, at the base of the skull.

"Entrance wound," she said.

She gently turned the skull over and, using her gloved index finger, brushed away the thin layer of dust which clung stubbornly to the top of the cranium. She brought the skull toward her face as if to sniff it, but instead pursed her lips and blew away the remaining dust, revealing an unbroken expanse of smooth bone.

"No exit wound," she announced.

Tommy stepped over and leaned in. "I told you she was the best," he said. He reached down onto the grass at his feet and produced a fine wire screen in a wooden frame. "Shake it out in here," he said.

I winced when Rebecca poked a gloved finger into the empty eye socket. She worked the packed sawdust loose around the front of the skull until the material suddenly dropped down into the screen in a damp clump. Tommy leaned in close as she used her palm to spread the sawdust over the face of the screen.

Tommy's eyes widened as he reached down into the screen and plucked something from the morass. He held it between the thumb and index finger of his right hand and blew away the remaining dust.

"Voila," he enthused. "Thirty-caliber."

"Thirty-two," Rebecca said.

Tommy shook his head and curled an eyebrow. "Lunch?"

"You're on," she said.

He produced a small glass vial and dropped the slug in with a click. "So much for cause of death," he said.

I demonstrated my unusually keen perception of the obvious.

"One shot to the back of the head," I said.

Tommy nodded. "You see 'em like this when they lay down on the floor and the perp puts the gun right up to the back of the head. It's the pro approach because it virtually eliminates blood spatter."

"An assassination," I said.

He tried to lighten things up. "Either that or the guy was murdered by a midget."

My smile must have been less than convincing. His eyes got big and he quickly stepped back out of arm's reach. Rebecca scowled and wagged a finger at me. After I nodded grudgingly, she bent at the waist and put the skull back where she'd found it and then straightened up. She looked deep into my eyes, sort of like when she wants something she knows I'm not going to want to give.

"Might not be the worst idea in the world to call Jed now," she said. "Just to be safe."

I shook my head. "Remember . . . he took Sarah to Paris for a second honeymoon," I said.

"That's right. Maybe we should call his service to see who's covering for him?"

"Let's hang tight and see what happens," I said.

She peeled the gloves from her hands and dropped them on the littered ground. We started toward the house together, when Tommy called out to one of the technicians. "Miller," he shouted. "Bring that thing over here and give it a runover before we box it."

I'd never seen this Miller guy before this evening. He was a short little specimen with a wiry halo of black hair surrounding an otherwise bald head. His yellow windbreaker rustled as he came trotting past us with a small gray metal detector thrust out before him like a lance. Rebecca threw an arm around my waist and spun me slowly around.

We watched in silence as he started down by the feet and got an immediate hit. A couple minutes of sifting through the debris yielded six small metal eyelets, which Tommy held in his palm.

"From his shoes," he announced with a toothy grin.

Before he was through congratulating himself, the machine emitted another series of electronic beeps, louder this time. It only took a second for Miller to reach in and come up with a rusted belt buckle, which joined the eyelets in Tommy's hand. Miller worked his way silently up the bones, until, just about level with the top of the rib cage, the metal detector went batshit, squealing almost continually, its little red and green lights blinking like an accident scene.

The noise brought the medical examiner himself trotting in from the darkness. When Byrne arrived, Tommy was bent over the area, running his hands through the remaining dust. Suddenly, Tommy stopped rummaging and looked up at his boss. A puzzled expression spread over his face as he pulled his hands from the dust. Because his back partially obscured the object in his hands, my brain discarded its first impression of what he was holding. It wasn't until he turned my way that I could see I had been right the first time. He had three hands. The two God gave him and the one he'd just fished out of my backyard.

Interestingly enough, it was the uncommunicative Mr. Byrne who got his wits together first and uttered the line which was to become a permanent part of Northwest folklore.

"Holy Christ, it's Peerless Price," he whispered.

5

OPINIONS DIFFER SHARPLY AS TO BOTH WHAT PEERLESS PRICE BE-
came and what became of Peerless Price. For a public life of
nearly three decades to end on such an uncertain and tremu-
lous note allowed for a wide range of speculation among
those familiar with the story, and thus, lacking the comfort
of ready answers, unwittingly provided the raw material of
legend. Although the phrase has surely fallen from use
among today's youth, few of whom are aware of anything
that transpired prior to their last tattoo, to many of us ancient
Northwesterners, the phrase "Pulling a Peerless" still referred
to getting lost in a hurry and staying that way.

Peerless Price was the only son of Tyler K. Price, a prominent local clothing manufacturer whose company, Peerless
Products, had grown prosperous outfitting starry-eyed miners
bound for the Klondike. After graduating from Stanford, ig-
noring his father's invitation to join the family firm, Peerless
Price instead joined the Marine Corps, where he distin-
guished himself in the Pacific theater of W.W. II. Peerless
assuaged his thwarted literary ambitions through frequent
letters to his father, vividly describing GI life and death on
the Pacific front.

Tyler Price was understandably proud of his son's contribution to the war effort, and during a businessmen's lun-
cheon at the Cascade Club one afternoon in nineteen forty-

three, he casually showed one of his son's letters to his long-time friend R. C. Gamble, who was, at that time, editor in chief of the *Seattle Post-Intelligencer*. Whether Gamble was greatly impressed by the young man's prose or whether he perhaps printed the letter merely as a favor to his old friend will never be known. Either way, reader response was immediate and overwhelmingly positive, and so, for the duration of the war, every Sunday, Peerless Price became Seattle's link to life on those faraway front lines.

Peerless Price returned to Seattle in the rainy winter of nineteen forty-five with a bronze star on his chest and a stainless steel hand at the end of his left arm. In the closing days of the war, only weeks before VJ Day, his luck deserted him when, in an unthinking moment, he tried to slip a booby-trapped codebook out from under the arm of a dead Japanese major. There are those who say that the remainder of his life could be traced directly back to the loss of his hand, but I'm not so sure. That he had returned disillusioned, embittered and no longer at peace did not significantly differentiate him from the thousands upon thousands of other young men and women who likewise shed their youth and enthusiasm on those same beaches. What can be said with some certainty, however, is that the war gave the young Peerless Price an insatiable appetite for contention and a political stance just slightly right of Atilla the Hun, both of which would serve as hallmarks for the remainder of his life and career.

R. C. Gamble, in his memoirs, would later claim that his offer of a full-time reporting job with the *Post-Intelligencer* had been purely a product of his great faith in the young Price's abilities rather than an act of patriotic Christian charity, as many suggested. Either way, old R. C. made out like a bandit.

Over the next ten or twelve years, Peerless Price ascended from an occasional features writer to the lead man in the metro section. From weekly first-person accounts of dog shows and charity auctions to a featured six-day-a-week column which was the first thing everyone in Seattle turned to over coffee. By nineteen fifty-four, he had his own logo. A caricature, really. A little drawing of him with an oversized head, sitting at an undersized desk, wearing an eyeshade, an old-fashioned fountain pen wedged behind his ear. Typing . . . with one hand.

As is often the case, his success was, to some degree, partially attributable to good timing. Peerless Price and the fifties were made for each other, or perhaps more likely, from each other. Like the strange decade which molded him, Peerless Price led a double life. On the outside, smug and self-satisfied, as only the victors of wars are permitted, but on the inside frustrated, perverse and paranoid. On one hand, fueled by an unquestioning belief in truth, justice and the American way. On the other hand, sufficiently self-righteous and fearful of change as to make one wonder if perhaps he didn't protest just a bit too much.

Although always a staunch defender of the status quo, Peerless didn't truly hit his stride until he encountered the proper enemy. Sure, he was a Red-baiter second only to Joe McCarthy. Sure he could find the makings for a Communist conspiracy at a PTA bake sale. Here was a guy who orchestrated a massive bonfire of rock and roll records, which were, he claimed, a cleverly disguised Russian mind-control technique intended to compromise the virtue of America's youth. All of that, however, was merely the pre-game warmup for the sixties.

As luck would have it, Tyler K. Price died in the spring of nineteen sixty-two leaving the family business to Peerless and his three younger sisters, Emily, Justine and Elizabeth. Having neither the necessary business acumen nor the slightest inclination to run a manufacturing operation, the children quickly sold out to a British firm. Each of the children received, after taxes, slightly less than three million dollars.

While his sisters used their wealth to ascend to the very apex of Seattle high society, Peerless lived simply. He had no interest in fast cars or fancy houses. Yachts held no fascination. He never married, or, for that matter, showed any interest whatsoever in the opposite sex. What fascinated Peerless Price was power, and toward that end, he invested his new-found fortune.

Although in most things an arch-traditionalist, Peerless Price was in one respect a forward thinker. Much like his avowed hero J. Edgar Hoover, Price realized early on that information was power and set about making sure that he always had more information than the next guy. Seattle in the early sixties was a city in a state of flux. The old-time systems of police payoffs and governmental influence pedaling were coming to an end. All aspects of the public sector had come under ever-increasing media scrutiny and were responding by mutating into the well-meaning but mostly incompetent organizations we've all come to know and distrust.

Peerless Price filled the graft vacuum. Every cop in town knew that a few extra bucks would miraculously appear every time he shared what he knew with Peerless Price. Every clerk in every city and county office knew where that new winter coat could be had. Every hooker, doorman, valet, bellhop, bartender, cabby and parking attendant knew exactly where talk *wasn't* cheap. And you didn't have to look the other way or drop your pants, either. All you had to look for was a phone booth, and all you had to drop was a dime.

The Vietnam War provided Peerless with precisely the sort of simpleminded dilemma best suited for his politics. He became the hawk's hawk and began a systematic character assassination of any public figure who dared express opposition to the conflict. To incur the wrath of Peerless Price was to have that long-ago affair with your secretary plastered all over the Thursday edition, or to find an exhaustive interview with your step-grandfather Ned, retired now and dabbling in bondage down in Scottsdale, Arizona. To some, Peerless Price became the last true defender of the faith. To others, he became the most feared and hated man in Seattle.

To his lasting consternation, the one guy Peerless Price could never make a dent in was my old man. By the time Peerless hit his stride, Wild Bill Waterman had been in office for sixteen years and twice run for mayor. Plenty of time for a man with Bill's nepotistic inclinations to have salted the bureaucratic mine with vast numbers of his family nuggets. While the rest of Seattle's movers and shakers cowered under a deluge of audits and investigations, the old man went about business as usual, just keeping it in the family, so to speak. Not only was he insulated from the nitpicking of Peerless Price, but he was also Seattle's most visible and insistent anti-war advocate. For most of the sixties, Peerless Price seldom referred to Wild Bill Waterman as anything except Hanoi Bill. If deflating those in power was to be Peerless Price's job, dethroning my old man became his obsession.

According to urban legend, their mutual animosity finally boiled over in nineteen sixty-eight when, after a heated shouting match in the Green Parrot Lounge, my old man called Peerless out. Said if he wanted to keep running his lip, why didn't he step outside in the alley for a minute and settle the matter in the time-honored manner of men.

Peerless Price, who basked in a well-deserved reputation as a barroom brawler, immediately picked up the gauntlet, and out into the alley they went. I remember the big bandage on my father's head and how, for weeks afterwards, he stayed at home, conducting business by phone in his darkened study. My old man always claimed that he got the twenty-three stitches in his forehead when Peerless sucker punched him with the stainless steel hand and that the beating which put Peerless in the hospital on thirty-day medical leave had been administered purely as an act of self-defense.

Just as an entire generation of Americans can remember precisely what they were doing when John F. Kennedy was killed, a great many Northwesterners can likewise recall what they were about when Peerless Price disappeared. It was easy. It was the Fourth of July weekend and, for the first time in its history, the city had issued permits for not one, but two holiday parades. While the traditional patriotic pageant was scheduled to be prancing downtown, a massive antiwar rally, led by none other than old Hanoi Bill himself, had been planned for Broadway.

I remember sitting between my parents on the stage in Volunteer Park on the night that Peerless Price disappeared, listening to speaker after speaker deride that faraway conflict and call for the immediate withdrawal of our troops. Sitting until the wee hours, dressed like a miniature FBI agent, until, finally, it was my father's turn to speak. I remember the harsh yellow light. And being too tired to follow his words and becoming lost in the sea of faces.

In the weeks preceding the holiday, Peerless had viciously attacked anyone and everyone he deemed responsible for issuing the demonstrators a permit to march, branding them as fags, traitors and Communist sympathizers. So incensed was Peerless Price that, against the wishes of his employers, he cast aside any vestige of journalistic impartiality and publicly proclaimed his intention to march at the head of the downtown parade, right next to the mayor. Needless to say, his failure to show up for the parade did not go unnoticed.

The initial police investigation revealed that he was last seen on the night before, July third, nineteen sixty-nine, at about eight o'clock in the evening when he used a credit card to pay for a meal at a Chinese restaurant in the International District. Two days later his car was found parked and locked in a pay lot on South King Street, a block and a half from where he had eaten his last meal.

Despite the Price family's public offer of a hundred-thousand-dollar reward for information regarding the whereabouts of their beloved brother, over the next two months, the largest manhunt in the history of the Pacific Northwest yielded absolutely nothing, and the disappearance of Peerless Price became the stuff of legend.

When the investigation was, at long last, drawn to an unsuccessful close, Bill Moody, the police commissioner, was asked by a reporter how it could be that the best investigators in the department had failed to turn up even a single suspect.

"Oh, we've got plenty of suspects," he said.

"Who?" pressed the reporter.

"Just open the phone book," Moody replied.

And to think, after nearly thirty years of rumors and speculation, of the insistent story of how he'd been poured into the foundations of the Kingdome, or paved over when they built the new freeway, or, my personal favorite, how he'd been shredded and sold for crab bait, all the while Peerless Price had been resting comfortably in my backyard. Dude.

6

IF WHAT I DID SATURDAY NIGHT COULD BE CALLED SLEEPING, THEN I guess what I did Sunday morning could be called waking up. After six hours of watching horror movies on the inside of my eyelids, I stumbled downstairs, feeling far worse than when I'd gone to bed. Instead of making my usual beeline for the kitchen, I crossed the living room and peeked out through the drapes. We were down to two TV trucks. I figured the other guys were off visiting the Hair Club for Men.

I'll admit it. I smiled when I saw the hairpiece on the kitchen counter. As a matter of fact I smiled all the way through my first cup of coffee. Right up until I opened the morning paper.

HOLY CH**ST, IT'S PEERLESS PRICE

Biggest typeface since Princess Di. I sailed the front page over into the corner of the room and concentrated on the sports section. The Sonics were about to open training camp. After an entire year of listening to Shawn Kemp complaining about his contract, George Karl was now bitching about his own contract. Go figure. I read the article three times and still had no idea exactly what Karl's problem was. I heaved a sigh and then waddled over and retrieved the front page.

The most enduring mystery in the history of the Pacific
Northwest was solved yesterday when the body of Peerless Price—

The story went on and on, covering half the front page and
all of page two. There was even a little box directing readers
to other related articles throughout the paper. Pictures of the
bones, of the front of the house, of me, of the old man, of
Peerless and of course of our beloved medical examiner Jeff
Byrne. I followed the various articles around the paper. They
had it all. They'd even dug up that old AP photo of Peerless
Price after he duked it out with the old man. The one where
his left eye was completely swollen shut and his nose was
over by his ear.

They never came right out and said that Peerless Price had
been offed by former city councilman Bill Waterman, or that
well-known politico Waterman buried the reporter in his
backyard, but they sure didn't leave their readers many other
choices. The way I read the articles, either my old man was
guilty, or we had us a case of alien abduction. I could feel
the blood rising to my face.

I thumbed my way back to the front page. The lead article
was by somebody named Brian Swanson. I followed directions back to page eighteen, and as I suspected, there at the
end of the article were both an E-mail address and a phone
number for this Swanson dweeb. What the hell. Why not start
the day by screaming into somebody's voice mail.

Fortunately, where cold reason failed, technology inter-
vened. When I plugged the phone back in, I got that pulsing
dial tone that meant I had messages. I dialed the access number and then my secret code. *Bong de de bing.* "*You have forty-
three new messages. To listen to new messages, push one. First
message . . . recorded last evening at . . .*"

It took the better part of an hour to work through all the
messages. I knew better than to move on to the next message
before the prior caller hung up. All that did was transfer the
damn things to the Saved Messages folder where they would
remain until Armageddon. All but two were from the media.

As the night wore on, the messages got shorter and shorter. The last few were hang-ups.

At seven-thirty this morning, Tommy Matsukawa had called for Rebecca. A preliminary check of dental records confirmed the identity of the bones. Rebecca had been right. The slug was a thirty-two. Tommy acknowledged his lunch debt. The other call was from my uncle Pat.

Patrick S. Waterman was the youngest of the three Waterman brothers, my father the oldest. In between were Edward, who died when I was a child, and the four sisters Karen, Hildy, May and Rochelle. Like everybody else in the family, Pat had lined his pockets buying real estate on my old man's inside information. For the past twenty years or so, he had been more or less a professional board member and social butterfly.

I called the number he left. The static told me he was in the car.

"Yeah."

"Pat. It's Leo."

"Don't you check your messages?"

As usual, his voice held an underlying tone of dissatisfaction. Sort of a "you cur" understood. And, as usual, it annoyed me.

Pat and I had never gotten along well. My mother used to claim it was because Pat had never married and wasn't accustomed to dealing with children, but, in my heart, I'd always known better. It was more than that. On some fundamental level, we saw the world in completely different terms. And unable to identify the source of the friction, we'd allowed it to slop over into all our dealings, creating an air of discord which, for the last thirty years, had drifted over the field of our linked lives like cannon smoke.

"I unplugged the phones. It's a fucking circus over here."

He was silent for a long moment. We both knew what came next. God knows we'd run through the scene enough times. Somehow it always happened when I talked to Pat. I knew he hated profanity, and although I had no conscious desire to offend him, something inside of me always had the uncontrollable urge to swear like a drill sergeant.

"Must you?" he intoned.

"I'm having a bad morning."

Above the static and road noise, I heard him sigh.

When I was younger, Pat and I used to compete for my father's attention, acting more like feuding brothers than like uncle and nephew. It took me twenty years of that foolishness to figure out that the old man fostered the rivalry between Pat and me as a means of controlling us, the way he controlled everything else in his universe, but, by that time, the bones of contention were buried too deep to be exhumed.

"Yeah. They've been all over me, too," he said. "I'm on my way back from the airport. I just put your aunt Rochelle on a plane to Portland. Sent her down to Ed's mother's place until this is over."

"Probably best," I agreed.

"She hasn't been the same since Ed died."

Roughly translated, this meant that I'd know about what was going on with my father's youngest sister if only I kept in better touch with the family, which I don't. *You cur.*

After my father's death, Pat slid noiselessly into the role of family patriarch. He was, after all, the sole living Waterman brother and, as such, the heir apparent to the mantle. For reasons I can't explain, something deep in my heart sorely begrudged him that role. Maybe it was because, in my family, the patriarch is the keeper of the family story. At least the one we tell in public. And Pat never told it the way I remembered it. That's why I stopped going to most of the big family gatherings. I was afraid that right in the middle of some otherwise joyous holiday moment, he was going to start holding forth about some Christmas or Easter past and I was going to lose it, spring to my feet and shout, "That's not it. That's not how it happened," and the whole slack-jawed multitude would gaze at me as if I'd just dropped my pants and crapped in the corner. Better to stay home, I figured.

I dreaded the next act, so I tried something noncommittal.

"Sorry to hear that."

I should have known better. It didn't matter how I responded. I could have said, "I'm on my way to the Polo Grounds to fuck Hitler's mother," and his response would have been exactly the same. With Pat and me, it was as if our conversations crouched behind our lips like predators, silently marking time until the moment of the kill.

"She was terribly upset when she saw the story on the news. She's not strong, you know." *You cur.*

What came next was the part where we worked out who was suffering more. Prizes were awarded in this category. Winner got a crown of thorns, and the right to assume the position; loser got the hair shirt and self-flagellation rights. I figured martyrdom was a dying business, so I cut to the chase.

"What do you need from me?"

Silence. This wasn't how it was supposed to go. *You cur.*

After a moment, he said, "How you guys holding up over there?"

"It's a ffffff . . . it's a state of siege."

I had him going now. He shifted gears.

"We need to get a lid on this."

"I don't think the toothpaste is going back in the tube, Pat."

"No, but we can certainly control the flow."

"How's that?"

"I've got a meeting set up for two o'clock this afternoon at the Cascade Club."

"A meeting with who?"

"Whom," he corrected.

"Yeah, so whom's gonna be there?"

I'm not sure, but I thought I heard him grinding his teeth.

"The PI's going to send their lawyer. I don't know who's coming to represent the Price family . . . probably another lawyer. Most likely Henry McColl."

"And you want *me* to come?"

He hesitated. "I thought you'd want to be there," he said. Roughly translated, this meant that since I'd been sufficiently thoughtless as to find the damn body, I had an obligation to suffer along with the rest of them. *You cur.*

"What are we going to meet about?"

Now I was sure I heard his teeth.

"What we're going to meet about, Leo, is how to keep this thing contained. How to keep the journalism responsible. How to keep this thing from disrupting our lives any more than is absolutely necessary. Of course, if you have no—"

I cut him off. "I'll be there," I said.

He jumped in quickly, before I could hang up. "And Leo . . ."

"Yeah?"

"You will wear a suit, won't you?" *You cur.*

"Fuckin' A," I said.

One second after I replaced the receiver, the phone began to ring. Since the voice mail had done such a fine job last evening, I couldn't think of a single reason why it shouldn't get another chance, so I unplugged the phone and headed for the shower.

On a good day, I can shower, shave and shinola in twenty minutes flat, start to finish, out the door. Today, it was a good thing I had a few hours. I had a bad case of the slows. I stood under the steaming shower until the hot water gave out and then cut myself twice while shaving.

When I padded back into the bedroom looking for clothes, Rebecca was gone and the bed was made. The choice of attire should have been simple. After all, I only owned one good suit. Nope. Turned out the only thing simple was me. I stood in the closet for a good twenty minutes pawing everything I owned and then finally selected—yup, you guessed it—my good suit.

By the time I got downstairs Rebecca had already finished a pot of coffee and read the entire Sunday paper.

"Oooh," she said. "Don't you look nice."

"I better," I said. "You look sloppy at the Cascade Club somebody'll hand you a mop."

"Really . . . the Cascade Club . . . dear me."

For want of an option, I told her about Pat's call and the meeting. What followed was a twenty-minute ceremony, wherein I swore oaths up and down, back and forth, sacred and profane, that I would not lose my head and disgrace myself and that, furthermore, if I should be so foolish as to lose my temper and act in an unseemly manner, the effect of such actions on my future romantic prospects would be tantamount to being shipwrecked on a desert island.

I was still mulling over that cheery prospect when I set the e-brake on the Fiat and hopped out into the driveway of the Cascade Club. The valet looked at the little car with undisguised disdain. I dropped the keys into his palm. "My other car is a piece of shit too," I said.

I'd only been inside once before. Back in college, I'd taken an architecture class and had toured the building. The place may have been made from fire-flashed clinker brick and topped with Dutch gables, but what really constructed the Cascade Club was money. And not new money either. No. In these halls, the only money that counted was hand-me-down money. Money from so far back the family no longer recalled who it was had made the dough in the first place. That kind.

That's how I knew to ask the ancient attendant for the Price party. While many of the Watermans were certainly not strapped for cash, the money was, to the mind of these sort of folks, not only entirely too recent, but, to an even greater extent, scandalously ill-gotten.

She led me down the long central hall of the building, past gold-framed portraits of stern men with chin whiskers, across a couple acres of floral carpet thick enough to pass for U.S. Open rough and then ushered me through the proverbial third door on the right.

A small banquet table had been set up at the back of the room. Gleaming silver urns of coffee and tea, plates of prepared fruit, decadent pastries and hors d'oeuvres, artfully arranged. Just your basic little Sunday morning meeting.

Pat was standing over by the leaded windows, holding a

white china cup in one hand and a saucer in the other, making conversation with a nice-looking young guy in a double-breasted blue blazer. Pat had that pink-all-over, fresh-scrubbed quality of my father's Scandinavian roots. He kept his remaining hair extremely short. He was straight and trim to a degree attainable only by those who have all day to spend at the gym. He placed the cup in the saucer, set them on the windowsill and crossed to my side.

He looked me up and down. "Glad you could make it," he said.

I reckoned how I was likewise thrilled.

"Fabulous suit," he said. "Been letting Rebecca do your shopping for you, haven't you?"

I'd have been less annoyed if it hadn't been true. I looked over his shoulder toward the linen-covered table in the center of the room, where Emily Price Morton sat sipping tea with her attorney H. R. McColl.

"The suit better be good. You neglected to tell me I'd be lunching with the queen."

He compressed his lips. "Quite surprising," he admitted, then took me by the elbow. "Come along," he whispered. "Let's get this show on the road."

As we approached the table, H. R. McColl got to his feet. McColl was the lawyer of choice for those who could pay the freight. Just this side of sixty, he was a tall man. His sharp cheekbones were framed by a shock of thick white hair, shaved nearly bald on the sides, worn in a short Marine brush cut on top—all sharp angles in a gray wool suit.

He extended his hand. "Pat," was all he said.

With a small nod of the head, Pat took his hand.

"Henry. You know Leo, I believe."

His hand now found its way into mine, but he kept talking to Pat.

"Oh, yes. Our paths have crossed before."

McColl let me go and turned toward his client, who sat motionless in an off-white silk suit, her hands in her lap, her wide-spaced blue eyes averted and unblinking. Emily Price

Morton was the better part of seventy, but you had to get up close to see. Her primary care physician was probably a plastic surgeon. Amazing what enough money could do. Sitting there with her ash-blonde hair twisted atop her head in an old-fashioned knot, she could have passed for a cynical fifty. Except for the mouth. Her wide, dissatisfied mouth gave her away. The series of lines rippling out from the corners served as silent testament to the current limits of plastic surgery. If they pulled the rest of her face back any tighter, she'd have been looking out to the sides like a fly.

McColl didn't bother with introductions. We were supposed to know who she was. He spoke to her. "You know Pat, of course."

She rattled her jewelry in assent.

Pat motioned my way. "And my nephew, Leo Waterman."

No rattle. She looked at me like I was wearing a dog shit suit.

The guy in the blue blazer was at my elbow now. He spoke directly to Emily. "Mark Forrester," he said, offering a hand. "I'm here representing the *Post-Intelligencer*."

No rattle. Not even the shit-suit look. I felt better.

Pat took the lead. "I know everyone has a busy schedule, so perhaps . . ." He swept his hands out over the chairs.

He waited for everyone to get settled before he continued.

"I'd like to thank Mrs. Morton for arranging a space for this get-together," he began. "And I want each of you to know I appreciate your taking time from your busy lives to be here with us today."

Emily Price Morton spoke for the first time.

"I arranged the room merely as a courtesy. To be quite frank, I am unable to imagine any profitable purpose to this meeting."

"I had hoped—" Pat began.

She cut him off. "You hoped to sweep this matter under the rug is what you hoped, Mr. Waterman."

Pat stayed calm. "I had hoped . . ." he repeated, ". . . that perhaps we could reach some sort of accord as to how to keep this unfortunate incident from affecting our lives and the lives of our loved ones any more than is absolutely necessary."

McColl jumped in. "What Mrs. Morton means to say . . ."

"Be quiet, Henry," she snapped. She fixed Pat with a granite stare. "Mrs. Morton said exactly what she meant, Mr. Waterman. My family and I intend to see blame properly ascribed and justice administered. We have lived with the pain and uncertainty for nearly thirty years. We intend to see this matter through to its conclusion, no matter what the cost or to whom."

She turned her stony gaze my way. "I hold you no personal animosity, young man," she said. "And I have no wish to foster the sins of the fathers off upon the children, but my family . . ."

My turn to interrupt.

"What sins would those be?"

In my peripheral vision, I could see Pat stiffen and raise himself to his full height along the seat back. "What Leo means to say . . ." he began.

I kept my eyes locked on hers. "Leo said what he meant to say."

She curled a perfectly lined lip at me. "You can't be serious. My brother's remains were found in your father's yard. What other conclusion could possibly be drawn?"

"I seem to recall something about people being innocent until proven guilty. And, with all due respect, Mrs. Morton, I don't recall my father even being charged with anything, much less convicted."

The looks on everyone's faces suggested that they were waiting for lightning to strike me dead. I figured, you know, what the hell, so I jerked a thumb at Mark Forrester who was sitting on my right. "Although I can certainly understand how you might have come to that conclusion if you've been reading that sensationalist piece of fish wrap these guys have the gall to call a newspaper."

The kid was smooth. "The *Post-Intelligencer* has complete

confidence in the veracity of its sources and the quality of its reporting."

"That's because you don't say anything," I said. "You imply; you infer; you stick things that have nothing to do with one another in the same paragraph together and let the readers do the rest."

"I didn't come here to debate the merits of the press, Mr. Waterman." He began to rise.

"Please," Pat entreated. He pressed down on the table with his palms as if it were about to take flight, and then shot a glance over my way. Forrester settled back into his seat. "Leo and I and the rest of the Waterman family want nothing more than a speedy resolution to this unfortunate matter. Like everyone else—"

H. R. McColl cut him off. "I'm not sure Leo is on board with you on that one, Pat."

Pat folded his hands and arched an eyebrow.

"How so?"

"As I understand it, last night, only hours after the discovery of the remains, your nephew refused to cooperate with the authorities."

Being talked about as if I weren't in the room was beginning to chap my hide, but I kept my temper.

"What do I have to cooperate about?" I asked evenly. "I was twelve years old when Peerless Price disappeared. Except for the past few months, I haven't lived in that house for over twenty years. What could I possibly know that would be of use?"

For the first time McColl addressed me directly.

"So you did indeed refuse to cooperate?"

"Big as life," I answered.

TWO COPS, one big, one little, one rumpled, one neat. Naturally, I knew the big rumpled one. Frank Wessels and I went way back. Oh yeah. We'd detested each other for decades. For a while, in the tenth grade, I'd dated his younger sister Jean. He was a big nasty bastard about ten years my senior. One of those throwbacks to the rubber hose days of law enforcement who liked to hurt people. I was pleased to see that the years had treated him badly. Since I'd seen him last, he'd put on thirty pounds and grown a veiny red nose with the texture of a golf ball.

I pulled open the door. Before I could open my mouth, the little neat one stuck a gold badge in my face and started to step over the threshold. I wedged an arm against the doorjamb about chin high and let him run into it. He staggered back two steps and nearly sat down in the geraniums.

"Somebody invite you in?" I asked.

He was about thirty-five, a good-looking little Hispanic guy with a thick head of black hair combed straight back. Just as neat as a pin in a blue silk suit, matching tie and pocket hankie and one of those custom-made shirts with the little rounded collars.

He readjusted his suit and stepped back up to me.

"What are you, blind?" he demanded, shaking the badge in my face. "We're SPD."

"So what," I said. "That doesn't give you the right to come walking into my house without an invitation."

He looked back over his shoulder at Wessels.

"You hear this guy?"

"I hear," Wessels said. "Leo's a laugh a minute."

I looked out over the little guy's head. No way these two guys worked together on a regular basis. I figured they sent Wessels along in case I got hostile with Little Lord Fauntleroy here.

"Hey, Frank. They eliminate the department height requirement or what?"

Wessels kept a straight face. "Affirmative action," he said.

I already knew the answer to the next question, because I ran into her once in a while up at the Coastal Kitchen on Capitol Hill, but I asked him anyway, just to piss him off.

"How's Jean?" I asked.

Wessels shrugged and shuffled his feet. "I don't have

nothin' to do with her anymore. She's a dyke. She and her gap-lapper girlfriend got them a condo up on the hill."

"Hope it wasn't something *I* said?"

He showed me a mouthful of yellow teeth.

"Probably that little tiny dick of yours is what did it."

Rebecca poked her head out from under my arm. "Why, Officer," she said in her best Blanche DuBois drawl. "Surely that must be some other Leo you're referring to. I assure you, sir, this man's appointments are second to none." And you wonder why I love this woman.

It was hard to tell, but I think maybe Wessels blushed.

She grabbed me by the belt and pulled me out of the doorway.

"Won't you gentlemen come in," she said.

Rebecca and I sat on one side of the dining room table. Detective Peter Trujillo removed a pencil and a small spiral-bound notepad from his suit jacket, hung the jacket on the back of a chair and then sat down directly across from us. Wessels lounged in the corner.

Beneath the rim of the table, Rebecca squeezed my knee. Hard. Using her nails. Years of dating the same woman had taught me to interpret a wide range of nonverbal signals. The nails were a dead giveaway. I knew this one. This was, of course, the old "if you start busting this guy's balls and make this take any longer than necessary, I'm going to disembowel you and feed your entrails to feral swine" squeeze. No doubt about it.

Several calls to Jed's answering service had failed to turn him up, so I was on my own. If things kept up the way they'd been going, Rebecca was going to cripple me, so I decided to put an end to the banter.

"I want to make a statement," I said. "And then you can take Wessels here back to the zoo." Nobody moved.

I pointed at the pencil on the table by his elbow.

"You might want to write this down, Sparky," I said. "I'm not going to be fielding questions afterward."

Reluctantly, Trujillo picked up the pencil.

"You ready?" I asked. "I'll try not to use any big words."

I opened my mouth to speak but stopped. An intermittent yellow light pulsed around the room. Wessels noticed too. He bumped himself off the wall, and we walked out through the archway and across the huge living room, with Trujillo and Rebecca in hot pursuit. I opened the front door and stepped out onto the porch. Not one, not two, but three mobile TV units were parked nose to tail out on Crockett Avenue in front of the house. I quickly stepped back over the threshold and slammed the door behind me.

"What in hell is this?" I demanded.

Trujillo grinned and shot his cuffs. "What did you expect? This is the story of the century, Waterman. You're about to have your fifteen minutes of fame. You're lucky *Sixty Minutes* isn't out there. The man who found Peerless Price."

Wessels began humming "The Man Who Shot Liberty Valance."

"We don't even know for sure it's Peerless Price," I countered.

I knew it was dumb the minute I said it, but I was way too pissed off to take it back. "It could be anybody," I added.

Trujillo laughed. "Yeah, it's that other missing dude with the stainless steel hand."

I started for him, but Wessels got between us. I could smell scotch on his breath. I leaned out around him, shouting at Trujillo.

"Did you call those assholes?"

Wessels pushed me out to arm's length and showed me his palms.

"Lighten up, fuckhead," he said. "We didn't call nobody. You better talk to her." He inclined his head toward Rebecca. "You better talk to her boss about that. Anybody called the press, it was him."

"Can we get on with this?" Trujillo whined.

I stepped around Wessels and put my face in his.

"What you can get . . . is the hell out of my house." I walked back into the dining room, retrieved his suit coat from the back of the chair and handed it to him. He draped it over his arm.

"Get out. I've got nothing to say to you. You want to talk to me, you call my attorney Jed James. He'll be back from Paris on the tenth of the month."

I pulled open the front door. Wessels and Trujillo stepped out into the night. Wessels fixed me with a long stare that was supposed to make me soil myself and then headed for the street, but Trujillo couldn't stand it; he just had to have the last word.

"We'll be back," he said.

"Oooh, stop it now, Detective Trujillo; you'll have me in such a tizzy I'll have to sleep with a night-light."

Pat began to wheedle. "I'm sure Leo was under a great deal of strain. I mean it's not every day one makes that sort of grisly discovery in one's own backyard, so to speak." He flicked another look my way. "I'm certain that now that he can see the spirit of goodwill inherent in this meeting, he will be more than happy to cooperate in any way possible."

Suddenly all eyes were on me. I took a deep breath.

"I would be more than willing to cooperate in any investigation that starts out with an open mind."

They all began to speak at once. I raised my voice.

"I will not, however, have anything to do with an investigation which blandly assumes that my father is in any way responsible for the death of Peerless Price."

Emily Morton's throat had begun to redden. "What other conclusion could possibly be drawn?" she demanded. "Considering the history of the two men," she continued, "considering your father's well-documented career as a professional thug . . ."

I held up a hand. "All we know for sure is when your brother disappeared and when he was found. That's it. As far as I'm concerned, everything else is purely speculation."

The four-part choral protesting began anew, so I got louder.

"I will also refuse to cooperate with any investigation

which is either unwilling or unable to respect the privacy of the people involved. This isn't a sound bite or a photo op. This is my life."

Emily Price Morton began a point-by-point recitation of my father's career. Pat began to make excuses. Forrester blabbered about the public's right to know. Things got so bad I wished I was doing yard work.

McColl waited for the din to subside. "I am given to understand that you have already had an altercation with a member of the local media. Is that so?"

"I invited a couple of them to get off of my property."

"I understand that you invited them . . . er . . . rather manually."

"I thought they were thieves. I was defending my property."

Forrester couldn't resist.

"And what was it you imagined they were stealing?"

Neither could I.

"My privacy."

TWO SECONDS after I slammed the door on Wessels and Trujillo, the phone began to ring. I picked it up. She didn't wait for me to speak.

"Leo, it's Bonnie Hart at KOMO. How about we—"

"Bye, Bonnie," I said as I depressed the button.

Bonnie Hart was the afternoon host on KOMO 1000, Talk Radio Seattle. She was a nice gal and damn good at what she did. She'd had me on the show a couple of times. I'd never realized how difficult radio was until I got a chance to see it for myself. Anyone who thinks it's easy to stay spunky while conducting two-hour interviews with amateurs, all the while fielding phone calls from listeners who sound like they're talking with rented lips, ought to try it sometime. Believe me, it's an art. I felt bad about hanging up on her, but not bad enough to take my finger off the button. Didn't matter anyway; the phone began ringing in my hand. I lifted my finger, counted to three and pushed down again. Rebecca stood in the dining room archway.

"I take it we're going incognito," she said.

"Big-time," I said.

I unplugged the phone in my hand and then made my way around in the front of the house, upstairs and down, dropping the Levelors, closing the drapes and unplugging the rest of the telephones. The phones were easy to find. They were all ringing.

When I got back downstairs, Rebecca hadn't moved. "This is going to be a mess," she said. "They're going to hound us."

"I know," I said. "I don't know why but I feel like I ought to apologize."

She shook her head.

"It's me who should apologize, Leo. I'm the one who wanted to live here. I'm the one who insisted. You never wanted any of this."

I walked over and gave her a long hug. I was still holding her when the darkness at the back of the house gave way to a bright white light. She felt me pull back and then read the expression on my face.

"What?" she said.

I took her by the hand, pulling her through the dining room into the kitchen. We stood in front of the sink, looking out into the backyard, where a TV cameraman stood in the middle of the area testing his lights. Closer to the house, on the near side of the old greenhouse, stood some guy with his back to us, a microphone in his hand, adjusting his sport coat and patting at his hair. I dropped her hand and started for the back door, muttering, "Son of a bitch."

"No," she said. "Don't go out that way. If you go out that way you'll walk right into the camera. Go out the side door."

She had a lot more experience ducking newsmen than I did. She was right. I'd end up on the morning news red-faced with steam coming out of my ears, which was pretty much the last thing on earth I wanted. I reversed field and headed back toward the living room and the side door. "Leo," she called after me. I stopped and turned back.

"Stay calm. Okay?" When I didn't answer, she said it again.

"Okay," I said.

"Promise."

I took a deep breath. "I promise to stay calm."

The lights in the street cast long shadows over the south side of the house. I stayed off the walk, instead moving as far to the right as possible, keeping my right shoulder against the hedge. I walked quietly until I was behind the cameraman and then crossed to his side in a hurry. No matter. The way he was squinting into the eyepiece, I could have been driving a bus.

"All right," I said. "This is private property. You're trespassing, both of you. I want you . . ."

The kid flipped on the bank of lights mounted on top of the camera and started to turn my way.

I straight-armed the lens back in the other direction, nearly knocking the camera from his shoulder.

I shook a finger in his face. "You point that goddamn thing at me and you're gonna need a proctologist to get it back."

He hesitated, looking over at the other guy who stood slack-jawed, looking like he was about to swallow the wireless mike.

"Get off my property. Now."

When the kid swung the camera back my way, I reached out with both hands. With one I grabbed the plastic carry strap on top of the camera and jerked it from his shoulder. With the other, I took ahold of his hair, bending his head down by his knees.

He began to scream. "Owww owwww Jesus owwww . . ."

I kept him in that position as I backed him up the walk and out toward the street. The brilliant lights bobbed all over the landscape like there was a prison break as I pulled him along. Rebecca was standing in the side door shaking her head. I pretended I didn't see her.

"Jesus . . . owwwww owwww . . ."

By the time I slung him over the curb by the hair, he was a mezzo-soprano, emitting notes high enough to open garage doors. He rolled over once and came to rest in the sitting position. I got both hands on the camera and made a perfect two-handed basketball pass. It hit him right in the chest, bowling him over backward, driving the wind from his lungs. Even as he lay gasping like a tubercular mule, he never let the camera hit the ground. Good training, I figured.

Mr. Newscaster in the lovely black cashmere blazer was about halfway up the walk, level with Rebecca and heading my way. When I got close he began to babble into the microphone.

"We're here at the home of—"

I reached over and flipped the little black button on the side of the mike and then jerked it from his hand.

"Wait a minute now . . ." he began.

I jammed the microphone down into the pocket of his blazer so hard that four inches of it protruded from the bottom. When he looked down at his jacket in horror, I reached out and grabbed him by the hair. The hair was thick, lustrous and easy to grasp. Unfortunately for him, however, it wasn't connected to his head.

The guy was both smarter and faster than he looked. Before I could decide what to do next, he hotfooted it up the walk and disappeared into the darkness. I turned to Rebecca and smiled.

"Good thing you stayed calm," she said.

I held the toupee out like an offering.

"Look what followed me home. Can we keep it?"

Emily Price Morton dabbed daintily at the corners of her mouth and then pushed herself to her feet. McColl, Forrester and Pat came up out of their seats like they had strings attached, standing now in front of their chairs like good little soldiers awaiting inspection. I stayed put.

She swept her eyes about the room and cleared her throat.

"Gentlemen," she began. "We've been at this for the better

part of an hour to little or no avail. I can see no practical purpose to further discourse. As far as I am concerned, this meeting is concluded."

She saved her final comment for me.

"Young man. On one hand, I find your loyalty to your father and his memory to be quite laudatory. Such old-fashioned notions as loyalty and family are all too often missing in this modern world."

When I nodded my agreement, she continued.

"On the other hand, however, I find your unwillingness to allow the facts to speak for themselves to be quite childish and vain."

"We don't have any facts," I said evenly. "When we do, I'll be sure to let them speak for themselves."

I think that if she'd had a pitcher and a bowl, she'd have washed her hands of me. Instead, she gave me a long stare, more of pity than of disdain, and then rustled off toward the door.

H. R. McColl and Mark Forrester trailed her across the room like a brace of dogs trained to heel. When the door clicked behind them, I turned to Pat. "What in hell is the matter with you?" I asked.

"Me?" He looked incredulous. "What's the matter with me?"

"Yeah. You. What in hell did you think you were doing?"

He stepped in closer. I could smell his breath mints.

"What I was—for your information—trying so desperately to accomplish was to get a handle on this thing. If you'd kept your big mouth shut . . ."

"If I'd shut up and let you handle it, you'd have copped a goddamn plea."

We were nose-to-nose now. He spread his arms.

"What did you expect? Your father's . . . my brother's worst enemy is found buried in his backyard with a bullet in his head . . ."

"I expect you to be defending my father . . . your brother, that's what I expect. Period. End of discussion."

"On what grounds? For pity's sake . . . what do you imagine I might claim? Coincidence? Syncronicity? Divine intervention? What sort of rationale did you have in mind, Leo?"

"You claim whatever it takes, man. You do whatever you have to do. You make sure a bunch of strangers don't get away with pissing on your brother's grave."

"Grow up, Leo. This isn't never-never land. We're never going to know what your father did or didn't do. That's the past. This thing is here and now and it's going to be played out on the field of public opinion. It's bad enough that you've been plastered all over the front page with this Brennan thing."

"What's bad about that?" I demanded.

He made his disgusted face. The one where it looks like sheep dip has just been passed beneath his nose.

"The press," he scoffed.

"I see your picture in the society pages about twice a week; you don't seem to have any objection to that."

"I don't suppose it's occurred to you that Brennan and your father used to do quite a bit of business with each other. Brennan knows where the bodies are buried, Leo. Lots of them. What if he reads the papers and decides he can trade a little inside information on your father's dealings for a plea bargain? What then?"

"He's a convicted murderer, Pat. His testimony and a buck will get you on the bus."

"Whatever lies he tells will still be on the front page."

"So what?"

He took several measured breaths.

"We have to appear reasonable. Possibly even contrite. If we do that, this thing will fade. Something else will catch the public fancy. Unreasonable denials will merely add fuel to the fire."

"Who says denials are unreasonable?"

"Denial merely prolongs the agony."

I poked him solidly in the chest with my index finger.

"Maybe you're willing to give him up as guilty, but I'm

not." I had a terrific urge to poke him again but instead lowered my voice. "You make one public statement that even sounds like you think he's guilty and Emily Morton and that shithouse newspaper and your precious social position will be the least of your fucking worries. I'll completely redefine agony for you, you little prick. If you don't feel like you can bring yourself to come to your brother's defense, then just shut the fuck up. You hear what I'm saying here, Pat?"

He took a short step backward and put his hands on his hips.

"Are you threatening me?"

"You bet your ass," I said.

He sneered. "Like father, like son."

7

I SUPPOSE THAT IF YOU WANTED TO BE A FANATIC ABOUT IT, YOU could maybe say I lied. But just maybe. And only a little. Technically speaking, I *had* kept my act together during the meeting. I hadn't yelled at anybody. I hadn't cursed or threatened. What happened with Pat afterward . . . well . . . the way I saw it . . . that was sorta like a whole different meeting altogether. Something more akin to private therapy than public theater. You know what I mean. Anyway, that's what I'd settled on for my story, and I was sticking to it.

Rebecca, possessed of that nurturing instinct found only among the fairest of the fairer sex, knew precisely what to say next.

"Pat's probably right," she offered. "Mucking around in this thing will just stir it up."

As far as I was concerned, the only thing Pat was right about was how I was more like my old man than I generally liked to admit. Mood I was in, though, I wasn't about to admit to that either.

"Et tu, Duvall?" I said in mock despair. "How sharp as the serpent's tooth the ungrateful significant other."

She brought her hand to her bosom and narrowed her eyes.

"Oh, Gomez . . . you know what poetry does to me . . ."

"It's not funny," I protested.

"Listen to yourself. Mr. Irrepressible telling me something's not funny." She walked over and threw an arm around my waist, drawing me tight against her. "Besides that, big fella . . ." She rubbed her breasts against me. ". . . who says I was kidding." She nuzzled her face into my neck and began kissing me.

"I'll give you a half an hour to stop that," I said.

When she redoubled her efforts, I gently pulled away.

The fact that I could practically hear my blood redistributing itself merely served to heighten my sense of gloom. Lately, the smug assurance of women as to the predictability of my reactions gives me the occasional urge to demur, as, if nothing else, a symbolic means of reclaiming some long-lost territory of my soul. At least, that's what I tell myself. Truth be told, however, despite my best intentions, even the slightest physical entreatment, real or imagined, sets into motion within me an urging engine, which drags my best intentions along in its wake like a rusted chain of burned-out cars. I used to beat myself up about it, but have come to see it as inevitable and merely an accident of the blood.

"Sorry," I said. "I guess I'm a little off my feed."

She leaned over and kissed me on the cheek.

"Can't say as I blame you. This is pretty rough."

I did the manly thing. I changed the subject.

"Have you seen the keys to the attic?"

"What's in the attic?"

"I was going to see if I could find my father's daybooks from about the time Peerless Price disappeared."

For much of his public life, the old man had weathered a veritable hail of independent investigations, fact findings, closed-door hearings and internal audits, all instigated by Peerless Price. The barrage of litigation had forced my father to document his each and every move. Every hour of his professional life, every reimbursable expense, every mile of official business driven by the city vehicle in his possession. All of it. My father kept track of this torrent of minutia in a series of small blue notebooks which were, when I look back at it now, the precursor to the day planner. He filled up three or four a year, marked the dates of their inclusion on the spine and then filed them chronologically, in preparation for the next audit. He called them his daybooks and never left home without one in his pocket.

I could tell from Rebecca's expression that she wanted to say something but was holding back.

"What?"

She jammed her hands into her pants pockets and shook her head.

"You think I'm being stupid, huh?"

"I think it's a thirty-year-old case," she sighed. "I think high-profile cases like this are like quicksand. The more you wiggle around in them, the faster you sink."

My turn to sigh.

"As you already so kindly pointed out, that was more or less Pat's point of view."

She shrugged. "Sorry," she said.

"I've got to do something."

"I know."

"I mean, it's not like I expect to find some little notation . . . you know . . . like . . . July third, nineteen sixty-nine, ten-thrity P.M., *kill Peerless Price*, or something like that. I just thought maybe I'd look and see what my father was doing and then maybe check with the paper and see what Peerless Price was working on and you know . . . see if . . ." I let it go.

"There's a big ring of those old skeleton keys in the front part of the drawer with the silverware. It's probably one of those."

When I didn't move, she stepped over and took me by the hand.

"Come on," she said. "I'll show you."

WHAT I REMEMBER *most about my parents' house was the silence. How, in every room, from floor to ceiling, for as long as I could remember, the butt ends of whatever they had to say to each other but couldn't bring themselves to utter had floated about like airborne dust. Even as a young boy, I had come to realize that something within that silent space had swallowed their love and ripped them asunder. Why? Who knows? I guess the answer depends on whether you're more inclined to believe in miracles or in mistakes.*

I stood at the bottom of the fold-down stairs, looking up into the semidarkness, brandishing a black rubber flashlight like a scepter.

"You wanna come up?" I asked.

"You want me to?"

"No," I said. "I know where they are. Shouldn't take long."

"You sure?"

I didn't like the expression on her face.

"What? You think I'm afraid of the dark?"

"I didn't say that."

I lifted one foot and placed it carefully on the first tread.

"I'll be right back," I said with a bit more bravado than I felt. I began to climb. I climbed fast and without looking back, putting one foot above the other, until I stood on the rough board floor at the head of the stairs. I turned and pointed the thin yellow beam back toward the square of light at my feet, and then I realized I'd been holding my breath. I took in some new air and looked around.

On my left, two small triangular windows flanked the chimney, throwing wide shafts of light out on the far end of the room. Behind me, the three gables of the front facade divided the remaining interior into alternating patches of dark and light. I switched off the flashlight.

I saw what I was looking for. The four brown file cabinets into which my father's life had been squeezed were huddled together down by the chimney. As I looked down the length of the room, it struck me that some unknown force in the attic had divided my parents' afterlives along precisely the same lines which they themselves had chosen to divide things during their tenure on earth.

On the left was the guy stuff. The folding Ping-Pong table. The croquet set and volleyball net. The bent basketball hoop that used to grace the front of the garage. And of course, all the boxes upon boxes of Christmas ornaments and lights, which, every holiday season, he and I had struggled to hang from every eave and bough on the property. When I was young, it was my father hanging from the ladder and crawling across the roof. My lot was merely to fetch and tote. Later, I did the high-wire part of the act, while he stood on the ground, smoking cigars and waving his long arms. Later still, in the years after she died, he hired it out, and we stood together on the frozen grass, shoulder to shoulder, drinking whiskey and stamping our feet while the workmen wrapped the place in Yuletide cheer.

On the right, a wide-hipped mannequin lorded over the wretched refuse like an indoor scarecrow. They'd removed the round mirror from her walnut dresser and pushed it back up under the eaves. The antique wicker baby carriage—she always called it a perambulator—sat atop a pile of old windows, next to an ornate wooden birdcage big enough for a California condor. We'd always had the cage. Never had a bird. But always had the cage.

My nose felt thick with dust. I started down the length of the room. As I passed the carriage, I glanced down into its interior. Lying there on the cracked little mattress was a child's toy. A brown and white monkey twisted and sewn from several pairs of socks, winking with a missing eye, its wide red lips puckered for a kiss. When I picked him up, the little bell on the top of his hat tinkled and instantly, I knew he was mine. Mikey the Monkey accompanied me down to the file cabinets. He wasn't much of a talker, but it beat hell out of going alone.

MY FEAR OF the darkness began to subside with the realization that the world outside my family's walls was, often as not, unlike anything I had known. That in other houses shouts and footsteps regularly rang through the halls, and windows were for something

*other than blinding with blinds and draping with drapes. Still later,
I came to see that the darkness always traveled with me and knew
that deep inside I had a keep, a flickering tunnel where absolutely
no one else was welcome. Not a dungeon—but a root cellar where
the refuse of my heart could be safely shielded from prying eyes and
pointing fingers, a place where everyone agreed that my inability to
conjure the faces of my doomsters merely made the threat more dire.*

Rebecca stifled a yawn with one hand and rubbed the back
of my neck with the other. "I'm going to bed," she said.

"What time is it?"

"Ten-forty." She yawned again. "I've got an early day tomorrow. Staff meeting."

I turned the little blue book over so I wouldn't lose my
place and stretched my arms up and back, pulling her
toward me.

"I'll be up in a while," I said. "Just want to finish going
through this one again."

I'd brought down the three books which covered nineteen
sixty-nine and left Mikey the Monkey to guard their place in
the file. Fourth of July weekend was near the end of the
middle book. I was making my third pass through that particular volume. Each successive pass brought further spasms of
lucidity, wherein I would suddenly understand what had up
until that point seemed nothing more than alphanumeric gib-
berish, so then I'd have to go back and read everything again.

She patted me on top of the head.

"You must be tired. You've been at it all day."

"It took me a long while to figure out his shorthand."

"Find anything?"

"Nothing I'd write home about."

She leaned over my shoulder. "What are the big numbers
at the bottom of each page?" It read: *15,789.*

"Mileage on the city car. The city only paid for mileage
when my father was actually in the car. He paid for Bermuda's mileage out of his own pocket. From the time Bermuda

left him off at night, to the time he picked him up again in the morning, those were personal miles."

For nearly twenty years, Ed "Bermuda" Schwartz had been my old man's personal driver and confidant. His promising career in the SPD had ended one night during a high-speed chase through the Rainier Valley, when Bermuda's police cruiser T-boned a garbage truck, killing his partner instantly and leaving the young officer Schwartz with a broken back and one mangled leg four inches shorter than the other.

Despite its tragic overtones, the situation had a couple of things going for it. First off, right about that time, one of my old man's many real estate scams had incurred the wrath of a couple of old-time land barons. The way they told the story, he'd used his official clout to lose some of their paperwork and then had appropriated their recently refurbished eight-story building on Third Avenue for little more than the price of back taxes. A ploy which, interestingly enough, turned out to be precisely how they'd gotten hold of the building in the first place. These were the kind of guys who were used to paying off politicians, not getting fleeced by them, so needless to say, they were miffed. So miffed, in fact, that they let it be known on the street that were my old man to appear suddenly before the headlights of the wrong automobile some dark and lonely night, he might well turn up late for supper.

Secondly, and of equal importance, Officer Ed Schwartz was, at that time, the SPD's sole and token Jew. Not only that but Schwartz didn't want to go on disability. He wanted to stay on the force. At a desk if he had to, but on the force. As any cop will tell you, you can't have a uniformed officer pushing a walker around the squad room. It's bad for morale. It's hard enough to put on the badge and go out every day, knowing that any routine traffic stop could well be your last act, without having to look at it every morning.

It was one of those sweet deals that politicians so love. The kind that works out all around. The police department got to look benevolent. Bermuda got to stay on active duty and work toward his pension; the city got to make good on its racial and ethnic guidelines and, most importantly perhaps, my old man got a full-time gofer with a gun. A fearful symmetry indeed.

I turned the page. "See . . . top of the next page. Car mileage first thing in the morning." *15,805.*

"Sixteen miles," she said.

"Right. Wherever Bermuda lived back then, it was sixteen miles round-trip from right here." I tapped the table and began to flip through the pages. "Every night, the same thing. He'd drop the old man off, drive home and then come back in the morning to get him."

I pointed down onto the page. "See . . . *B-CAR, seven forty-five p.m. 16,432.*" I turned the page. *"CAR Official seven fifty-five a.m. 16,449."*

"What's B-CAR?"

"It means Bermuda had the car for the night."

"Which he did every night."

"Mostly," I hedged. "That's the only inconsistency I can see. Other than that these guys were like clockwork."

"What's that?"

I checked the notepad at my elbow. "There may be more, but so far, between the middle of May nineteen sixty-nine and the end of June of the same year, just prior to when Peerless Price disappeared, there are two occasions when my father took the city car home for the night."

"So?"

"Those are the only times, during the whole year, when that happened. Twice during that six-week period."

"So?"

"He had a car at home."

"Maybe it was in the shop."

"For six weeks?"

I thumbed ahead in the book. *CAR-ME Per.* "And look, both times he takes the car, he gives Bermuda fifty bucks in personal money. Probably for cab fare home and then back in the morning." *B-$50 per.*

"So?"

"It's just odd, that's all. Picture it. They're downtown somewhere." I flipped the page and pointed at the next day's mileage. Only a five-mile difference. Wherever my father had gone, it was somewhere downtown. I flipped back. *11:15 p.m.* "It's the end of the day. He hands Bermuda, who, by the way, walks with two canes, fifty bucks and tells him to take a cab home. I mean . . . why would he do that?"

She thought it over. "Sounds like he had something to do that he didn't want Mr. Schwartz to know about."

"That's exactly what got my attention. I mean what could he possibly be doing that he didn't want Bermuda to know about? They'd been together for years. Bermuda knew where all the bodies were buried." I stopped myself. "Figuratively speaking, of course."

"Why don't you ask Mr. Schwartz?"

"I don't even know if he's still alive," I said.

"How old would he be?"

"I'm not sure. Maybe seventy-five, eighty or so."

I rolled the chair backward toward the counter and pulled the phone book out of the bread drawer. She watched with a wry grin.

"The amazing tricks you gumshoes know."

I ignored the jibe. Ninety-eight out of every hundred people are listed in the phone book. Way back when, I'd once looked for a guy for a day and a half before a brainstorm sent me to the white pages.

No Edward Albert Schwartz. No E Schwartz of any kind. I lobbed the book back into the drawer and rolled it closed with my foot.

"It's like Sherlock said. First you eliminate the obvious; then you get weird from there."

"Those were his exact words?"

"More or less."

"Did Mr. Schwartz have a family? A wife? Kiddies?"

"I don't know," I said.

She started for the door. "Well, Sherlock, I'll be upstairs whenever you get through sleuthing."

I closed my eyes, listening to the sound of her footsteps on the stairs and wondering how I could recall so little about the life of a man who knew so much about mine. Other than tooling around in the city car with my father, Bermuda's main task had been toting me around. I mean, my mother didn't drive—hell, for the most part, she didn't even go out—and it wasn't like either of them was going to sit through Little League baseball games or anything. Fat chance. But I always knew that before the game was over, Bermuda would show up to get me, in that long black car. Rain or shine, he'd always try to make as much of the game as he could. No matter where I was on the field, I'd hear him clanking up into the stands with those aluminum canes of his, wearing that same black suit with the jacket buttoned. Always in the front row, sitting like a rock, right next to the over-involved, maniac parents, because that was as high as he could climb. I remembered how he never had a word or an opinion about anything unless you asked him directly, and then he had words and opinions about everything, because he cover-to-covered three newspapers a day, and did all the crossword puzzles while he was sitting on his duff waiting for my old man. Half the useless crap running around in my head, I'd learned from Bermuda Schwartz, and all I could recall was his satchel face, his big red hands and the silly name everybody called him. Go figure.

8

In a pulp novel, an erstwhile local private dick like me, faced with finding an old ex-cop, would simply call his cynical, weather-beaten buddy on the police force. He'd have the buddy see if the pension check was still going out, and, if so, where to. Wham bam thank you ma'am. Problem was, I didn't have a buddy on the police force. Quite the contrary. As a matter of fact, it was generally agreed that one of the quickest and surest paths to a lifetime of obscurity on the Seattle Police Department was to have anything to do with me. That's because my ex-wife Annette was now working her marital magic on a certain Seattle police captain named Henry Monroe. He'd started out cheerful enough. Henry the Magnanimous, always greeting me loudly and clapping me on the back, in the assured manner of a man who feels certain he's grabbed the brass ring. Not for long, though. No . . . a couple of years of connubial bliss and, without so much as a word, he'd started having me removed from the Public Safety Building whenever he saw me in the halls. Couldn't say as I blamed him either. I figured it was one of those unfortunate "Friends don't let friends . . ." kind of things. Love may be blind, but marriage is a real eye-opener.

I'd met Claire Wells right after my divorce, when well-meaning friends had fixed us up on a blind date. She'd recently separated from some guy named Joe. Yeah, I knew better, but in those days my urges usually got the upper hand, so to speak. I'd taken her to Ristorante Isabella, an atmospheric Italian joint on Third Avenue. You know, a little wine, a little pasta, a couple of choruses of "Volare." *Whoa oh.* You never know. It could happen.

Not this time though. Hell, we never even made it through the salad. Half a glass of wine and twenty minutes of inane conversation later, she looked out over the rim of a nice glass of Estancia Chardonnay, narrowed her slate-gray eyes and popped the question.

"Are you having a good time?"

Usually, answering a question such as this is easy, because, unless you're a barbarian, your options are limited. As I see it, you either pass the buck with a question of your own such as "Are you?" A pathetic, shopworn ruse lacking in both style and originality. Or you try to change the subject to something . . . anything less threatening than your own feelings. "How's the wine?" for instance. The problem with this sort of random segue is that, à la Groucho Marx, anybody who'd fall for it wouldn't be somebody with whom you'd want to be sharing a meal. So you're pretty much left doing what everybody does in a moment like that, you tell 'em what it is you think they want to hear. "Oh, yeah. Real good." It's like après sex. I mean, what the hell are you going to tell somebody you've just been doing the hokey pokey with when they look over and give you some variation of the old "It was good for me; was it good for you?" I mean, it's not like you can yawn into the back of your hand and reckon how, all in all, you'd rather have been pulling weeds in the front yard. No sir. You can't even sidestep the issue with something like "I especially liked the part where you moved." No . . . no. Unless you want to be short-listed for the Goth of the Month Award, you come up with something life-affirming. Period. No matter what anybody says, some situations do not cry out for candor.

That's why the words that escaped my lips so startled me. "Not a bit," I said.

Claire Wells smiled. "So . . . it's not just me," she began. "I was afraid that maybe I wasn't ready for something like this. That maybe it was just too soon for me." She took another sip. "But it's not that, is it? We don't agree on anything, do we?"

I figured in for a penny, in for a pound, so I spoke up.

"Near as I can tell, you and I couldn't agree on so much as the weather or the time of day."

She drew a hand to her throat, closed her eyes and took several deep breaths.

"I feel so much better."

"Me too," I offered. "Can we go home now?"

"You mean like separately?"

I gave the Scout's honor sign.

"Absolutely."

"In a minute." She forked in half the salad and then washed it down with a healthy slurp of wine. When she finished swallowing, she said, "You know . . . if you're going to make a go at this dating thing, Leo, you're going to have to get rid of those bleeding-heart, man-of-the-people politics of yours. There's no future in that. Women hear that stuff, they start picturing life in a mobile home."

A strong man, an assertive man, a man in complete charge of his faculties would have smiled knowingly and said nothing. At least that's what I figure. If I ever meet one, I'll ask him.

"Oh, yeah? Well, what about your elitist, spoiled-little-rich-girl, fresh-out-of-journalism-school politics? Nobody with a brain bigger than a lima bean or a heart bigger than a gnat will listen to that 'them and us' crap for a minute."

She chewed and swallowed the last of the salad and then began to wave her fork in my general direction.

"And that corny, cynical private-eye stuff."

"Ohhhhh so insensitive . . ." I scoffed. ". . . and thus doubly offensive to an assertive, fork-waving woman such as yourself."

She grinned madly and nodded.

"Exactly."

We both burst out laughing. She had a piece of lettuce on her front tooth. I raised my glass. "To us," I toasted. We downed our wine. We hadn't yet ordered entrees, so I threw forty bucks on the table, rescued her coat from the coatroom and drove her directly home. No kisses. No hugs. Just enough of a smile to assure the lettuce was still locked in place and an awkward handshake. An odd night to be sure, but, if nothing else, it cured me of blind dates, once and for all.

Interestingly enough, over the next ten years, fate and those same mutual friends kept throwing Claire Wells and me back together. We kept running into one another at Christmas parties, political fund-raisers and summer birthday bashes. She was working her way up the corporate ladder with the *Post-Intelligencer*. For a while, she'd tried her hand at newswriting, but had eventually decided she was more interested in telling people what to do, so she went into financial administration. I was scratching out a living serving legal papers. Dashin' for cash, we used to call it. Maybe it was because neither of us was having much luck with our dating lives, but, after that, whenever we found ourselves in the same room, we'd invariably gravitate toward some empty corner where we'd gossip about our partners of old and our companions du jour, and eventually we'd get around to reliving that strange night long ago, and then we'd again attempt to unravel the knot of how that aborted evening had, in some peculiar way, cemented a lasting bond between us.

That's how I knew that if I showed up on Monday morning, down at the security desk at the *Post-Intelligencer*, she'd come down and rescue me. Friends don't leave friends at the security desk. I told the guard my name was Randy Metzger and asked him to inform Claire Wells that I was in the lobby.

I was hiding in a copy of *Outdoor Life*, learning to hunt mule deer from a tree stand, when I heard her heels on the floor. There was no mistaking the sound. Claire Wells was the fastest walker in the world. Even handicapped by a pair of four-inch heels and a tight red skirt, she'd leave all those wiggly-ass Olympic-style walkers in the dust.

She clicked to a halt, about a foot from my shins. She was a slender woman of about forty, five-eight or so, wearing a black silk blouse and shoes to match the skirt. Her thick brown hair was shorter and not quite the shade I remembered, but she had those same gray eyes. She tapped the toe of one red shoe and then spoke, barely moving her lips.

"The name thing. Was that supposed to be funny?"

"I couldn't very well give him my own name, could I?"

She paced around in a small circle, her hands on her hips. "Make my day, Leo. Tell me you're here to give the paper an exclusive on this Peerless Price thing."

I shrugged. "You wouldn't want me to start lying to you now, would you, Claire? Not after all these years."

She raised her voice. "The hat and the glasses are supposed to make you invisible, is that it?"

"Shhh. I'm undercover."

She smirked. "What makes you think I'm going to let you stay that way? Huh? You can run out of here with your coat over your head and we'll still be miles ahead of the competition."

"You wouldn't do that."

"Why not? You're the hottest story in town. Right now, you're the only story in town."

" 'Cause, first off, you're not that kind of girl."

She opened her mouth, but I cut her off.

"Besides which, you're a bean counter, not a newshound."

"So what? Regardless of my function, I work for a newspaper. What do you suppose my bosses would think if they knew you were here, and I didn't tell anyone?"

I ignored the question, instead taking the offensive.

"Besides that, you owe me."

"For what?" she demanded.

I tried to look hurt. "How quickly they forget." She wasn't giving an inch. "Howsabout the aforementioned Randy Metzger?"

She winced. "I can't believe you'd stoop so low."

"If I recall correctly, my dear Claire, it was you who was about to do the stooping."

About five years ago, Claire had gotten engaged to a guy named Randy Metzger. Good-looking blond guy about her age from Mukiteo. Some sort of high-priced software engineer for Boeing. At least that's what he claimed. I ran into the happy couple coming out of the Metropolitan Grill one Friday night, and, even though we spent no more than five minutes trading banalities on the sidewalk, something about the guy bothered me. In my business, I get lied to a lot. Lies have a certain rhythm of their own, as if in some odd way they slip out from between the lips more easily than the truth. Two minutes into the conversation, Randy Metzger had my bull-shit meter reading maximum, but, at a time like that, what was I going to say? "Nice to see you again, Claire. Boy, is this guy you're going to marry next month full of shit." Naaah. I don't think so.

A couple of weeks later, I was up at Boeing's manufacturing facility in Everett trying to run down a former avionics engineer who'd skipped on a thirty-thousand-dollar bond. After I came up empty on the bail jumper, something clicked somewhere in my mind, and I asked my source to run the name Randy Metzger through her computer. Came up—not currently employed by the Boeing Company. Do not rehire. Not only that, but, a couple of years hence, when he *had* briefly been employed, it was in the capacity of an apprentice airframe mechanic, not a code writer. Not only that, but gosh and b'golly, my inquiry on Randy Metzger was not the first. No, Mr. Metzger was also currently being sought by authorities in Sandpoint, Idaho, where he still had a wife whom he had severely battered and three children whom he was accused of having sexually molested.

I'd mulled the news over for a couple of days and then called Claire. Like I figured, her first instinct was to shoot the messenger. She went postal on me, calling me a no-good busybody motherfucker, saying I was jealous of her happiness and all that. As I recall, she also questioned the fiber of my morality, the validity of my parentage and the quality of my tumescence before finally hanging up in my ear.

A couple of weeks later, she'd called me and come as close to saying thanks as she was able. She'd made a few calls, found out I was right and then turned Randy in to the Washington State Police, who'd promptly extradited his butt back to Idaho. Funny though, when she got through telling me of the lame excuses she'd been forced to make to her family and how embarrassed she was about the whole thing, she'd hung up in my ear all over again. Dude.

She swiveled her neck, taking in the lobby, and then flipped the magazine over. "Oh . . . nice . . . *Outdoor Life*. Goes with the disguise."

"I need your help."

She put her hands on her hips. "Oh, stop it. I hate it when you give me that puppy-dog look. It may have worked on your mother, but it doesn't work on me."

"It didn't work on her either," I confessed.

Again, she peered furtively around the crowded lobby. "I can't take you to my office without a badge, and I can't get you a badge without ID," she muttered.

I shrugged.

"Come over here," she said, motioning to the hall which led to the public restrooms. "Before somebody sees you."

I jogged along behind as she clicked across the lobby and down the uncarpeted hall. She led me down to the end, past the restroom doors, to a small bench with a black plastic cushion. I sat.

"What do you want?"

"Peerless Price . . ." I began.

"The cops took it all this morning. They had a court order for all of it."

"All what?"

"Said the case had been officially reopened. Backed a truck right up to the shipping dock and loaded the stuff in. Boom. They're gone."

"What stuff?"

"The whole Peerless Price archive. The whole kit."

"What archive?"

"We kept all his stuff together down in the basement, instead of putting it on microfilm. That way, every time somebody wanted a copy, we didn't have to go looking for it."

I must have looked baffled.

"We get asked for Peerless Price material all the time, Leo. Almost daily. Counting for labor and materials, we spent nine thousand dollars last year sending out Peerless Price information to other news agencies. Nine thousand dollars. He's the Jimmy Hoffa of the Northwest. Heck, we've even got a standard press kit we send out as bulk mail."

A short East Indian woman came down the hall toward us, the rubber soles of her shoes squeaking with every step. She wore a shiny silver blouse outside a pair of black stretch pants.

Claire looked back over her shoulder. "Hello, Bharti," she said.

The woman's black eyes moved back and forth between us.

"Hi, Claire. How are you doing?"

"Fine."

She straight-armed the door to the women's room and disappeared inside. The door eased shut.

"Does it have his last columns?" I asked.

"The last month or so. It's got a bio and family background. You know, all the standard crap."

"Can I have one?"

She was skeptical. "That's it?"

"No. I need something else." I hesitated. "And I need it to be just between us."

"You mean like . . ."

I didn't let her finish.

"Kind of like Randy Metzger. That kind of just between us."

Suddenly the air between us grew thicker.

"Are you threatening me, Leo? Are you suggesting . . ."

I wasn't sure whether she meant it, or whether she was pulling an end run on me, so I interrupted.

"No," I said quickly. "You misunderstood me, Claire. What's between us is between us and always will be. Anything else would be a breach of trust. I'm just calling in my marker is all."

Her eyes searched my face and came up empty.

"It's a guy thing," I added. "Accountability."

The door to the women's room hissed open. The roaring of a hand dryer arrived in the corridor before Bharti, who stepped out, gave each of us a quizzical smile and then squeaked her way back up the hall. Claire waited until the woman was out of sight.

"I'm sorry. I don't know what made me say that. That was a rotten thing to say."

"Yeah. It was."

"I haven't heard that name in a long time. When the guard called . . ." She stopped herself. "What do you need?"

I pulled a yellow piece of paper from the pocket of my jacket and handed it to her. "I need you to check with circulation. I need an address for this guy."

"Edward Albert Schwartz," she read. "Who's he?"

I shook my head.

"What makes you think this guy reads the paper?"

"If he's still alive and living around here, he gets the paper."

Claire folded the yellow paper twice and slipped it between her fingers. She heaved a sigh.

"Where are you parked?"

"In front. Out on Elliott."

"You still drive that little green . . ." She searched for a word.

"Yeah."

"I'll meet you out there," she said.

When she'd clicked off, I ambled back through the lobby and out into the parking lot. I didn't need a weatherman. It was as dark as dusk. To the east, steel clouds cut off the tops of the hills on the far side of Western Avenue. To the west, out over the water, a blanket of gray had swallowed the mountains whole. The front of the storm was over Bainbridge Island and running hard this way, its diaphanous curtains of rain sweeping and weaving before it like ghostly dancers.

Ten minutes later, the storm had rolled halfway across the sound and was bearing down on the city like a locomotive. Claire Wells came clicking out the side door and across the street at about fifteen miles an hour. In her left hand, she held a spiral-bound booklet with a clear plastic cover. When she got close, I reached for the booklet, but she quickly pulled it back.

"Did you really pull Stone Sanders's wig off?"

"What kind of name is that anyway? Stone."

"What's wrong with Stone? We had a Rock."

"Hell, we had a Pebbles and a Bamm Bamm. But Stone? Jesus."

"And Cliff," she added. "Don't forget Cliff."

I reckoned how I should have known better than to start with her.

She kept the papers out of reach. "Did you?"

I nodded. "I left it with the security guard over at KTZZ before I came over here this morning."

She smirked and handed me the booklet. "I wrote Mr. Schwartz's address on the first page," she said. "Weekdays, he gets three papers. Two on Sunday. You were right."

"Thanks," I said.

The damp breeze shimmied through her black blouse. She hugged herself and looked out over the sound, where the surface of the black water roiled like braided serpents. She brushed her hair from her face. "What do you want out of this, Leo?"

I thought it over. "I think I'm pretty much trying not to think about that," I said finally.

"Not knowing what you want is very dangerous."

I allowed how I was aware of that fact.

"I hope you're not looking to prove your father's innocence or something really stupid like that."

"Funny, I kinda figured he was innocent. I had this weird idea that was how the system worked."

She gave me the fish-eye. "You don't really believe that, do you?"

When I didn't answer, she turned her face to the wind. A volley of huge raindrops spattered about us, slapping down onto hoods and windshields. She held out her hand as if to catch one.

"Back then, when we used to run into each other a lot, you know . . . those were the unhappiest days of my life."

"Gee, thanks."

She laughed. "That disaster with Randy. I mean . . . that was the last straw. Something about that whole mess . . . something finally told me I was trying way too hard. Gave me my first real look at what a desperate creature I was." She massaged the back of her neck. "There didn't seem to be anything to do but back up and get straight with myself."

As I waited, the rain stopped splattering and the wind suddenly died. Like I figured, she wasn't through.

"I was unhappy because I didn't know what I wanted. I thought I wanted . . ." She used her fingers to etch quotation marks in the air. ". . . a relationship, you know . . . like everybody else wanted, and it used to drive me crazy thinking that there was something wrong with me. Like I was the most relationship-challenged person on the planet. It was like, no matter how good things started out, after I slept with a guy about five times, I was always looking at my watch, wishing he'd go home."

"So what did you do?"

"I finally figured out that a . . ." Quotation marks again. ". . . relationship was what my mother wanted and what my aunts wanted and my sisters. I'd just sort of inherited the idea. What *I* actually wanted was a whole lot easier to find than a relationship." She bapped herself in the side of the head with her fingertips. "Turns out I just like to get laid on a regular basis."

She read the expression on my face.

"So shoot me. I mean, it's not like I'm an uncaring person or anything. I like me. You like me. Lots of people like me. I'm just not emotionally equipped to actually live with anybody."

"So?"

"So, now I'm happy as a clam, Leo. I keep a steady stream of hard-bodied twenty-somethings running in and out of my life." She dug me in the ribs and winked. "If you'll permit me the unmixed metaphor. No bullshit, no promises, no over-nighters, just a healthy little poke in the whiskers and hit the road, Jack."

Something deep within me, something middle-aged, was offended. I could tell, because I said something incredibly stupid.

"I'll bet they're dazzling conversationalists."

She chuckled and bopped me on the shoulder. "We don't talk much, Leo. We just get naked and *do* all night long what it takes guys your age all night long to *do*. Now get the hell out of here before I change my mind and sic the newsdogs on you."

9

I HEADED UP ELLIOT, GOT LUCKY AT THE LIGHT ON THE CORNER of Western Avenue and turned left, rolling north past a ramshackle collection of old lumberyards, plumbing wholesalers and machine shops that littered the length of the narrow valley between Queen Anne Hill and the Magnolia Bluffs.

My luck held as I drove toward Ballard. I made the lights all the way past the Magnolia Bridge, getting nearly to Fisherman's Terminal before the sky unloaded. Within a minute, the little split in the convertible top that I'd been promising myself I'd fix was channeling a steady trickle of water into the hollow of the passenger seat. A sudden gust of wind moved the car a half a lane to the right. Quickly, I checked the mirror. Couldn't see a thing. Gritting my teeth, I eased the Fiat all the way into the right lane and slowed to thirty.

I was leaning forward out over the steering wheel, peering through the intermittent little fans scraped clear by the wipers. Outside, trees thrashed about in the gale, and the air was filled with debris and the last leaves of fall, torn loose now and riding on the back of the fifty-mile-an-hour breeze. I kept both hands on the wheel.

The little car buzzed and wobbled on the metal grating as I crossed the Ballard Bridge. On either side of the roadway, a tangled maze of boat rigging and antennas trembled gray and gaunt like a drowned forest. I used my sleeve to clear the windshield, put on my signal, said a silent prayer and moved one lane to the left.

The traffic light at the corner of Western and Northwest Market swung in the wind like a lantern as the rain fell in volleys, line after silver line blowing in from the west. All around me, the rush of traffic created a moving shroud of mist, which slid along above the sodden street, reducing visibility to dim taillights in a half-erased pencil drawing.

Northwest Fifty-eighth Street was a middle-class neighborhood. Small postwar homes, one and two bedrooms, no two quite alike, their well-tended lawns and hand-painted mailboxes separated only by narrow concrete driveways. I rolled down the window. The driving rain splattered my face as I eased up the narrow street, looking for numbers. Even numbers on the left. Odd on the right. It was the kind of neighborhood where nuclear families used to live, before Seattle became Uncle Bill's land of latte.

Thirty sixty-four was halfway up the block, a neat little one-story house, freshly painted white with forest-green trim and shutters. To the right of the front door, a seasonal arrangement of colorful gourds and Indian corn was being guarded by a brown ceramic squirrel, while all along the front of the house, a hardy bed of red and white impatiens defiantly shook the last of its colorful blossoms in the face of the storm.

I slid the Fiat to the curb and turned the engine off. I sat for a moment counting my breath as it fogged the windshield, listening to the pounding of the rain and hoping for a break in the weather. Yeah. Sure. Sometime late next May. I took a deep breath, shouldered the door open and went sloshing across the street and up onto the porch.

I pulled open the green screen door and knocked on the solid white one underneath. It wasn't latched and opened a crack as I struck it.

"That you, Amy?" a voice called.

"No," I said.

A gust of wind blew the white door all the way inward

and I could see him sitting in a leather rocker over on the far side of the living room, over by the picture window on the west wall. His aluminum canes hung from the window-sill, next to his glasses. The white walls of the corner were covered with an array of framed photographs. Even from where I stood, I could pick out my father in most of them. I closed both doors behind me and stepped into the room.

The years had sunken Bermuda's thick chest, pushing whatever remained down beneath his wide black belt, leaving his upper torso nearly childlike. It looked as if, with no effort at all, he could rest his chin on his silver belt buckle. His hair was white and disheveled, kind of that Einstein at Princeton look. He wore a blue cardigan sweater over a loud flannel shirt. His left hand groped about the windowsill, searching for his glasses. He found them and brought them to his face. Larry King glasses, huge and black, with lenses so thick that, from my side, they reduced his pupils to pinpricks.

"I thought you were Amy," he said.

"Whoever Amy is, Bermuda, I hope for your sake she's a lot better-looking woman than I am."

"Does things around here for me . . ." he started.

He pushed his glasses up on his nose, blinked several times and then broke into a huge grin.

"I'll be goddamned. Look at you, kid," he exclaimed. "Damn shame you got so old. How'd that happen?"

I stood on the rose-colored carpet and looked myself up and down.

"I don't know what happened, Bermuda. Last thing I recall, I was twenty and gonna set the world on fire. Remember?"

"Oh, I remember." He tapped his temple. "Nothing wrong up here, kid. I remember real good. Legs don't work any-more, but the rest of me is working just fine."

"Glad to hear it," I said.

I checked out the room. In the main section, a brown leather sofa and matching chair surrounded a glass-topped coffee table. Several color-coordinated floral prints adorned the walls. A fireplace dominated the east end, its green tile front reflecting the blue gas flames out onto the floor. From where I stood, the area seemed foreign and unused, as if a decorator had stolen in at night, leaving Bermuda only the corner by the window to call his own.

By the time I looked back, he was staring out the window.

"Where did it go, kid? Where did it all get to?"

"I'll tell you, Bermuda, I had any idea where it went, I'd go there and bring it back for the both of us."

A rueful smile bent his lips.

"Would that we could, kid."

"Somebody once said that life is what happens while you're busy making other plans."

"John Lennon," he said quickly. "John Lennon said that."

His head swiveled my way and his eyes narrowed. "I knew somebody'd find me," he said. "Soon as I saw the papers. Figured some bright young media type would do his homework and find his way to my door. Didn't imagine it would be you though."

I crossed the room and sat down in the ladder-backed chair which had been pushed over next to his rocker.

"The papers are making like my father killed him. Like it's cut and dried. No question about it."

He rolled his eyes. "It's what they do," he said. "They sell papers."

"'The SPD has officially reopened the investigation."

"So I heard."

"The Price family is going to bring big-time pressure. They're gonna play this one for all it's worth."

"No doubt about it," he said. "So the question becomes how're *you* gonna handle it?"

He was leading me down a familiar and unwelcome path.

"I can't stand around and do nothing, Bermuda. It may be the smart thing to do, but it's not the Leo thing to do. One of the things I've learned along the way is to recognize what I can and can't live with, and I've got some serious doubts about living with doing nothing here."

He showed another grin. "Then you do what you gotta do, Leo."

He reached over and put a hand on my shoulder.

"You always hung in there, kid. It was your gift. Didn't matter whether your team was way ahead or way behind; you were always givin' it your all. Full bore till the final bell." He licked his lips. "With you, it never had anything to do with the score. It's why I liked watching you play."

I put my hand on top of his hand and then leaned over and gently rested my forehead on his. We stayed that way for a moment.

"Thanks, Bermuda," I said. "For all of it."

"Don't mention it, kid. It was my pleasure. Not everybody gets the pleasure of watching somebody that hardheaded."

I sat back. "So you know me, man. You know, I'm gonna have to thrash around in this a bit. Like you said, it's my nature."

He folded his arms across his narrow chest. "Which is, I presume, how come I am now blessed with the honor of your company . . . after all these years."

I ignored the dig and plowed on.

"I figured if anybody would know anything it would be you, Bermuda. You guys spent most of your waking hours together."

The rain ticked like gravel on the window. As he turned his head toward the sound, the light streaming through the glass highlighted the wispy texture of his hair and the indefinite line of his profile. He spoke without turning my way.

"And what if I did know something, kid. What then? Suppose I could say to you that I knew how Peerless Price ended up planted in your father's backyard." He leaned back in the chair and caught my eye. "Are you sure you'd really want to know? You ever think of that? What if the truth was something you didn't want to hear about?"

"Like what?"

He put his index finger to his temple and cocked his thumb. "Like how about if old Peerless pissed your father off one time too many and how about we took him down in the tide flats and put one in his ear." He dropped his thumb. "What about that?"

"Is that what happened?"

"Nope," he said. "I'm just trying to make a point here, Leo."

"What point is that?"

"That what's done is done. Peerless Price is gone. Your father, God rest his soul, is gone. Even if I knew something, what could I do now? You think I'd show your father so little honor as to violate his trust?" He spread his hands in disbelief. "After all these years?"

"No. I don't figure you would."

He smiled. "I worked for the man for eighteen years, Leo. It wasn't for him I'd have ended up on a creeper selling pencils." He swept a hand about the room. "He had a part in everything I got, kid. I got nothing but good things to say about Bill Waterman."

"And you've got no idea how Peerless Price ended up in my old man's backyard?"

"None," he said. "Damnedest thing I ever heard of." He wagged a finger at me. "Tell you one thing, though, kid . . ."

"What's that?"

"Your old man had wanted to pop a cap on somebody, believe you me, he'da done it right. Whoever it was sure as hell wouldn'ta ended up planted in Bill's own backyard, and wherever he was planted, they wouldn'ta found him." He cut the air with the side of his hand. "Not ever."

"That's why I came to you, Bermuda. I never for a second thought you'd sell my father out. No way. But this thing doesn't make sense to me, either. Like you just said, nobody pops his worst enemy and buries him in his own backyard."

Bermuda shook his big head.

"Peerless Price had a lot of enemies, kid. So did the Boss . . . your father. But Price, now, that son of a bitch had a real knack for making enemies." He straightened himself in the chair. "Could be somebody was looking to kill two birds with one stone. Everybody knew about the bad blood between them. Everybody seen that picture they ran yesterday in the *PI*. The one where your dad rearranged Price's mug for him. Wouldn't take a genius to put two and two together, pop Price and try to pin it on Bill Waterman."

"So why not wait a month and then call the cops? How come the body ends up there for almost thirty years?"

"You got me, Leo. I knew that . . . I'd sell it to the *National Enquirer*. Move to the Bahamas."

The old house creaked and groaned from the onslaught of the wind. Somewhere in the back of the building, a tree branch was sweeping back and forth across the roof like long fingernails.

I sat back in my chair, ran a hand over my face and pulled my notebook from my pants pocket.

He had a faraway look in his eyes as he began to speak. "Your father . . ." he looked over my way. "Now there was a man, Leo. When I first met him, I was . . ."

I tuned him out. I'd heard all the stories before and none of them sounded like anybody I knew. The way I saw it, either they were exaggerating everything or they weren't making people like they used to anymore. I sat back, set the notebook on my knee and waited for him to finish. It took him about ten minutes to work his way up to the present.

"I was going through my father's daybooks for nineteen sixty-nine," I began.

"Among the finest pieces of fiction ever penned."

"Everything?" I asked. "None of it's accurate?"

He smiled. "Well, must be some of it's the truth. Only a fool would lie when he don't have to."

"It's about the car mileage."

He chuckled. "How he hated having to keep track of all that shit." He spread his big hands. "But what was he gonna do? Price had every city agency running audits on him. Didn't want to go down for something stupid like expenses."

I flipped open the notebook. "If I'm reading this right," I began, "you guys operated pretty much like clockwork.

You'd drop him off at night and then pick him up every morning before eight."

"Seven forty-five sharp. Monday through Friday."

"Except . . ." I flipped back a couple of pages. "Except for May eighteenth and June first, nineteen sixty-nine."

He looked confused. "Except what?"

"According to his daybooks, on those nights he gave you cab fare and took the car himself."

He answered quickly. "If you say so, kid."

"What's interesting is that those are the only nights in the whole year when he took the car home."

"If you say so," he said again.

"You mean you don't remember?"

He jerked his head back and pulled off his glasses.

"I told you, kid, I remember just fine."

"Well?" I prodded.

"Well what? Like I'm supposed to remember what I was doin' on a specific night thirty years ago? Gimme a break here, Leo."

"If you don't remember, you don't remember."

He slid his glasses back onto his face and pinned me with a stare.

"I hope that's not as subtle as you get, kid."

I smiled. "Like you said before, Bermuda, subtlety's not my strong point. I'm more the balls-to-the-wall type."

"Your father always had an angle."

"I've got one too. Straight ahead."

"I mean, you know, kid . . . you and me . . . we gonna get into that amateur psychology stuff, we gonna have to stomp around in that Freudian crap about you spendin' your life trying to fill your father's shoes." Behind the thick lenses, his eyes nearly disappeared.

"I'm not trying to fill his shoes, Bermuda, I'm just trying to scrape a little shit off them."

He folded his arms over what remained of his chest and rocked all the way back in the chair. "You sure?" he asked finally.

"Believe me, if I hadn't given up trying to live up to other people's expectations, I'd be dead by now."

He thrust his lower lip out onto his chin and nodded.

"He did cast a hell of a shadow," he said.

"Don't I know it, man. I spent about ten years getting myself twisted so I wouldn't have to look at it."

"And look at what a fine figure of a man you've become."

His lips formed a thin smile, but his tone invited me to take his words any way I wanted.

"Thanks," I said.

He pushed his glasses back up on his nose.

"Old men like me . . ." he started. ". . . we're always stuck in the past, lookin' at the world in the rearview mirror, 'cause there's not much highway left out in front of us no more." He sighed and waved his hand. "No point in it for you, though. Your future is all out in front of you, kid. Only good thing about the past is it's over."

I shook my head. "It's over for him. Maybe it's over for you. But it's not over for me."

He turned his face toward the window and began to rock. A spring somewhere inside the chair groaned every time he moved forward. Above the squeaking of the chair and the hissing of the gas fire, a car door slammed and then came the sounds of feet slapping the water in the street and the screen door groaning open. A head poked into the room.

"Hey, Ed," she yelled.

She was about twenty and very fair. A thickset girl in a bright yellow raincoat, she stepped inside and pulled the yellow hood from her head. She had thick, wiry blonde hair and a mouthful of bad teeth. She spotted me.

"Oh . . . I'm sorry . . ." She looked over at Bermuda. "I could come back, Ed. No prob . . ."

"Amy," he said. "No, don't go. This is Leo Waterman."

She shook the water from herself and came my way. I stood up and offered a hand. "Nice to meet you, Amy."

Her grip was damp but strong.

"I come over to make Ed some lunch." She eyed me.

"Waterman . . . Waterman . . . Wasn't that the name of the guy Ed used to work for?"

"My father," I said.

She kept pumping my hand and nodding. "Cool," she said. "I think we got some turkey and some pita bread left. Got some chips, too. How 'bout I make you a sandwich too, Leo? Won't be no trouble."

"Thanks, Amy, but I'm gonna run here in a minute."

"You sure?"

"Thanks anyway."

Satisfied, she ducked through the swinging door into the kitchen beyond. I heard the rubbery suck of the refrigerator being opened and the clink of glass before he spoke.

"I don't know what he was doing with the car, Leo. All of a sudden he just had a bug up his ass that he needed the car. Both times on a Friday night, too, so I was stuck taking the bus all goddamn weekend. Seemed like every Friday night there for a while, he'd tell me to pull over on First Avenue in front of the old Chase Hotel. He'd slip me a fifty, tell me to take a cab both ways and that he'd see me on Monday."

"He went into the hotel?"

"Nope. I know that for sure 'cause that's where I always went to have a drink and call a cab. Only place in the neighborhood." He closed his eyes. "Place had a real nice bar those days. Real money. City tore it down back in the early eighties. Tore down the whole block. Put up a damn parking garage." His eyes opened. "Your dad, he drove off."

"Which way?"

"He'd go up one block to Marion and then go down the hill. Toward Alaska. Same thing both times."

I knew he meant Alaskan Way, not the state.

"And you have no idea . . . ?"

"Wasn't none of my business, Leo. Wasn't like I was gonna ask him or anything. The Boss wants the car, he gets the car." He sat forward in the chair. "I'll tell ya something else, kid.

Whatever he was doing cost some scratch. He always had a roll on those nights.''

I opened my mouth but he waved me off. ''He never carried no money, Leo. The Boss . . . your dad, he didn't need money. This was his town. Wasn't hardly nobody would take his money from him in this town. Those nights, though . . . he had a pocketful of coin.''

Amy backed through the swinging door carrying a metal folding tray which she set over Bermuda's legs. She looked my way.

''Last chance,'' she teased.

''I'm watching my girlish figure,'' I said.

She gave it about twice as much laugh as it was worth and bustled back into the kitchen.

I pocketed my notebook and got to my feet.

''Great to see you again, Bermuda. Thanks for the help.''

''Wish there was somethin' more I coulda done for you, kid.''

''You already did more than your share for me, Bermuda.''

Something in me wanted to make a speech. I didn't know what it was I wanted to say, but I knew it concerned the past, and I knew from experience that I was the only one who'd end up feeling better for its having been said, so I shut up.

A fresh fusilade of rain raked the window. He put the fingertips of his left hand on the pane, tracing the drops. I pulled a business card out and walked over and put it on the windowsill.

''In case you think of anything else.''

He nodded.

''See ya, huh?'' I said.

He nodded again. I let myself out.

10

I CONFESS. I'M THE LAST HUMAN BEING IN AMERICA OVER THE AGE of nine who doesn't own a cellular phone. Not only that but— gird your loins now—I don't have any intention of owning one, either. Not only that, but you know that bumper sticker? YOU'D PROBABLY DRIVE BETTER WITH THAT CELL PHONE UP YOUR ASS. Granted, it's a bit crude, but I've driven behind those people, and so have you. Need I say more? As far as I'm concerned, cellular phones and beepers are to human beings what leashes and choke chains are to dogs. In spite of this, however, there have been several occasions when, to be quite honest, I've cursed my own cussedness and longed for the convenience of such postindustrial marvels. And *this* most definitely was one of those times.

Twenty minutes after leaving Bermuda, I was standing in a phone booth on Forty-fifth Street. The rain had calmed to a mere typhoon. The inside of the booth was awash with a swirling armada of cigarette butts and pop tops about three inches deep. My feet were soaked. Half a baloney sandwich on whole wheat bobbed contentedly about my ankles. On top of that, I was having one of those phone days. The ones where nobody you call is in, or, if they are in, they can't come to the phone at this time, and either way it doesn't matter because you're getting nothing but machines who regret that So-and-so isn't home or at his desk and would you please leave your message after the beep. *Beep.*

I fed another quarter into the box and dialed Rebecca at work. Even if Duvall was in a meeting, I knew the intern, Tyanne Cummings, would answer the phone. I'd already decided. If I got another machine, I was using my last quarter to call Dr. Laura for advice.

"King County Medical Examiner."

"Hi, Tyanne. Is Rebecca available?"

I heard her catch her breath.

"Oh . . . Leo . . . you still don't know, huh?"

I hate it when conversations begin like this. Already, I was beginning to pine for an answering machine.

"Know what?"

"The police. She left. They served her with a warrant this morning about eleven-thirty."

"What kind of warrant?"

"A search warrant."

"For what?"

"For her . . . your . . . the house where you guys live."

I don't remember whether I thanked her or not. As a matter of fact, the whole ride back to the house was pretty much a blur. I don't recall anything until I slid around the corner on Crockett and bounced up into the driveway next to the blue-and-white SPD truck.

I used the booklet I'd gotten from Claire Wells as a hat, setting it directly on my head as I stepped out into the driveway. The slanting rain slapped down onto the clear plastic cover, adding its irregular tapping to the hissing sound of water moving everywhere around me.

I peeked into the truck on the way by. Inside, strapped two to a side, stood the four file cabinets from the attic. Strapped to the back wall was the two-drawer oak model from my office. On the right, in the cabinet closest to me, the middle drawer had been closed on Mikey the Monkey's brown tail. When I turned toward the house, a small river ran down my collar and I shuddered. A blue plastic carpet runner ran from the back of the truck straight into the garage. I stepped onto the plastic path and headed off in search of Rebecca.

She was sitting at the kitchen table drinking coffee and reading the lifestyles section of the paper. On the table, by her elbow, the headline screamed the question BLOOD FEUD? directly above side-by-side shots of Peerless Price and Wild Bill Waterman. I could hear voices and footsteps up on the second floor. Sitting there, holding her head in one hand while she read, Rebecca looked as tired as I'd ever seen her.

"Hey," I said.

She looked up from the paper and smiled.

"Hey yourself."

"Tyanne said . . ."

She lifted the front page from the table. I crossed the room, dropped the dripping booklet onto the table and picked up the warrant. Judge Ellen Gardner, in and for the county of King, in the state of Washington, had decreed that duly appointed members of the Seattle Police Department should be entitled to search the residence at two twenty-four Crockett Avenue for any and all documents pertaining to the public career of William G. Waterman. Including, but not limited to . . . yadda yadda yadda. Two pages' worth.

I flipped the warrant back at the table where it landed face-down.

"These assholes served you at the office?"

She used her foot to push the chair across from her out from the table. "Sit," she said. "I can see you working yourself up here, Leo. They could have jimmied the front door. Legally, they have the right. Coming to the office first was a courtesy."

I began pulling sections of the paper from the table.

"Did they . . ." I whispered.

"The three blue books you left here on the table?"

"Shhh."

She waved a hand at me. "They found those first thing. That's how come I had to tell them about the rest of the stuff upstairs."

"Shit."

I could hear the sound of footsteps on the stairs.

Detective Trujillo was natty in a gold sport jacket and deep brown slacks. Matching tie and hanky again. Custom-made shirt, too. Brown tasseled shoes this time. He pranced into the room and pushed a clipboard under my nose. A blue pen hung from a metal chain attached to the top of the board.

"Nice you could make it," he offered.

I couldn't come up with a sentence that didn't include the word "motherfucker," so I kept my mouth shut. He jiggled the board.

"Here's the inventory of what we took. You want to come out and check this against what we got in the truck, feel free."

When neither of us moved, he went on. "Sign on the bottom two lines. Initials where I've got the X's."

I took the clipboard and followed directions, scribbling my way to the bottom of the page.

"When can I expect my property back?" I asked.

"When we're finished with it," he snapped. "We've got a six-man task force set to go through the material. When they get through with it, you'll get it back."

I held on to the clipboard. "Why do I find that less than informative, Detective Trujillo?"

He reached over and plucked the clipboard from my hand. He tore a perforated strip from the bottom of the page, wiggled out a yellow copy and handed it to me. "You had your chance to cooperate, Waterman. You wanted to be the smart guy. Now you take what that gets you."

"Are you finished?" I asked.

Trujillo smirked. "I'll let you know when we're finished, Waterman. In the meantime, do us both a favor and try to stay out of the way."

"Don't let the door hit you in the ass, Trujillo."

He turned on his heel and followed the runner out into the garage.

Frank Wessels stood in the doorway grinning. "Gee, Leo,"

he said. "Way to leave the little lady to handle it by herself there, Hercules. A real stud superhero you are, leaving your girlfriend here to clean up your family's dirty laundry."

I was still deciding which hand to hit him with and where, when Rebecca materialized at my elbow. "Detective Wessels," she said, stepping around me. "I am neither a little lady nor a girl." He started to open his mouth, but she moved right up into his face. I could tell he wasn't used to women who were as tall as he was. She practically had her nose on his. "And if you ever refer to me either publicly or privately as anything other than 'Dr. Duvall' again, I will bring departmental sexual harassment charges against you so fast it will make your head spin. And you know, I don't think you want to find out which of us is considered more indispensable by King County, do you, Officer Wessels?"

He shifted his weight from foot to foot and checked his shoes for laces. "No," he said finally. "My apologies for any misunderstanding."

"Apology noted, Officer. Now why don't you follow my *boyfriend's* suggestion and watch out for that proverbial door."

He didn't need to be told twice. He threw me a quick sneer and headed out through the garage. Rebecca walked over to the doorway and watched him go. "I believe I could develop a real dislike for that man."

"You'll have to get in line and take a number," I said.

Two uniforms came by, rolling the plastic runner before them. I heard them close the door to the garage behind themselves. I threw an arm around Rebecca and pulled her close. I could feel her anger. In the driveway, the police van started and backed out, the throbbing of its exhaust finally fading into silence.

"What was that guy's name who worked for the U? The guy who borrowed all my father's stuff so they could copy it for their archives?"

No answer. She looked blank.

"What?"

"Remember? The Seattle history guy. The one who came here to the house that time right after we moved in."

"Oh," she said. "The little man with the red beard and the elbow patches on everything."

"And the loud bow ties," I offered.

She knit her brow. "Fitz something."

"Patrick."

"No."

"Henry."

"Not Henry either."

"Roy," I said. "Fitzroy."

She nodded. "That's it. Dr. Milton Fitzroy. I remember we figured he was the type to wear tailored pajamas and that they probably had leather patches, too. What do you want with him?"

I told her about finding Bermuda and what he'd said about my father taking the car. "I thought maybe Fitzroy would know what was in that neighborhood way back when."

"How do you know that whatever he was doing was in that neighborhood? He had the car, Leo. He could have gone anywhere."

"Because of the mileage. When Bermuda got to the house on the following Monday mornings, the mileage difference was always five miles."

"So?"

"So, from downtown to the house here is damn near five miles. Wherever he went, it wasn't very damn far from where he left Bermuda off."

"Presuming the mileage is correct."

"It's like Bermuda said. Only an idiot lies about anything he doesn't have to."

She didn't seem convinced.

"At least, I'm working from that presumption," I added.

She said, "That guy Fitzroy left a business card. I think I stapled it into the Rolodex in your office." She kissed me on the cheek. "I need to get back to work." She retrieved her green rain jacket from the back of the chair. "Don't wait up.

Everybody else is working on Peerless Price. So, I'm stuck with the rest of it. I'm up to my armpits in stiffs."

I walked her out to her car. She got in and started the engine. Her window slid down. "I don't suppose there's anything I could say that would induce you to let this thing go, is there?"

I shook my head. "Now it's personal."

"Oh?"

"They took my monkey."

She threw the Explorer in gear and backed out into the street.

11

Dr. Milton Fitzroy answered his phone on the first ring.

"History Department, Fitzroy."

"Dr. Fitzroy," I began, "this is Leo Waterman. I don't know if you recall but a few months ago . . ."

"Of course I recall, Mr. Waterman." He cleared his throat. "So sorry about the . . . er . . . the recent turn of events."

"Thanks," I said. "I was hoping maybe you could help me with something."

"By all means. Anything. I am most assuredly in your debt. I don't know whether you realize it, but the information which you provided me was of incalculable value to an over-all understanding of the sociopolitical infrastructure of the city prior to nineteen eighty."

I was terrified he'd explain it to me, so I lied and allowed how I was aware of my substantial contribution to his work.

"What can I do for you?"

"If I wanted to know what was open for business in a certain section of the city, in a certain year, could you provide me with that information?"

It was a long shot, and I knew it. All I had going for me was that whatever my father was about had to be of sufficient importance that he felt impelled to leave Bermuda out of it, and it had to be somewhere right there in that neighborhood. That, and whatever it was, had required him to be, uncharacteristically, in possession of folding money.

He thought it over. "Certainly. Of course, we would only have access to legitimate business, for which a license had been issued and from whom taxes were being collected. Such things as sidewalk stands and after-hours clubs, and . . . er . . . anything illegal or illicit would, of course, escape our scrutiny."

"What I had in mind was everything below First Avenue, from Pike Street on the north to Yesler on the south. That whole area of Alaskan Way and Western Avenue between First Avenue and the sound. I need to know what was there that would possibly be open on a Friday night. Would that be possible?"

"I don't see why not," he said. "That particular portion of the city should, in all probability, be relatively easy to plot. I suspect that its composition was much as it is now. What year did you say?"

"The summer of nineteen sixty-nine. And I'm looking for things that would be open on a Friday night, which works great for what you said about legitimate businesses. It's too late for sidewalk business and too early for after-hours clubs."

He coughed again. "Yes, of course. Of course. Quite. Nineteen sixty-nine, you say."

I could hear him mumbling to himself. "Of course, for an accurate picture, I would have to cross-reference the plat maps with business licenses and liquor licenses in order to determine hours of operation."

"Of course."

"And of course, we would have no way of plotting anything residential."

"How long do you think it would take for you to come up with the information?"

"Oh . . . well, no more than a day or so, I should say."

I explained that circumstances had forced us to leave the phones unplugged and asked him to leave me a message

when he had the information collected. He assured me he
would.

Two hours and two pots of coffee later, my scalp was beginning to tingle from the caffeine, and I'd had to break out
that pair of glasses I don't need. The *Post-Intelligencer* press
packet had been copied so many times the letters looked like
ancient runes and the pictures had taken on the amorphous
quality of Rorschach renderings.

During the last days of Peerless Price's professional life, he
had written on only three subjects: the Yellow Peril and the
Red Menace, which, fashion considerations notwithstanding,
were the same thing, as far as Peerless Price was concerned.
Next was the, and I quote, "rot at the center of American
morals" as personified by the recent proliferation of gay and
lesbian clubs in the Seattle area. And finally, he wrote inces-
santly about the upcoming Fourth of July parades, which, of
course, was where my old man got mixed into the pudding.

According to Price, antiwar activists should be held personally accountable for each and every American death, should
be prosecuted for aiding and abetting the enemy, meted out
lengthy jail terms and then, upon release, should be sum-
marily deported to those countries with whom they had chosen to cast their lot. And those were the lucky ones.

For my old man and the others who had consistently spo-
ken out against the conflict and who had finagled the permit
for the antiwar demonstration, Price was willing to skip all
that tiresome law and order stuff and get right down to a
series of public executions, a myth-making spectacle which
he was convinced would considerably stiffen the city's, if not
the nation's, badly wavering moral fiber.

According to Peerless Price, this moral rot was most visible
in the phenomenon commonly known as the "sexual revolution." In his view, every citizen of the state was put at risk
by the half dozen, and I quote again, "pervo palaces" which
had sprung up throughout the city, catering to the recently
radicalized element of the gay and lesbian communities,

whose members he considered to be "abnormal abominations" and "an affront to both man and God."

Particularly galling to Price was the SPD's refusal to enforce a turn-of-the-century city ordinance which made it a crime for members of the same sex to engaged in any type of physical display or contact whatsoever. Unable to budge the SPD hierarchy on the issue, Peerless Price had taken matters into his own hands. He'd coerced a rummy SPD lieutenant named Bailey into pulling a raid on one of the downtown gay bars. A place called the Garden of Eden. According to Price, the raid had netted a bevy of Seattle's best and brightest citizens engaged in acts of such perversity as to make a Roman orgy seem like a Lutheran coffee social.

At last, Peerless Price had them right where he wanted them, or so it seemed. Problem was that by noon the next day, not only had they all made bail, but every shred of documentation pertaining to their arrest and booking had miraculously disappeared from the Downtown Precinct house, never to be seen again.

Bailey was suspended indefinitely and eventually opted to retire rather than face departmental charges. Publicly prodded by Peerless Price, the SPD staged a perfunctory investigation into the missing paperwork, but nothing ever came of it, because, once again according to PP, strings had been pulled at the very highest levels of city government. In the week prior to his death, Peerless Price had promised his readers that he was about to name those public officials responsible for sweeping the matter under the rug.

The third subject dear to Peerless Price at the time of his disappearance was the wave of Asian refugees who were flooding into the city. Old Peerless made no distinction among the various Asian communities, labeling them all as "wogs" and demanding that they be immediately shipped back from whence they had come. To Price, the increased pace of immigration from that part of the world was little more than a thinly disguised attempt to undermine us from within. Not only were thousands of these inferior beings using our overly permissive laws against us, but we were also besieged by another silent wave of illegal immigrants whose insidious plan to infiltrate both our nation and our gene pool constituted "the most severe threat to our national sovereignty since the War of 1812."

Peerless was convinced that the Seattle waterfront was a major port of entry for Chinese refugees fleeing the atrocities of the Cultural Revolution. In his final column of July third, Peerless Price had promised his readers that those responsible were about to be unmasked.

The last article in the booklet was not written by Peerless Price. As a matter of fact, it wasn't even from the *Post-Intelligencer*, but from the rival *Seattle Times*, written by one Judi Hunt, who was identified in the byline as a *Times* staff reporter. It was dated July ninth, nineteen sixty-nine. Six days after Peerless Price's disappearance, a customs inspector named Gaylord LaFontaine was summoned to Pier Sixteen by an unnamed yard boss, who was concerned about the ungodly odor emanating from an unmarked and unclaimed shipping container sitting alone on the far side of his yard. LaFontaine used a borrowed bolt cutter to pop the lock and, much to his revulsion and dismay, found the decomposing bodies of fourteen Chinese nationals, including four children, huddled together on the ribbed metal floor of the box. It was almost a shame that Peerless Price hadn't been around to say, "I told you so." Almost.

I dialed the *Seattle Times*.

"Judi Hunt, please."

I could hear her pushing buttons. "I'm sorry, sir, but I'm not showing a listing for a Judi Hunt."

"Could you give me the metro desk, then."

"Yes, sir. Thank you."

Three clicks and "Metro." A deep man's voice.

I went for the cheery good ol' boy approach.

"What's a guy gotta do to reach Judi Hunt?"

"You'd either see a priest or you'd call the Psychic Hotline."

"Oh?"

"Judi died in eighty-four or -five. Ovarian cancer."

I mumbled a thanks, but, mercifully, he was already gone. Undaunted, I rolled backward and pulled the phone book out of the bread drawer, thumbed my way back to the L's and followed my finger down the page. The *Times* article said Mr. LaFontaine was twenty-nine years old at the time of his grisly discovery, so I was guessing he was still with us. Yep. Gaylord LaFontaine. Twenty-nine seventy-four Fifteenth Avenue East. Three two nine, sixty-four eighty. With a name like that I figured there couldn't be two of them, so I dialed the number.

"Yah."

I could hear the sound of children's voices in the background.

"Is this Mr. Gaylord LaFontaine?"

"Yah. Wadda ya need?"

"Are you with U.S. Customs?"

"Used to be. Who is this?"

Before I could respond, the background voices grew shrill and he said, "Wait a sec." And was gone.

"Anyway," he said when he came back. "Sorry about that. Who did you say you were?"

"My name is Leo Waterman." I waited to see if he'd been reading the papers. Apparently, he hadn't.

"Wadda ya need, Mr. Waterman?"

I wasn't sure how to express it. It came out like "I wanted to ask you some questions about nineteen sixty-nine. That container."

No hesitation. "What about it?"

"I'm a private detective. I'm looking into something that may or may not be connected to that tragedy."

"If you don't mind me saying, Mr. Waterman, whatever trail you're following must be pretty damn cold by now. That was a hell of a long time ago."

"Yeah," I said. "that's why I was hoping—"

"Hang on," he said again. The phone clattered in my ear.

I could hear his voice in the background but couldn't make out the words. He was gone for a couple of minutes. When he returned, he sounded short of breath, and I could hear crying in the background.

"Sorry about that. Listen. I got a minor emergency here I gotta take care of. You wanna come over, I'll tell you whatever I can, but you've got to be quick about it 'cause I promised the kids a movie at four-fifteen." I checked the clock— two forty-five—got directions from LaFontaine and headed for the door.

The rain had turned to an insistent mist which seemed to wet everything at once, rather than a drop at a time. I sprinted for the Fiat, threw myself into the driver's seat and then . . . son of a bitch! For the second time today, my feet were completely awash. The rain had soaked its way through the passenger seat and filled the foot well with six inches of greasy-looking water upon which several petrified McDonald's French fries now floated. I eased the car forward into the garage.

I got out, found a bucket and an old margarine container and bailed out the floor of the car. Then dragged the shop vac over and sucked up the rest of it. While I was inside changing my shoes and socks, I appropriated one of the old towels from the laundry room and a roll of duct tape from the kitchen drawer. You know what they say. If you can't fix it with duct tape, that sucker can't be fixed.

What in better weather had seemed a mere slit had somehow mutated into an eighteen-inch gash in the rough black fabric. I dried the area off as best I could and used up half a roll of the silver tape to put the top back together. Okay, so it looked like hell. I made a mental note to go out and buy some black tape as soon as the weather cleared.

By the time I pulled to the curb in front of twenty-nine seventy-four Fifteenth Avenue East, I was feeling pretty smug. My roof repair had allowed nary a drop into the car, which was a good thing, because the minute I'd flipped on the heater, an acrid fog had begun to rise from the sodden carpet, reducing visibility inside the car to something akin to midnight on the moors. I had to drive with the windows down.

The house sat high above the street. Dark brick on the bottom, light blue stucco on the top, in kind of a neo-Tudor motif. Two sets of stairs up to the house. Six, then four. The wide porch was covered in blue Astroturf. The window to the right of the door displayed a yellow Neighborhood Watch insignia. I gave the bell a pair of assertive rings.

She was about three, with brown hair cut straight across the front and held on the sides by a pair of red plastic barrettes. She held her tiny hand up for me to see. Her small index finger was nearly covered by a Flintstones Band-Aid. Her blue eyes were still wet around the edges.

"Did you hurt your finger?" I asked.

She nodded and stuck the damaged digit in her mouth.

I heard the tapping of feet and a clone appeared at her elbow. A boy, this time. Same age; same face. Either twins or acid flashbacks.

"Is this your brother?" I asked her.

Another nod. Another finger in the mouth.

"Jason," he chirped. "Megan got a owee."

"She showed me," I said.

The door swung all the way open. Gaylord LaFontaine was a wiry five-ten, about a hundred sixty pounds. He had a round, open face with big features set apart from one another. He'd grown his twelve remaining hairs long and wrapped them around his dome a couple of times in a last-ditch attempt to forestall the inevitable. He was drying his hands with a black-and-white dish towel.

"You'd be Waterman," he said.

"The very same," I assured him.

He turned his attention to the twins.

"What have I told you two about answering the door?"

The pair began to recite in two-part harmony. "Never open the door to strangers. Never . . ."

When they finished, he said, "All right, you two. You go

in the den and watch cartoons for a bit while I'm talking to Mr. Waterman. Then we'll get dressed and go to the movie."

The deadly duo didn't require further prompting. In an instant, they went tearing around the corner together and were lost from sight.

"Cartoooooooooooooooooooooooooooons."

He ran the dish towel over his face and neck.

"It's murder when the weather's like this and they can't go out," he said. "Come on back to the kitchen. I've got a few things to do."

I followed him back to the kitchen. He talked as we walked.

"You know, I've been thinking about that day ever since you called. Haven't thought about it in years, but since you called, you know . . . I can't get it off of my mind."

He steered me into an oak chair at his kitchen table, poured us both a cup of coffee and sat down across from me.

He looked out over my head toward a blank spot on the wall, and took a sip of the coffee. "There's certain pictures . . . you know, images that are gonna be with me forever. Things I'm gonna see when I close my eyes, right up till they put me in the ground. That family there in the container . . ." He took a deep breath.

"Family?"

"Oh, yeah. They were all related. Four generations of the same family. Fourteen of 'em. Four kids."

"What killed them?"

"The heat," he said. "It was ninety-eight, a hundred all that week. The docs figured it was probably a hundred and sixty inside the container. They never had a chance."

"And the yard was closed for the holiday," I added.

"A full four days. The Fourth was on a Thursday. Everybody had the whole weekend off." He shook his head. "Wasn't even anybody around to hear 'em scream. Hell, they'd be lucky to last four hours in that kind of heat, let alone four days."

We shared a belated moment of silence before I asked, "And nobody ever went down for it?"

"Nah. Down on the docks, nobody ever goes down for nothing." His eyes narrowed. "It's dumb kids doing the hard time. The kind of people bring people over here in containers, everybody knows who they are, but they don't do time."

"What do you mean, 'everybody knows who they are'?"

"Just what I said. Wasn't any problem knowing what was going on. It had been going on for years and it's probably still going on now. Problem was proving it."

"How's that?"

"Listen. In those days, you got four companies using the Pier Eighteen yard. Two American, one Japanese, one Chinese. I mean . . . I don't know about you, and I don't want to sound like a bigot here, but I don't see Safeway, Costco or Panasonic branching out into the illegal Chinese immigration business."

"If it was that obvious—" I started.

"The fix was in. They had big-time juice. They had somebody downtown and somebody in the Port of Seattle both. Somebody high up who could assign them to a commercial yard. Somebody who could fix it that a couple of containers here and there wouldn't be missed from time to time."

He read my expression. "Hey . . . I'm telling ya. When I first come on, you know, I was green and eager, so I asked the port supervisor, went marching right into his office—and this guy was high up—I said . . . 'Hey, what's this little piss-ant company doing down here on the commercial end? How come it's not down at Harbor Island with the rest of the ham-and-eggers where we can keep better track of it?' 'Cause you know, Customs doesn't pay a hell of a lot of attention to the big commercial yards. Between you, me and the wall, the bureau figures a Panasonic container contains whatever Panasonic says it contains. It's the mom-and-pop importers like Seven Rivers you got to watch like a hawk. Know what the port guy told me?"

"What?"

"He said if I was planning on making pension, I oughta just do my job and keep my mouth shut. Said if he was me, he'd just sort of forget about Seven Rivers Trading altogether. Said Seven Rivers was political."

"Political how?"

He shrugged. "I always figured he could have meant it one of two ways. Either he was saying the fix was in . . . You know . . . that somebody in government was throwing his weight around for a piece of the action."

"Or?"

"Or . . . you know . . . that the whole refugee thing was political. Had a lot of people in those days didn't see anything wrong with people trying to get out of places like Red China. Made those poor souls in that box out to be like martyrs, and whoever tried to bring 'em into the country into some sort of humanitarians or something."

"The underground railway."

"You got it. Either way, somebody higher up decided it wasn't something for little old me to be messing around in. Soon as it was clear they were illegal, INS took over the investigation and boom, the bureau transferred me down to the airport. Two days' notice. No explanation. No nothing. Just down to the airport."

"You said before you figured it was still going on."

"Why not? Last time I looked, they were still down on Eighteen. Change the name every year or so, but it's still the same people. They've got an open door into the country. Why should they stop? I wouldn't."

"You think they're still bringing people into the country?"

He thought it over. "I think . . . if you took two dozen INS agents and made a sweep through the International District you'd need a fleet of school buses to haul off the illegals. It's the same in every major city in America." He dropped his hands to his sides. "They gotta come from somewhere."

You couldn't argue with that, so I didn't.

He checked his watch. "Gotta go," he said. "Movie's clear up in Lynnwood at the dollar theater."

"Baby-sitting?"

He looked bemused. "You could say that."

I thought he was going to let it go, but I was wrong.

"They're my grandkids," he announced suddenly and with a certain amount of pride. "I guess ya could say we're kinda stuck with each other."

Unless I was mistaken, we were approaching another of those conversational moments when it didn't matter what you said next, so I kept it simple. "Cute kids," I said.

He spoke as if he were reciting a catechism.

"My boy . . . their father . . . he's out on McNeil Island. Went down for armed robbery . . . got four more years before he comes eligible."

"Sorry to hear that."

"He'd be takin' care of his kids, if he could."

I tried to look like I knew that to be true.

"What about the mother?"

He gave a short, dry laugh. "If it ain't got anything to do with a crack pipe, it ain't got anything to do with Jolene." His eyes took on a new life. "That's how it happened, you know. Davey was just tryin' to get money to feed her habit. Davey never had that monkey on his back. It was her. No . . . right now, at least until Davey comes eligible, I guess I'm about all those kids got."

"They're lucky to have you."

"First the state wanted to send them to Jolene's trailer-trash family. Can't even take care of their own. Then they wanted to put 'em in foster homes, but I mean, what am I gonna do, send 'em off to strangers? I read about what goes on in those places. I couldn't let that happen. They're family."

"Lotta kids don't have anybody like you," I said.

He stuck his hands in his pants pockets and leaned back against the kitchen counter.

"Not exactly what I had in mind for my retirement. I'd sorta been thinkin' about cabin cruisers and grateful widows."

We shared a small chuckle.

"Who knows," I said. "Maybe you're lucky to have them, too."

His eyes twinkled. "Well, if nothin' else, they keep me runnin' all day. I'll probably live longer that way." He smiled. "Could be you're right."

He crossed the room and leaned into the front room. "Okay, you two, you get your jackets . . . the ones with the hoods, you get 'em from the hall closet and meet me by the front door."

They shrieked in unison and ran from the room.

"Yeeeeeeeeeeeeeeeeeeeeeeeeeeeeeeeeeeah."

"*The Little Mermaid*," he said. "We've seen it before."

He and I ambled across the room and out to the front door. "Thanks for your time, Mr. LaFontaine."

"My pleasure. Don't get to talk to other adults much these days," he said. "Hope whatever you're working on works out for you."

"Yeeeeeeeeeeeeeeeeeeeeeeeeeeeeeeeeeeah."

The kids were back, carrying matching red raincoats. I let myself out while Gaylord LaFontaine helped them on with the coats.

12

PIER EIGHTEEN SITS IN THE PERPETUAL SHADOW OF THE WEST SE-attle Bridge, nearly at the original mouth of the Duwamish River. That was before they rerouted its flow, tore Harbor Island from its bottom, and lined its banks with heavy industry. Way back then, it was actually a river. Nowadays, they call it a waterway. That's bureau-speak for "river they screwed up on purpose."

I lined up behind three container carriers waiting at the Pier Eighteen guard gate. I had my LEO WATERMAN, SENIOR INSURANCE ESTIMATOR, PRUDENTIAL INSURANCE COMPANY business card out and my rap ready. Something about the picture of that blue rock on the card. Never fails.

Didn't fail this time, either, because the guard just waved me through when the big eighteen-wheeler in front of me went roaring off across the yard. I guess they figured that if whatever you were driving wasn't big enough to load a container into or onto, you couldn't be much of a threat. A white sign stood in a small traffic island just inside the gate. Costco and Eagle Hardware to the right, Safeway straight ahead. Triad Trading and Western Cold Storage to the left. Ahead and to the right, huge concrete buildings lined the edge of the waterway, each bearing a famous logo. To the left, nothing was in sight. It was like LaFontaine said. Didn't take a rocket scientist.

The yard was crammed with orange containers with the

word HANJIN painted on their sides in bold white letters. Stacked four high, they ran row upon row, seemingly to the horizon, forming a corrugated canyon whose ribbed walls nearly erased the sky above the car. I kept it in first gear and drove slowly down the long central aisle for the better part of a half mile before I came to a perpendicular artery, where I turned left, toward the water. I figured I'd keep going until I got to the water and then reconnoiter. No need.

Triad Trading Company ran low along the bank, directly under the bridge. A rippled wooden structure from another era, whose loose collection of add-ons meandered its way in stages from the container yard down to the riverbank fifteen feet below. Ahead of me in the gloom, a mobile construction shed with the word OFFICE stenciled on the front stood dark and empty. To its right a sagging metal warehouse loomed up into the darkening sky like a monument to rust.

No lights. No cars. No nothing.

I pulled the Fiat into the narrow alley between the office shed and the warehouse and rolled nearly out to the end. In front of the car, ten feet of gravel driveway sloped precipitately down toward the river. I jammed the Fiat in reverse, pulled up on the e-brake for all I was worth and then turned off the engine and stepped out.

The evening sky was the color of a bad bruise, and it was ten degrees colder here by the water. My breath plumed out in front of me like steam. Pushed by the wet wind, the rain felt like it could cut my face and the cold, rather than being external, seemed to emanate from deep within my bones.

I walked past the front of the car and looked down into the black water, watching the raindrops pit the glittering surface and then disappear into the flow. Two hundred feet away, across the Duwamish, a green-and-white Washington State ferry was in dry dock. A motorized scaffold hung from the side. Two welders and two sets of tanks were sending dual showers of sparks spewing down into the water below. Above the sparkling streams, the lighted decks were alive with workers in green rain gear and yellow hard hats.

I pulled my jacket tighter around me and walked back up the alley to the office. The sticker on the steel door declared that the building was protected by a Brinks Security System and that trespassers would be prosecuted to the fullest extent of the law. In the window, a hand-lettered sign said: IN CASE OF EMERGENCY CALL 624-7765. I pulled out my notebook and wrote the number down.

I crossed the alley to the big sliding door on the side of the building and found it fastened with a serious new lock and chain. I started making my way around to the front, trying to stay close to the building and out of the rain, keeping my inside hand on the rough metal siding. I kept my eyes on my feet, stepping carefully over and around the dangerous collection of shattered pallets, twisted rebar and discarded metal banding material which the years had deposited along the sides of the structure.

I slid along the front of the building, walking past a huge pair of electronically operated roll-up doors, all the way to the far end, where I peeked around the corner. Right in front of my face was a small concrete landing leading to a blue metal door. Just for fun I reached out and tried the knob. It wasn't locked. I swiveled my head around to make sure I was alone in the yard, took several deep breaths, pulled open the door and casually stepped inside.

High in the ceiling, a double line of fluorescent lights ran down the length of the warehouse, bathing the center of the room in a murky green glow, while leaving the periphery in near darkness. The room was filled with shipping containers about half the size of those out in the yard. Blue, with TRIAD TRADING stenciled on the side. In the narrow central aisle, a pair of yellow Hyster forklifts were parked back-to-back.

Against the back wall, what I imagined to be the warehouse supervisor's office had been built high up off the floor above a pair of restrooms. The interesting part was that the lights were on upstairs. I stood still, my hand resting on the doorknob. At the far end, inside the office, the light wavered once and then a moment later, moved again. Unless I was mistaken, somebody was moving around in there. I eased the door closed behind me and started for the light.

I slipped between the forklifts and walked all the way down to the far end. On the right, a rickety-looking set of stairs rose in two sections to the office above. I fished the Prudential card out from my jacket pocket and started up. I figured I'd make like I was lost. Tell whoever was up there that I was looking for their neighbor Western Cold Storage. Maybe have me a little look around while I was at it. Us private dicks are real tricky that way.

It wasn't like I was tiptoeing or anything, and it's sure not as if the stairs didn't make any noise. On the contrary, the ancient risers creaked and groaned with my every step. I definitely wasn't looking to surprise anybody. Folks can get downright dangerous if you scare the hell out of them. I figured for sure whoever was up there was going to hear me coming from a mile away. That's because I figured whoever was up there probably had ears. Silly me.

He was sitting at a yellow Formica table reading the newspaper, following the lines with his finger, his lips moving as he read his way down the page. He was tall for a Chinese. Maybe six foot five or so. His narrow eyes were set close to a bumpy red nose. The area around his mouth was chapped and dry, and he had a serious split in his lower lip. About sixty, he'd grown his salt and pepper hair unusually long, into what I believe used to be called a pageboy hairdo. Kind of looked like Sonny Bono back in the heyday of Sonny and Cher. Back when Sonny still had hair and Cher still had a nose.

I was ruminating on his retro look when he reached up to scratch the back of his neck. In the process, his hand moved the thick curl of hair hiding the side of his head, and I could see that he didn't have an ear on this side. Just a scabrous black hole in the side of his head, red and puckered, pulling at the surrounding skin, creating the sense that the whole side of his face was about to disappear down the hole. Unsure now, I shuddered and stepped back out of the puddle of light at the top of the stairs.

I looked to my left, and thought about backing all the way down the stairs. And I might have done it, too, but in that instant, some primitive inner sense alerted him. Suddenly, his eyes grew wide and his mouth dropped open. He looked up from the paper, directly at me, and our eyes locked. I smiled and held up the business card. Never fails. A piece of the rock. Well . . . almost never.

He recoiled in terror. Throwing himself over backward in the chair and then crabbing down the narrow hall on all fours and sliding the accordion door closed behind him.

I pushed open the office door and stepped partially inside. I went for the understated approach.

"Sorry if I scared you," I said.

I could hear things being thrown around in the next room. "I'm from—" I started.

The door slid back and he burst back into the room. He wore a long knit cap pulled down over his head nearly to the line of his lower jaw. He brandished a large rubber mallet, the kind they use in auto body shops to pound out dents. Up close, I could see that he had the scarlet cheeks of a rummy and I could tell from the way the hat lay on his head that he didn't have an ear on the other side either. I showed him my empty hands.

"Whoa," I said. "Sorry. I didn't mean to—"

"You come here to spy on me," he screamed. A string of white spittle escaped from the corner of his mouth.

I cursed myself for being unarmed. After weeks of walking around armed to the teeth, waiting for the judge's shooters to have a go at me, I'd been relishing not carrying anything heavier than a pen. Bad move.

"No," I said. "I'm looking for Western Cold Storage."

He began to shift from foot to foot and wave the hammer around. "You get a good look? You happy now? You get a good look?"

As a matter of fact, I didn't like the look of it at all. This guy was out there. Whatever smoldered inside him wasn't something I wanted to deal with right now. If I wasn't careful, he'd scramble my brains. I showed him my palms again. "I'm going to go," I said. "I'm going to leave this card . . ." I waved it at him. ". . . right here on the table, and then I'm going to go. Sorry."

"You happy now?" he screamed again. His eyes were wet and filled with a look of horror usually only seen in war photos. For a moment, I thought he might cry.

I kept my eyes glued on the hammer as I leaned over and placed the card on the edge of the table. I groped behind my back and found the knob. "Sorry," I said again as I backed out of the room. I did the first set of stairs backward keeping my eyes locked on the door and then, when I got to the landing, turned and hustled down to ground level.

When I turned and looked back up at the office, he was standing in the middle of the room with my business card in his hand, his lips moving as he read. When he finished, he walked over to the window and glared down at me; the expression on his face sent a shiver trickling down my spine. I'd seen its like before, but only on cornered animals. Cue the *Twilight Zone* theme. I turned on my heel and started double-timing it for the door.

I got about halfway to the Hysters when the lights went out.

I stood still in the velvet black, keeping my breath steady and even. Behind and above me, I heard the office door scrape open.

"Come on, man," I said to the darkness. "No need for this."

I waited for my eyes to adjust and listened to the creaking and groaning that meant he was coming down the stairs. The building was tight. No strips of light along the roofline or around the doors.

I felt my throat tighten. No way I was playing blindman's bluff with this guy. I could hear the slide of his feet on the floor somewhere behind me and the hair rose on the back of my neck. Now a low grunt.

I opted for speed instead of stealth, walking quickly forward with my hands thrust out in front of me like feelers, figuring as long as I stayed in the middle, I was bound to run into the Hysters before long.

Then I heard the noise. He was walking on top of the containers, jumping the gaps as he hopped progressively closer. I stood still and held my breath, hoping to get a bearing on him, but suddenly, he was silent, too. I had the eerie feeling that he could see me in the dark whereas I couldn't see my hand in front of my face.

I moved quickly to my right, walking at a normal rate with my hands thrust out before me until I collided with a container. I put my back to the cold metal and listened. Nothing. I figured I'd stay put and wait for my eyes to adjust to the inky darkness. With the container at my back, he either had to come at me from the front or over the top. I kept my eyes glued to the front. I figured I'd feel the vibrations in the metal if he walked along the top of the box. I waited.

My neck stiffened as I heard his feet slap the concrete floor. I could now make out the outlines of the containers lining the other side of the aisle. Inside my head, my breathing sounded like a fire siren.

I worked at long silent breaths of the same length, in and out, one to ten, one nostril and then the other, one to ten, focusing, taming my metabolism, until I could feel my heartbeat returning to normal.

I took one measured step at a time, carefully placing my foot and then bringing the rest of my weight over, trying to prevent the slap of a sole or the rustle of clothing. Using this method, I slowly sidestepped to the far end of the container. More breathing.

Satisfied that I was under control, I hopped silently across the dark empty space and rested my back along the next row of boxes. The ribbed metal felt cold and gritty against my shoulders. I estimated I was three or four containers from the forklifts. The way I remembered it, the front half of the warehouse was virtually empty. If I could get on the other side of the Hyster blockade, I could make an all-out sprint for the door. He knew the place better than I did, but was twenty years my senior. The way I saw it, my best chance was to make it a footrace instead of a game of hide-and-seek in the dark. Even if he was waiting for me at the door, I'd be moving his way at full speed, which is pretty much what you want to do when the other guy has a club. You want to get inside the power arc as quickly as possible, like a baseball pitcher coming inside with his hard stuff, trying to get you to hit the ball off the handle. Secret was to keep your head off the sweet spot in the bat.

Turned out it wasn't a problem. He quick-pitched me. As I sidled to the edge of the metal box and groped around the corner with my hand, some vestigial sense within me felt a whisper of air and I knew beyond doubt that he was close. Instinctively, I twisted to my left. As I turned toward the whisper, I had the oddest notion that I heard a sob.

I think I may have even raised my arm and said, "No."

And then I was back in the upstairs hall, wearing slipper-socks and that stupid plaid bathrobe, staying off the carpet runner and its three squeaky boards, creeping all the way past my mother's room to the back stairs, where the rumble of the voices drew me downward toward the kitchen below, to the men who sat sipping whiskey and smoking cigars, to the talk of votes and variances and to that last dark stair, where, after everyone had gone and the glasses were rinsed, my father would find me sleeping and carry me back to my room.

In my business it's pretty much an occupational hazard, but I've always hated getting hit in the face. In retrospect, the aversion probably saved my life. The impact must have thrown me face-first into the steering wheel. I awoke from my dream with hot blood running down my face and cold water running up my legs. For a second, I was giddy. I thought I'd fallen asleep at the wheel and was having one of those terror-filled "holy guacamole, I'm doing seventy, and don't remember the last five miles" moments, but no . . . it was my nose . . . something was emptying out over my upper lip and running down my chin, and I couldn't stand it. I pawed at my face and then held my hand out in front of my eyes for inspection. In the darkness, the blood gleamed nearly black. For some odd reason, I brought the stained hand to my face and licked it. Yup. It was official. I was bleeding. I staged a search for my other hand and located it over on the left, locked to the steering wheel. I blinked in wonder and then raised my eyes to the windshield just in time to see the side of the ferry and then a wave breaking over the hood.

Instinctively, I brought both hands to the wheel and tried to steer, but the little car merely rotated slowly in a circle. The numbing cold had rolled up and over my waist, nearly paralyzing me. My teeth chattered, and I began to shake violently.

At that moment, the extra weight of the engine in the front of the car stood the Fiat on its nose. Straight up and down, that ass-in-the-air, last-moment-of-the-*Titanic* pose. I was hanging from my seat belt harness, steering straight down into oblivion when the cold came rolling down my neck. I shuddered violently and gasped just as the car sank beneath the surface, and as I swung gently to the left in the wet blackness, steering happily away, it came to me that I was drowning.

I'd like to tell you how I remained calm. How I held my breath there in the darkness, coolly analyzed my options and realized that if I merely allowed the car to fill with water, the pressure inside would soon equalize with the pressure outside, allowing me to open the doors and waltz out. I'd like to tell you that, but it wouldn't be true.

I lost it. Completely. The only thing going through my head was music. I had this tune running through my head, and it wouldn't stop. Not a song really, more like a fanfare that I

kept humming over and over, louder and louder as if to remind myself that I was still alive.

I popped my seat belt and began to thrash about in the
narrow confines of the car, punching and kicking, trying desperately to break out a window or push open a door. The air
in my chest was on fire, and my limbs were cold and clumsy.
I put my back against the steering wheel and kicked hard at
the passenger side window. Nothing. A second wild kick
went off course, and I put my foot completely through the
convertible top. I grabbed my leg with both hands and pulled
it back through the fabric, then righted myself, grabbed the
hole and tugged for all I was worth.

The top split right along the rip I'd fixed this afternoon. I
got my feet under me, stuck one arm up through the hole
and then used my legs to force my shoulders up and through.
The music was screaming as I shook free of the car and began
to float slowly upward.

The sound stopped abruptly a moment later when I
couldn't help but open my mouth and replace the burning
air in my lungs with sweet cool water. I remember my chest
convulsing once and then again and then the twin rivers of
sparks. The rest, as they say, was strictly fade to black.

13

"ARE YOU SATISFIED NOW?" REBECCA ASKED.

Let's face it, when you're lying in a hospital bed, from whence a team of seemingly competent doctors has decreed thou shall not rise for several days, and you got there by doing precisely what everyone on the planet has been telling you *not* to do, this is not a fair question.

If my throat hadn't been raw from the collection of tubes they'd been running up and down it all night, I'd have defended myself. As it was, I had bigger problems. She'd brought visual aids. I pointed at the folded newspaper she carried beneath her arm and shook my head. The movement nearly rendered me unconscious.

"You don't want to see it?"

"No," I croaked.

"Oh, I really think you should see this."

"Uh-uh."

"You sound like Scooby Doo."

She unfolded the paper twice, but kept the front page facing in her direction. She tried to look disgusted but only managed to smirk.

"There's good news and bad news, Leo."

It's a truly loathsome woman who'll hit a guy when he's down. She didn't even wait for me to do my end of the good-news-bad-news joke. "The good news is that the pictures of your dad and Peerless Price are much smaller this morning.''

I groaned and tried to turn away, but even the slightest movement of my head sent my vision swirling. My head felt as if it were stuffed with steel wool. They'd given me enough Tylenol for a vasectomy, but it was barely keeping the brain-tumor headache at bay.

"The bad news is that the other two pictures are of you on a stretcher and your car on a hook.'' She turned the front page my way, holding it before her like a banner. "See.''

She was right. There I was in living color being wheeled to the wagon by a couple of EMTs. Thank God for the oxygen mask. The Fiat wasn't so lucky. In the picture, it hung on a hook like a dead fish, streaming water from its every pore, its once-rakish ragtop peeled back like a cheap toupee. A sad sight indeed.

"Where's the car?'' I whispered.

"I had them tow it to Mario's. Bobby says it's a goner.''

I shook my head and immediately wished I hadn't.

"No way.''

I figured I could get her off on the old "why in God's name do you keep that car'' tangent. That one always works. Would have worked this time too, except at that moment the door opened and Trujillo and Wessels came blowing into the room.

Wessels took one look at Duvall and headed for the far wall, over by the john. Trujillo strode over to the side of the bed.

"Dr. Duvall.''

"Detective Trujillo.''

"You guys catch him yet?'' I whispered.

Trujillo made a dismissive noise with his lips.

"You should count yourself lucky, Waterman. The owner doesn't want to drop a trespassing charge on you.''

I cleared my throat. My head was pounding. "What about speeding? I'll bet the car was going like hell on its way down to the river.''

He walked over and handed Rebecca a piece of paper.

"That's a bill from the Matson Crane Company. Eleven hundred bucks for pulling the car out of the waterway."

"Wouldn't that be littering?" she inquired.

"No. With that car it would be more like toxic dumping. But we've been thinking about maybe charging him with filing a false police report, haven't we, Frank."

Wessels grinned but kept his mouth shut.

"Oh, I get it," I said. "You bozos can't even come up with a lead on a guy with no ears?"

Trujillo flipped open his notebook. "Let's see here. We interviewed the president of Triad, who assured us that no one fitting your description is in any way associated with Triad Trading. Frank and I, we're very thorough, you know, so double-checked with both payroll and personnel . . ." He gave me a wink. "You know, just to be on the safe side. Same deal. No such person. Then we spoke with every guard who works the gate on Pier Eighteen. None of whom, incidentally, recall a man with no ears."

"Not even a one-eared guy," Wessels added.

Trujillo licked his finger and turned a page. "We spoke with security for the cold-storage company next door and guess what . . ." he waited. "You guessed it. They'd never seen anyone even remotely like that either." He flipped another page. "Finally, we even asked the crew working on the ferry on the other side of the river. The ones who hustled around and saved your butt, and lo and behold, they didn't know a thing about a guy with no ears either." He snapped the notebook closed and returned it to his pocket.

"So . . . unless you've got something else you'd like to share with us . . . this is about as far as it goes."

"Some lunatic attacks me, throws me and my car in the river and you're going to forget about it."

He smiled. "You know, considering that nobody but you has ever seen this earless guy and the doctors tell us you don't have a mark on you after this guy supposedly cold-cocked you . . ." He let it ride. "I hope you won't mind if we don't exhaust our entire investigative arsenal on this one."

"He hit me with a rubber mallet," I said.

Trujillo nodded with mock gravity. "*Boing,*" he said.

"The man with no ears thumps the man with no brain who found the man with no hand." Wessels chortled from the corner. "I think there's a definite pattern here, Trujillo."

It was hard to argue with. I seemed to be developing a disturbing penchant for people with missing parts.

"Is that all?"

Trujillo walked over to the side of the bed. "No . . . as a matter of fact it's not." He looked over at Duvall and then turned back to me. "I have been requested by my superior, Lieutenant Franklin, to tell you that the Seattle Police Department is currently conducting an open investigation into the death of Peerless Price and that your assistance will be neither required nor tolerated." He fixed me with a long baleful stare. "We don't know what you were doing on Pier Eighteen, but we don't like the smell of it. There's general agreement that you're inclined to poke your nose in where it doesn't belong. We figure this whole thing with Price is going to be too much of a temptation for a guy like you, Waterman. So, as an aid to your recuperation, as of this moment, we're pulling your PI license and both of your gun-carry permits until further notice." He dropped a single sheet of folded paper into my lap, executed a crisp military turn and headed for the door. Wessels gave me a toodles wave on the way out.

I tried to sit up. The sudden flow of blood to my head made me dizzy. I closed my eyes. Just for a second.

When I opened my eyes again, the light in the room had shifted. Duvall was gone and Patrick Waterman was standing in the middle of the room looking about as uncomfortable as I'd ever seen him look.

"You look dreadful," he said.

"You ought to see it from this side."

"Everyone's very worried about you." *You cur.*

"I was a little concerned there for a while myself."

He made a quick inspection tour of the room.

"Catholic hospitals even smell differently," he said. "I think it's the piety." I figured he'd beat around the bush, but he surprised me and got to the point.

"I'm certain I speak for the rest of the family when I say we're relieved to see that you're all right, and we all certainly hope a lesson has been taken here." *You cur.*

I reached over to the bedside table and got my water glass with the nifty articulated straw. I took a long sip and then put it back.

"What sort of lesson did you have in mind?"

"That perhaps sleeping dogs should be allowed to lie." He lifted the newspaper from the chair and held the front page up for me to see. "This would have been over by Friday. The carrion eaters would have latched onto some other poor family and their tragedy and we could have gotten on with our lives. Surely this . . ." He rattled the paper and then returned it to the chair. ". . . must suggest to you that some measure of discretion is called for here." *You cur.*

When I didn't answer, he went into the prepared section of his presentation. "Has it ever occurred to you, Leo, that perhaps we were never intended to know our parents in the way we know other people."

"Can't say it has."

He hooked a thumb under his chin, ran his index finger up the side of his face and tilted his head.

"Have you ever pictured your parents making love?" he asked.

"Mercifully no," I said.

I started to laugh, but it hurt my head.

He smiled. "Notice how you answered. You said 'mercifully.' You couldn't keep a straight face. I have precisely the same reaction. That's because the picture of our parents in the throes of passion is more than we can imagine. Our parents aren't people in the normal sense. At least, not to us. To us, they're characters of mythic proportions. Far above the tawdry demands of biology."

I figured there was a lesson in here somewhere and I figured he'd sure as hell get to it. He didn't disappoint. "Your father was a complicated man who led a complicated life, Leo."

I started to speak, but he raised his voice and kept talking.

"You have no context, Leo. The social forces which shaped your father, the times, the entire context is lost now. There's nothing you can do for him. The only people who are affected by actions such as yesterday's debacle are your family. I implore you, Leo. Please don't make this any more painful for us than it has to be."

I had the urge to sit straighter in the bed but couldn't muster the strength. I settled for another sip of water.

"So," I said, holding the cup on my chest with both hands. "Let me see if I've got this straight. Because I can't conjure up a picture of my father hunched up behind my mother doggie-style, I ought to stand around doing nothing while everybody in the city talks about how he murdered a newspaper reporter thirty years ago and planted him in his own backyard. Is that it? Am I getting warm here, Pat?"

"There's no need to be objectionable. I should think your recent testimony in the Brennan case would have salved your need for the public eye. I fail to see . . ."

"Brennan?" I said. "Why do you keep bringing up Brennan? What's he got to do with . . ."

It felt like a small animal was trying to dig its way out of my head. I closed my eyes. Just for a minute.

"I'm tellin' ya, he's crapped," the familiar voice said.

I cracked one eye. The bed had been lowered. I was lying on my side, and it was dark outside. I rolled to my back and looked out over my feet. George and Harold were passing a pint of vodka back and forth between them, smacking their lips as they took in the room.

"Hey . . . hey," George said. "The king lives."

I groped around until I found the electronic control for the bed and then brought myself about halfway to sitting up.

"How'd you two get in here?"

"Fire stairs," said Harold.

George took a sip and then wiped his mouth with his sleeve.

"We come earlier but that goddamn blue-nose uncle of yours told the nurse you was sleeping and shouldn't be disturbed."

"Where's Ralph and Normal?"

"You know Normal," Harold said. "He don't like these places. He kinda got this thing that if he comes in one of these places they're just naturally gonna keep him."

"And Ralph?" I pressed.

George passed the bottle to Harold. He spoke without looking my way. "You know how Ralphie is, Leo. We all shared the dough we got from you with him. He's been knee-walkin' hammered ever since."

"A fool and his money are soon partying," added Harold, just a bit too quickly.

Something in the way they refused to meet my eyes made me nervous, but I didn't have the strength to wring it out of them.

George must have sensed what I was feeling. He suddenly became animated, waving the bottle in the air. "A little nip?"

"I'll pass on the vodka," I said. "But I'd love some fresh water out of that pitcher." I pointed to the sweating metal container on the table by the bed. "I'm dying of thirst."

These were guys who knew about thirst. They bustled around and came up with a fresh glass filled with fresh water and a brand new flex-straw. Couldn't leave a guy parched, after all.

"The whole crew was worried about you, Leo," Harold said.

"The pictures on the news looked real bad. Couldn't hardly tell it was you they was stuffin' in the meat wagon," said George.

"Tell everybody I'm okay. They say I'll be out of here on Friday. I'll stop by the Zoo and see everybody."

"What happened?" Harold asked. "How'd you end up in the drink?"

"I had a bad Tuesday."

"Ain't no other kind," said George grimly.

"You know . . ." Harold mused. "Tuesday's a shitty way to have to spend one-seventh of your life."

My head throbbed. They were working their way through the rest of the week when I closed my eyes. Just for a minute.

14

YOU KNOW WHAT THEY SAY: WHEN THE CHIPS ARE DOWN, THE buffalo's empty. And the chips were definitely down. They sent me home on Friday morning with three bottles of pills and a list of "thou shall nots" that would have made a Jesuit blush. Near as I could tell, for the next week or so, my activities were limited to low-impact needlepoint and the contemplation of my navel. At least, that's what I promised.

I lasted for about forty-five minutes after Rebecca went to work. Then I made the mistake of plugging the phone back in. Wedged in among the interview requests and sales pitches was a message from Bobby Alston, my mechanic down at Mario's Foreign Auto Repair. According to Bobby, they'd dried the Fiat out as best they could but needed the keys so they could see if it would start. I mean, what was I gonna do? Leave my car down there with strangers?

Dr. Fitzroy had called also. It took him a full five minutes to hem and haw his way to saying that he thought he had the information I had requested . . . documentation suggests . . . only preliminary . . . future research might well reveal . . . conclusions might be hasty at this time. The guy could overqualify a nocturnal emission.

The secret of getting around while concussed, I'd discovered, was moving slowly. As long as I didn't make any sudden moves, I felt decent and my vision more or less kept up with the movement of my head.

I shuffled over to the kitchen counter and shook out the manila envelope containing my personal belongings. The watch, the keys and the spare change were sandy but undamaged. My pocket notebook was soaked through and bleeding ink onto the counter. My wallet came out with a wet plop and lay dripping on the counter like a shelled mollusk.

I rinsed and dried the watch, keys and change, put the watch on my wrist and the keys in my pocket. The wallet and notebook, on the other hand, needed serious work.

I peeled the various folds of the wallet apart, rescued my driver's license and the credit cards and then spread the notebook, the wallet and all of its sodden contents around the heat registers in the kitchen floor, weighed them down with a pair of slippers and turned up the heat. Then I called my aunt Karen in County Records.

"Records."

"Karen. It's Leo."

"You're not supposed to be using the phone."

If information circled the globe at half the speed it moves through my family there'd be no need for satellites.

"Who says?" I demanded.

"Rebecca called Betty last night."

Much as it pained me, I had to admit it was a canny move on Duvall's part. Let your fingers do the walking. One-stop gossipmongering at its finest. Calling my cousin Betty was the civilian equivalent of issuing an all-points bulletin. Today Betty, tomorrow the world. When *America's Most Wanted* came up empty, they called Betty. She reminded me of that old blues song about how "Your Mind Is on Vacation, But Your Mouth Is Working Overtime."

"I'm feeling okay," I said.

"You're supposed to be resting. Do you know how worried we all were about you?"

Karen, unlike her brother Patrick, wasn't asshole enough to

start a guilt fest with me so I said, "Tell everybody I'm fine. A little fuzzy, but fine."

"Well, kiddo, that picture of you on the front page the other day didn't look any too fine." She laughed. "And heck, Leo, you've been a little fuzzy since the late sixties."

"That's precisely why I need your help."

"You're not supposed to be working."

"I'm not working. I'm just sitting home being nosy."

I heard her sigh. "About what?"

"About an import company named Triad Trading."

She asked me to spell it. I did.

"What did you want to know?"

"Mostly who owns it, but I'd be interested in anything else you had lying around."

"I'll see what I can do, but I'm not going to be able to get to it for a while. Call me later this afternoon."

"You're such a dear," I cooed.

"Oh, stuff it," she said. "And you better not tell Rebecca that I did this for you. She'll have me on a slab."

"I pledge my troth."

"What's troth, anyway?" she asked.

"No idea."

Click.

I called the university. Fitzroy wasn't available to come to the phone, but he had office hours from one till three in Denny Hall.

Click.

I pulled a fresh notebook from the top drawer and called a cab.

EVERY MECHANIC in the place stood around the Fiat in a loose semi-circle. "What?" I demanded. "These guys don't have any cars to work on? For what they get, they ought to at least pretend."

"Mario took his old lady to Mazatlan for the week," Bobby Alston said as we crossed the garage together. "We got a pool going. Actually several of them."

"On what?"

"On whether or not it will start. On whether the salvage guy will give us anything for it or whether we'll have to pay him to take it. On whether or not weird stuff is going to come out of the tailpipe. That sort of stuff."

"It'll start," I said, without believing it.

Quite frankly, the Fiat looked better than usual. It was cleaner and the convertible top, in spite of now being ripped in two directions, looked far better for having been mended with matching black tape.

"We done what we could," Bobby said. "I took the fuel and ignition systems apart and dried them out. Last two nights we took it over to the body shop next door and left it overnight in the oven they use to cure the paint jobs." He shrugged. "When they been underwater, you never know," he said. "They can be a little squirrely."

A low murmur rose from the assembled multitude as I strode to the side of the car and pulled open the door.

"Where's the 'it won't start' money?" I demanded.

A big blond guy with a flattop stepped forward. The red embroidery on his coveralls read YURI.

"How much?" he asked.

"I got twenty says it starts right up."

He wiped his hands on a coarse red rag.

"What's right up?"

"Before the battery goes dead."

"Even money?"

"Yep."

"You're on."

Of course I was on. Twenty bucks meant nothing to these foreign-car repair guys. These guys made more than U.S. senators. They drove newer and better cars than their clientele. They took longer and better vacations. If I ever have children, I'm not wasting my money or their time on college. I'm training them as BMW mechanics.

I slid into the seat, being extra-careful not to bump my head on the way down. I slipped the key into the ignition, pumped the gas pedal twice and turned the key. The engine ground once around, coughed . . . and sprang to life, purring right along as if nothing had ever happened.

Above the engine noise, I could hear shouts and whistles. I gunned it a few times. It ran great. Outside the car, money was changing hands; men were spreading out over the garage. I left the car running and got out. The blond guy was fishing behind his coveralls for his wallet. He produced a twenty. "I don't believe it," he said.

I gave him a grin. "You wouldn't mind getting the door for me, would you, Yuri?" I asked.

He matched me tooth for tooth. "My pleasure," he said.

I high-fived Bobby on my way by and got back in the car. With a squeal of the tires and toot of the horn, I bounced out onto Twelfth Avenue and headed north toward the University of Washington, with an ache in my head but a song in my heart. I almost made it, too.

I was coming up Pacific Avenue about four blocks south of the main campus, feeling better than I had in several days. I had the radio going. Del Shannon was singing "Runaway." It wasn't raining.

The car stopped running. No coughing, no sputtering, no missing or lurching. Just running one minute and shut down the next. I coasted to the curb in a bus stop, set the e-brake and turned the key. Nothing. Not a sound. I checked my watch. One-thirty. I waited five minutes and tried the car again. Dead as a doornail.

I released the brake and coasted the car downhill toward the back of the bus stop, about as far out of the way as I could get it. I locked up and started trudging up University Avenue toward the campus. One of the nice things about owning a Fiat is that if you park it illegally, most folks assume it's broken down and cut you some slack.

DR. MILTON FITZROY tore another strip of masking tape from the roll and attached the last corner of the plat map to the blackboard.

"There," he said, surveying his work.

I stepped to the front of the room and took a look. He'd enlarged the entire section of the city into a four-by-six-foot blueprint. Everything below First Avenue from Pike down to Yesler in July of nineteen sixty-nine inscribed in bright blue.

He pulled one of those flashlight pointers out of his pocket and stepped back. "Where to begin," he said. He looked my way. His eyes were bright. "What say we begin with restaurants," he said.

"Why not."

Follow along with the little red dot of light.

"On the waterfront, at that time, there were but two. Elliott's and Ivar's." He looked at me as if to ask whether he should go into greater detail. There was no need. Both restaurants had been in operation since the beginning of time and would probably still be dispensing clams and oysters to the tourists long after I was gone. The thing that brings locals to that part of town is visiting relatives from the Midwest. The waterfront was far too public for anything the old man would have felt necessary to hide from Bermuda.

"No," I said. "Nothing touristy."

He was taken aback. "Well . . . you realize, of course, that . . ." he puffed, ". . . well, that very nearly eliminates everything in the area. As I told you earlier, the composition of that area was then, much as it is now, industrial-commercial. I most certainly wish you had told me," he sputtered. "I could have saved myself considerable effort."

Fitzroy was right on both counts. I should have told him he could leave out the tourist stuff. And, if you subtracted that crap, there really wasn't much down there. The area was a no-man's-land, a buffer between the land of the tourists down on the central waterfront and the real business of the city taking place further up the hill.

When the founding fathers and a hundred thousand Chinese laborers washed the tops of the hills down onto the tide flats, they created most of the terra firma which today is downtown Seattle. Unfortunately, they never envisioned the automobile.

By the early sixties, downtown traffic had become so choked and motionless that the city fathers had little choice but to act. The only flat and thus practical route by which to channel traffic up and away from the downtown core was along the waterfront. So they built the Alaskan Way Viaduct, a piggyback elevated roadway whose massive concrete edifice rose not twenty feet in front of the buildings along Alaska Way, blocking any view of the sound and creating an area of perpetual shade in a city of perpetual rain. Nowadays it's all metered parking and lowlife. Late at night, under the viaduct is as good a place to get yourself killed as anywhere in downtown Seattle.

"Sorry, Doctor," I said. "Please forgive me. I'm feeling my way along here. I don't really know what I'm looking for."

He harrumphed a couple of times and then pointed his little flashlight. "Well then, I suppose the Chase Hotel would have to be considered the epicenter of the area."

He cast a quick glance in my direction. I didn't have the heart to tell him that the Chase was the only place I knew for sure my old man didn't go, so I let him do his number. I let him go through everything else he'd come up with. I shut up and took notes. Floral Expressions halfway down the hill on Marion. Open till eleven on Friday nights. Two coffee shops along Western Avenue, Danny's Western Grill and the Soundview Diner, both open till eleven Monday through Saturday. Warehouses, packing companies, a couple of lunch-only joints. It went on and on. Nothing rang a bell. Nothing held the slightest clue as to what my father might have been doing in that desolate part of the city.

When he finished, I asked, "That's it?"

He clicked off his light and stuck a finger in his collar.

"There were two others."

I waited. Mistake. He started in on the no-verbs rambling.

"I hesitate to suggest that a man of your father's prominence would . . . for a moment . . . the idea is of course ridiculous . . . a completely different element of society . . . which is not to suggest . . . far be it from me . . . the last one to judge . . . changing societal attitudes . . ."

If I let him keep talking I was going to be here all night.

"What two others?"

He looked uncomfortable.

"At the corner of Madison and Western during that time period . . ." He hesitated, swallowed once and spit it out. "The Western Steam Baths. Open twenty-four hours a day."

I grinned and tried to picture the old man sitting around in the fog with a bunch of other guys in towels. Maybe it was that same defense mechanism Pat spoke of the other day, but I could no more work up an image of my father having a suds party with somebody named Pete than I could picture my parents doing the horizontal bop.

"I don't think so," I said.

"And, of course, the Garden of Eden."

I knew I'd heard the name lately, but couldn't put my finger on where.

"What's that?"

"An . . . er . . . a nightclub." He started babbling again. My head began to pound. ". . . entertainment . . . would now be considered quite tame . . . less tolerant attitudes . . . status-quo morality . . ."

I massaged the bridge of my nose. The action merely spread the pain over a wider area of my head.

"What is it? A whorehouse or something?" I blurted.

He straightened himself. "Oh . . . no . . . by no means. No. Quite the contrary." He giggled at his little joke. "It was a gay bar."

"A gay bar?"

"Rather famous . . . or infamous, I suppose, depending upon one's outlook. Live entertainment. Female impersonators. And . . ."

Suddenly, it came to me. Peerless Price's final columns. The Garden of Eden was the place that the cops raided and the records disappeared. If memory served, Peerless recommended the place be burnt to the ground—preferably with its customers inside.

"And what?" I prodded.

"Well, most coincidentally to our inquiry, it happens that the Garden of Eden was open only on Friday nights. According to the liquor license, from eight until closing at two, every Friday evening."

"Really?"

"Indeed."

I eyed him closely. "Did you ever . . ." I began . . . "I mean, have you personally . . ."

"Oh, no," he said emphatically. "Although I must say that I personally harbor no . . ."

I wasn't sure where I'd imagined my little fishing expedition was going when I'd started poking my nose into the past a couple of days ago, but gay bars and steam baths had certainly not been on the agenda.

"Famous how?"

"Oh, several academic studies have been made of the Garden of Eden and one rather famous book was written on the . . . er . . . social scene surrounding the club and the baths . . . which, as I recall, were . . . I suppose 'linked' would be a proper term . . . by . . . a pivotal period . . . a seminal period . . . sociologically speaking of course . . ."

I checked my notes. "So, what we've got then, excluding the tourist joints on the waterfront, is a florist, two coffee shops, a steam bath and a gay bar."

"Precisely."

He seemed pleased. That made one of us.

"Of course, this excludes the residential consideration," he added. Excluding it was just what I had in mind.

The only person I'd ever known who'd lived down under the viaduct had been a guy named Charlie Boxer. Charlie had been a full-time hustler and part-time private eye around Seattle for forty years. During one of his drunk and disorderly periods, between wives, he'd rented a loft on Western from an elderly Korean gentleman named Walter Lee.

I remember because Charlie used to love to tell the story of how, after moving in, he discovered he was sharing the space with half a dozen rats the size of llamas. He told of going to Walter Lee to complain that not only was he forced to sleep with all the lights on, but, despite the full hundred-and-fifty-watt glare, the critters had eaten his shoes while he was in the shower. The old man listened until Charlie finished raving, nodding sympathetically at each turn of the story.

At this point in the tale, Charlie would go into character, assuming the manner and speech of the elderly Korean. He'd stoop low and squint his eyes.

"I tol you, Mista Boxer . . . No pets! You hava pets, you gotta go!" At least, that's how Charlie told the story.

Fitzroy produced a stack of papers stapled in the upper left-hand corner. "I had my TA . . . uh . . . a summary . . . incomplete of course . . . standard bibliography . . ." I thanked Fitzroy for his trouble and for the hard copy of the report, shared several promises about keeping in touch and then effected my escape.

I turned right out of Denny Hall and walked downhill. I felt spacy, as if I'd been smoking pot. Everything seemed just a bit more interesting and complex than usual. The roots of the massive oaks had cracked and buckled the sidewalk into a rolling concrete mosaic. Overhead, the nervous trees waved about in the wind. I turned my collar up around my ears and headed for the street.

When I reached Fifteenth Avenue, I stopped and rested for a moment. From where I stood, the downtown skyscrapers peeped up over the north flank of Capitol Hill like candles on a birthday cake.

I walked along next to the moss-covered cement wall that worked its way in serrated sections down the hill. Ahead of me at the bus stop, four Asian girls in big bell-bottom pants and huge clunky shoes milled about the kiosk, whispering quietly but laughing loudly.

I let gravity pull me past them. Something about me sent

them into peals of laughter, but I couldn't work up anything even close to caring. I kept one hand on the wall as I walked down the hill past the Henry Art Gallery and the underground parking garage, closing in on the car. I'd already made up my mind. If the Fiat didn't start, I was calling AAA to tow it back to Mario's and then calling a cab for myself. I'd had all the excitement I could stand. My head felt as big as Charlie Brown's. I needed a nap.

When the car started on the first turn of the key, I was a bit disappointed. I guess I'd been looking forward to the surety of the cab ride. Anyway, the street was empty, so I pulled a U-turn and started down Pacific Avenue toward the Montlake Bridge, rolling along parallel to the ship canal past the University Health Center until the huge steel chevrons of Husky Stadium bracketed the sky, and then turned right, over the bridge and down the ramp toward the freeway and home.

ACCORDING TO KAREN, Triad Trading was a division of Pacific Rim Trading, which, in turn was a wholly owned subsidiary of Eastern Expediting, doing business as a limited partnership between Fortune Enterprises and Canton Carriers, which, as the name inferred, was a shipping company based out of Taipei, Taiwan.

"What's all of that mean?" I asked.

"It means you better not want to sue these guys."

She started to say something and then stopped. I waited.

"Fortune Enterprises . . ." she said after a moment.

"What about it?"

She took a deep breath.

"That's Judy Chen."

"Really?"

Judy Chen owned the International District. In my mind's eye I could see her picture in the newspaper, cutting ribbons and accepting awards. Over the past thirty-five years, she'd systematically purchased nearly all the property in what had once been known as Japtown. That's what they'd called the International District back before the war. Before they shipped their Japanese neighbors off to desert concentration camps and appropriated their hard-earned lives. Judy Chen had her finger in a lot of potstickers. If it came into Chinatown, it went through Judy Chen and some of it ended up in her pocket. You could say she was the Asian version of my old man. Sort of like Szechwan, half a dozen of the other.

"You want to hear what Judy Chen owns?"

I picked up my notebook. "Go for it."

She ran it by me. At great length. It took a full five minutes. Restaurants, bakeries, warehouses, laundries, produce companies, a beer distributorship, insurance offices, travel agents, video stores, two bars and, if I counted correctly, just over twenty buildings.

"Quite the Horatio Alger story, huh?" she said.

I played along. "Judy Chen is either a very astute businesswoman or very lucky . . . or both."

"Well," she began, "there was always that persistent rumor that Judy Chen had friends in high places."

"Makes sense," I said.

Usually she makes me work like a galley slave for these tidbits, but today she came right out with it.

"They always said she had your father in her pocket."

"Who always said?"

"Everybody. The wags, Peerless Price. Everybody. It was always the talk that he was her rabbi."

"Was it true?"

She hesitated for a long moment. "You really want to know? You know, kid, sometimes it's better to let bygones be bygones."

I was losing my sense of humor about that particular piece of advice. "Was it?" I snapped.

"Yes," she said.

"You sure?"

"Absolutely positive. I worked for the assessor back then. The word was that whatever Judy Chen wanted, Judy Chen got."

I mulled it over, remembering what LaFontaine said about

somebody having a lot of city pull down on the docks. I didn't like it a bit. The idea that my father could be even indirectly connected to fourteen dead people was more than I was willing to consider. I almost liked the gay bar and the steam bath better than this. Almost.

She sensed my discomfort. "It was a long time ago, Leo. In those days it was pretty much standard operating procedure. It was just the way business was done. Nobody thought anything about it. Nowadays, it's the city that cuts itself in on the action. They just eliminated the middleman is all."

"Why would he do that for her?" I asked.

"There's a lot of money to be made on the docks," she said quickly. Too quickly. Almost like it was a prepared statement.

"There's a lot of money to be made a lot of places," I countered. "Why there? Why her?"

I heard her sigh again. Her discomfort was palpable.

"Hang on for a second," she said in a weary voice.

I said I would. I could hear her heels as she crossed the room and closed the door to her office and then walked back to the phone.

She came out of left field. "You remember . . . I'm sure . . . that your mother and I . . . we didn't . . ."

I helped her out. "You didn't get along."

"No," she said. "We didn't. But Lord knows Bill . . . your father . . . was a long way from perfect."

I held the phone tight to my ear and waited for her to work it out.

"She had this air . . . as if the whole lot of us were beneath her station," she said. "I was young and proud, and I had a big mouth." I could almost hear her shrug. "Things got said. The kind of things that can't be taken back."

"What's that got to do with Judy Chen?" I prodded.

She thought it over for quite a while. "I guess what it's got to do with Judy Chen is that my relationship with your mother gives me pause to question my own motives here, Leo."

The phone company was right. You could hear a pin drop.

"They always said . . ." She stopped.

"They who? Same 'they' as before?"

"Yes."

"Yeah."

"They always said . . . that they . . . your father and Judy Chen . . . had a . . . were a . . . an item."

"You mean . . . ?"

"Uh-huh."

"When was this?"

"For years and years. Till the end," she added.

"Right up until he died?"

"Yeah."

She tried to lighten things up.

"You know, Leo, I don't think the Waterman men have the marriage gene," she said. "Look at Edward. The way I hear it he and Joan didn't speak to one another in private for the last five years of his life. Pat never married. You had that cup-of-coffee marriage with Annette way back when . . . Your father and mother . . . well . . ." She showed some restraint and let it hang.

We both knew their marriage bore little or no resemblance to the Partridge Family. From about the time I was seven, I couldn't remember a time when they'd slept in the same room or eaten together at the same table. Other than that, things were quite cheery around the house.

"Did my mother know?"

"Oh, sure," she said. "She'd never admit it, of course. That wasn't her way. But she knew. She had to."

I was angry. Not about my father and mother, either. What passed between them was past. No, I was angry that I hadn't known of any of this and angry that he hadn't seen fit to tell me. And most of all I was angry about all the people who, over all the years, I'd offhandedly dismissed when they spoke of my father. Turned out, they might have known more about him than I did. Maybe Pat was right. Maybe everybody was right.

I thanked her. Mercifully, Karen was every bit as uncomfortable as I was and made it easy to get off the phone. I could feel the blood under the skin of my face, and my head had begun to throb in earnest. I pushed myself to my feet and headed for the couch. Nap time.

15

AT FIRST, I THOUGHT I WAS PARALYZED. I AWOKE AT NINE-FIFTEEN Friday morning in exactly the same position on the couch that I'd assumed fifteen hours earlier. Sometime during the night, Rebecca had stuffed a pillow under my head and covered me with the red plaid blanket we took to Husky football games. I was so stiff I could barely lever myself into the sitting position. My neck felt like I'd been hung. Arrrgh.

After ten minutes of massaging myself and groaning, I got to my feet and shuffled into the kitchen like I was walking on broken glass.

Rebecca had left a note on the table.

Since you're obviously well enough to be driving around, why don't you meet me at the Coastal at one. Lunch is on you. If you can't make it, leave a message with Tyanne. R.

She'd also been thoughtful enough to leave the morning paper propped open on the counter so I couldn't miss it. The three stooges stared out from the front page in black and white. This time, I was in the middle. The Larry Fine position. LEGACY OF VIOLENCE?

I extracted the sports page and threw the rest of the paper in the garbage can. I put together a cup of coffee and settled in at the table. The Sonics were off to a great start. Other than squandering a twenty-point lead to Dallas in the final quarter on Thursday night, they were undefeated and blowing opponents out by an average of fifteen points. The Seahawks were right where they always were—mediocre and considering a coaching change. As for me, other than the fact that my father may have been gay, or at least partially responsible for the deaths of fourteen people, or both, I was just peachy.

By the time I'd worked my way through three cups of coffee and the girls' basketball scores, I was beginning to feel human, so I ransacked the kitchen, came up with a week-old hockey-puck bagel and some cream cheese that was still reasonably white. On the theory that stale and toasted are somewhat akin, I toasted the bagel, stirred the viscous liquid back into the cream cheese, spread one upon the other and wolfed them down. *Bon appétit.*

FORTUNE ENTERPRISES occupied a white two-story stucco building on South Lane Street, directly across from the International Children's Park. I rolled the Fiat to the curb right next to the blue dragon slide, locked up and started across the street. From the Lane Street side, trucks drove up a ramp to the second-floor loading docks. A red-and-white sign with an arrow said the offices were down around the corner on Fifth Avenue South. I'm hell with directions.

Having failed so miserably at stealth, I decided to try the direct approach this time. The receptionist was a good-looking blonde woman with thin black eyebrows. About thirty, she wore a tight yellow blouse and black stretch pants. Behind her desk, the large open office area had been divided into about twenty cubicles. The maze hummed with activity. Voices chattered away in several languages.

"Can I help you, sir?" she asked.

"I'd like to see Judy Chen," I said.

She folded her arms across her ample chest and narrowed her eyes. Her facial expression suggested that I'd just asked if I could use her underwear to make soup.

"Whatever you're selling . . ." she began.

I pulled a business card from my pocket and handed it over. She read it carefully and then checked the back side.

"You're the guy . . ." She looked up. "Down at the warehouse."

"Yup," I said. "I'm the one."

She checked both sides of the card again, and then motioned toward the three folding chairs along the front wall.

"If you'll have a seat for a moment, I'll see if I can't find someone to help you."

She stepped out from behind the desk, walked down the hall to a door marked PRIVATE and knocked tentatively. Someone must have answered, because she stuck her head inside for a moment and then stepped back against the wall. She motioned me forward.

As soon as I stepped into the room, he got languidly to his feet. Must have been my week for tall Chinese guys. He was about six-three and thin. A little bit long on hair and short on chin. About a hundred eighty pounds in an immaculate blue silk suit and one of those collarless, nineties Nehru shirts, he held my card gingerly, at the edges, as one holds a squashed bug.

He didn't waste any time on introductions.

"Does this concern the incident at our warehouse the other night?" he asked. "Our attorneys assure us . . ."

I stuck out my hand. "Leo Waterman," I said.

He didn't even look at it, much less shake it. He kept flicking his black gravel eyes from the card to my face and back.

Unbidden, I took a seat in the red leather visitor's chair and tried to look comfortable. He stared at me for a long moment and then, with dramatized reluctance, seated himself behind his desk.

"I'm looking for Judy Chen," I said.

He cocked an eyebrow at me. "So you said."

"I'll say it again if you like."

He kept his face as still as stone.

"My mother no longer takes an active part in the business."

"This isn't business. It's personal."

"You are acquainted with my mother?"

"No," I said, "but my father was."

A subtle tightening around his jawline told me he knew exactly what I was talking about. So much for inscrutability.

"My mother does not see visitors."

"She'll see me."

He sat back in the chair, rested his elbows on the padded arms and steepled his fingers in front of him.

"What business do you have with my mother?"

"I told you. It's personal."

He turned his hands palms up.

"And I told you; my mother does not see visitors."

"Well then, feel free to think of me as an old family friend, rather than as a visitor."

He made a weak attempt at a smile. "Well then . . . as you're an old friend . . ." The smile got bigger. ". . . perhaps you will do me the honor of allowing me to assist you."

I made like I was thinking it over. "Okay . . ." I began. I tapped my temple. "Excuse me, but I can't for the life of me recall your name."

He went back to his Mr. Stone Face.

"Gordon Chen," he said after a moment.

"Okay then, since we're old friends, Gordo, howsabout you tell me what you know about a guy with no ears who was camped out down at your warehouse on Pier Eighteen."

He emitted a short dry laugh. "A little guy in pajamas, right? A little pigtail? Was he carrying a little hatchet?" He cut the air several times with the side of his hand. "Chop, chop."

"No pajamas. Actually, he was about your height, and it was a rubber mallet." I smiled. "He did have long hair, though."

He leaned out over the desk and gave me a conspiratorial leer.

"What really happened? You get drunk and drive in the river? Is that it? You don't want the little woman to know, so you're making up this cock-and-bull story about a man with no ears?"

I snapped my fingers. "You see right through me," I said. "Have you always been this insightful?"

He sat back and took a deep breath. We had a pin-drop moment.

"For reasons I fail to understand, you suddenly keep popping up in my life, Mr. Waterman. It is my sincerest hope that this disturbing trend can be brought to an immediate end."

He paused. I favored him with a shrug.

"So . . ." He wagged a long finger at me. ". . . just for the record, I'm going to tell you the same thing I told the authorities. No such person is, or ever has been, associated with this business." He fixed me with a stare. "Am I making myself clear here? Is there any part of that statement which you did not understand?"

He wasn't expecting an answer, so I didn't give him one.

He rocked back in the chair. "You know, Mr. Waterman, if you don't mind me saying . . ."

"And even if I do," I interrupted.

He smiled. "As you wish, " he said. "Considering all that's going on with your father and all of that, I should think you would have better things to do than make up tall tales about men with missing ears."

"What would you be doing?"

For the first time, I had him going.

"What?" he said.

"If it were your father who was in all the papers, what would you be doing?"

I was hoping that maybe I could get him talking. Hoping if I lightened up the banter, maybe he'd relax a bit. No such luck. The words were hardly out of my mouth when his brow furrowed and his face began to flush. I watched as his fingers dug into the padded armrests of his chair. Now I knew what it looked like to a dentist who accidentally drills into a nerve. Without being exactly sure how I'd managed it, I really had the guy going. Interesting.

I opened my mouth to speak, but it was too late. Suddenly, he jumped to his feet and leaned out over the desk at me.

"Perhaps you have time to waste, Mr. Waterman, but unfortunately, I do not. I have a business to run." He gestured toward the door. "If you don't mind, I have a great deal to do."

I stayed put. "I don't mind a bit."

"Get out," he said. "Or should I call the police?"

"That's not very hospitable to an old friend."

"Get out," he repeated.

"Listen, Junior," I said. "I'm going to see your mother whether you like it or not. Today . . . tomorrow. I'm not sure exactly when. But I'm going to see her."

He came around the desk fast and stood looming over me. I checked myself for hangnails and then smiled up at him.

"Nice suit," I said.

He thought about reaching down and hauling me from the chair, but sanity prevailed. I outweighed him by fifty pounds. He was seriously pissed off, but he wasn't that stupid. Instead, he turned and leaned low over the desk phone. He pushed the red button.

"Darlene . . . call the police."

I got to my feet and stood nose-to-nose with him.

"You know, Junior," I said, "a suspicious man could get the impression you've got something to hide."

He clapped me on the shoulder. On his wrist, he wore a thin stainless steel watch with a mesh band. "Of course I do." He winked. "We all do. Opium dens. Illegal mahjong parlors. Dog farms. The mysterious secrets of the Orient and all that."

His hand remained on my shoulder.

I shook a finger at him. "You know, with all this racial stuff, you're starting to sound like a bigot. If I were you, I'd watch that. These are very politically correct times."

He dug in hard with his fingers and tried to turn me toward the door. I stayed put and then reached up and gently removed his hand. He tried to pull away, but I held his wrist. The guy was vibrating like a tuning fork. I had this sudden vision of Arte Johnson doing the Nazi on *Laugh-In*. Veeeery interesting.

I kept my smile in place and my voice level.

"And if you touch me again, Sparky, you're going to have to learn to wipe your ass left-handed," I said.

I let go of his wrist; his hand fell to his side, with a slap.

He stared at me for a long moment, walked over to the door and pulled it wide.

Darlene held the phone pressed to her ear. Her pencil-thin eyebrows rode high on her forehead like dueling question marks.

"They put me on hold, Mr. Chen," she said.

I stepped around him and started quickly down the aisle toward Darlene. Her eyes were wide; her mouth formed a bright red circle.

"Don't bother," I said on the way by. "I'll be going now."

I pulled open the door and stepped out into the street. To the West, the Kingdome squatted like a concrete toadstool. I gave myself a mental boot in the ass for letting him piss me off. It not only was unprofessional, but I'd accomplished nothing. I didn't know any more about Fortune Enterprises or Judy Chen than I had this morning.

I was still beating myself up as I walked back past the loading docks to the Fiat, got in and turned the key. Nothing. Not a sound. Tried it again. Still nothing. I pulled the hood release and got back out of the car. I released the latch, propped the hood open and stuck my head down into the engine cavity. I checked the wire connections to the distributor coil and spark plugs. Everything was tight. I checked the battery terminals for a loose connection. Nothing.

I heaved a sigh and began to close the hood. Then I saw him. Young Mr. Chen had donned a gray wool topcoat and had apparently developed a sudden urge for a stroll on a blustery fall afternoon. I stepped back behind the upraised hood and then peeked out around the passenger side. He looked neither to the left nor the right as he strode purposely up South Lane Street, the wind twirling his hair and rustling the tails of his coat.

I let him get a half a block up the street and then eased the hood down, locked the car and started after him. I stayed on the opposite side of the street, easing in and out of doorways and slipping behind parked cars, until three blocks later, right as he got to the Sun Ya Restaurant, he angled across the street to my side and disappeared around the corner of Seventh Avenue South.

I sprinted up the sidewalk and poked my head around the corner just in time to see him pull a key from his pants pocket, thrust it out before him and then step from view.

I counted ten and then started up the street, keeping close to the building, easing past a travel agent and a Chinese herb store, until I came to an unmarked blue steel door. A small surveillance camera was mounted high over the hinges, allowing a full view of anyone in the doorway. I averted my face and backed up a half dozen steps.

I crossed the street, over to what used to be the old Shanghai Hotel, and then turned back and looked at the building. I'd walked by it a thousand times but had never really seen it. Built of blood-red brick, its three-story edifice occupied the entire center of the block. While the ground floor was commercial, the upper two stories apparently were not.

A pagoda-roofed portico both separated the ground-floor businesses from whatever was above and also provided the necessary support for the second-floor balcony which ran the length of the building. Three sets of heavily curtained French doors were spaced along the wall.

What caught my eye, however, was the roof. From this angle, I could see that the roof had been converted into a garden of some sort. I could make out the dry stalks of tall plants and the top of a trellis or an arbor.

I recrossed Seventh Avenue South and ensconced myself in the doorway of the Sea Garden, my favorite Chinese restaurant. I was two-thirds of a block from where Gordon Chen had entered. If he went back the way he'd come, I was golden. If he came this way, I'd step into the restaurant. Maybe have some Singapore noodles or prawns in black bean sauce. It could be worse.

I spent the next twenty-three minutes as an unofficial doorman, opening the door for arriving customers, waving bye-bye to babies, smiling and nodding, trying to seem inconspicuous. At eleven-ten, Gordon Chen stepped out onto the sidewalk, cast his eyes quickly up and down the street, and went striding back toward the office. I waited until he was out of sight and then sauntered down to the doorway.

The door was dark green and solid steel. Nothing short of a blowtorch and a sledgehammer was going to so much as make a dent. A small white button was mounted directly into the brick. The second I pushed it, the surveillance camera began to pan slowly across the area, its electronic eye adjusting to focus, its electric motor whirling in the cold air. The voice came from a small grated speaker mounted high up over the door.

"Jes."

"I'd like to see Judy Chen, please," I said.

The electronic voice was female and Hispanic.

"Mees Chen does no receive visitors."

"Please tell her Leo Waterman would like to speak to her."

She didn't say yes or no. The speaker rattled once, and she was gone. I leaned back against the south side of the entranceway and waited, trying to give the impression that I was either confident of my chances or prepared to wait for as long as it took. It took about five minutes.

When I heard the handle being turned from the inside, I stepped out into the street, figuring that anybody who guarded their privacy this zealously just might have a leg-breaker on retainer. The door opened to reveal a woman in a gray maid's uniform. She was about fifty, short and stout, with a thick head of wiry salt and pepper hair held in place by a white plastic headband. She dried her hands on her white apron. I felt pretty certain I could whip her, so I stepped back up to the door.

"Jew come wid me, please," she said.

When the door swung wide, I realized she was standing in a narrow elevator car. I stepped in next to her. The sole adornment to the interior was a current elevator inspection certificate screwed to the back wall. She pushed the uppermost button, and we began to move silently upward. As we ascended, the maid looked me up and down several times, as if my presence had some sort of miraculous quality.

The door slid back. We were on the roof. The maid held her finger on the DOOR OPEN button, but did not move. She looked up at me with big liquid brown eyes. "Mees Chen see jew here. Jew go."

I stepped out of the car and began to look around. The scene before my eyes was something out of space and time, as if some remnant of an earlier age had been transported intact to the present and plopped down on top of the building. The entire roof of the building had been transformed into a formal garden, complete with hedges and flagstone paths. The breeze carried the sound of running water to my ears. Behind me, the door slid shut and I could hear the grinding sound of the elevator mechanism as it descended.

From my present vantage, I could see that the building ran completely across the block to the west, providing what I imagined to be the better part of half an acre of roof garden. Either the building had been built to withstand an incredible amount of weight on the roof, or somebody had put one hell of a lot of money into a structural remodel.

Along three sides of the roof, stands of tall bamboo swayed and rustled in the breeze. A central path of irregular flagstone ran toward an ornate wooden gazebo which seemed to mark the center of the space. On either side of the path, flower beds had been raked clean for the winter and covered with black plastic. To my right, twisted grapevines covered a redwood arbor with leathery yellow leaves.

On my right, next to the elevator, two pair of rubber boots rested on a bamboo mat. One pair small, almost childlike.

The other pair big enough for me. It was like I'd figured; old Gordo lived with his mama.

She was down at the far end on the right, on her knees, digging. I walked down the path and around the gazebo until I was about eight feet from her and stopped. Her hands said she was about seventy, her hair gone silver beneath a Mariners baseball cap. She wore blue jeans and a gray Husky sweatshirt. She used her thumbs to separate bulbs. I stood quietly as she wiped the last of the dirt from the bulbs in her hand and then got to her feet. She used the wrist of her empty hand to wipe the hair from her face and then took me in from head to toe with a level gaze.

"You favor your father," she said.

"So I'm told."

She was still beautiful. Like the pictures I remembered from the newspaper. Her almond-shaped eyes were clear and her skin nearly flawless. Her mouth was small and tight, like the bud of a miniature rose. Only her hands and the lines around her eyes suggested age.

She motioned for me to follow as she moved down the path to the right, toward a brown basket which rested on the flagstones down by the south edge of the roof. We walked side by side. She moved with the lithe grace of a young girl.

"I presume you've seen the papers," I began.

"I haven't read a newspaper or watched the news in nearly ten years," she said. "Not since I retired."

I told her the story. The strange saga of Peerless Price. Five hundred words or less. She never even blinked.

"You can imagine what they're saying about my father."

She stopped walking and looked up at me.

"He wouldn't mind," she said flatly.

"You're sure?" I asked.

"I'm certain," she said without hesitation.

She began walking again. As I hustled to catch up, I had the feeling she was right.

"I mind," I said.

She stooped low over the basket and dropped the handful

of bulbs in with several dozen others. I stood still and listened as the wind rattled the dry bamboo. In the distance, a car alarm began to chirp like an urban cricket. She straightened back up, dusting her hands together.

"Is that what you were doing down at my warehouse? Protecting your father's honor?"

"I thought you didn't read the paper."

"Gordon told me of your unfortunate experience. Is it? Is that what you were doing?"

"Something like that," I hedged. "I was looking for something that might have pushed my father into killing Peerless Price."

She looked mildly amused.

"At my warehouse?" she scoffed.

"Fourteen dead people make an excellent motive for murder."

She compressed her lips into something thin enough to pass for a scar. "And you think your father was, in some way, connected to that tragedy?" She cocked her head. "You've confused me, Leo. Just a moment ago, you said your intention was to protect his honor."

I changed the subject. "They say that you and my father were . . ." I searched for a phrase but came up short.

"Were what?" she prodded.

"Lovers," I said.

Her eyes took me in all over again.

"And if I were to say to you, yes, that is true . . . what then? Would you not then find it necessary to defend your mother's honor?"

"My mother's face isn't all over the front page."

"You should be careful what you ask old women. The older we get, the more likely we become to tell you the truth."

"The truth is what I came for."

She thought it over, looked at me as if to say I'd been warned, and said, "Then . . . yes, since you insist, the truth is what you shall have. It's true. Your father and I were business associates and lovers for many years."

"Did my mother know?"

"Yes," she said.

As I sat there rolling it around in my head, she made a face and continued.

"In those days, the world of business was not open to little China girls. In order to do business, I had to find a . . ."

Now it was her turn to search for a word.

"A patron," I said.

"Yes. A good word. A patron. Your father was my patron. Your father had what they call today clout. He opened a great many doors for me, and . . . I would like to think . . . was amply rewarded for his efforts on my behalf."

I swiveled my head around.

"Looks like you made out pretty well too."

Her eyes grew darker and her voice took on an edge. "This may be difficult for you, but what I have is the result of my efforts and no one else's. As I said, your father opened doors. It was I who walked in."

I switched gears again.

"People say it was your company that was bringing those people who died into the country."

She made a resigned face but didn't speak.

"Was it?"

"And if it were? What then? Would it be so terrible to assist others in the quest for a better life? When I do it here, they call it 'giving back to the community.' A public service. They give me plaques." Her eyes narrowed. "Or perhaps it's just that bothersome feeling that we Asians don't value life as do you Occidentals. What with there being so many of us and all."

"Now I know where Gordon learned the trick."

"What trick would that be?"

"Throwing the race card whenever you get pushed. Just sort of segueing into bigotry at random."

"Perhaps you are on the wrong side of the issue to be making judgments such as that."

"What side of the issue was that family in the container on?"

"The inside," she said.

She adjusted the cap on her head and looked up at me.

"Do you honestly think those people were unaware of the risk they were taking?"

"They probably didn't plan on dying."

"Neither life nor business is without inherent risks."

"You seem to have played your cards right," I said.

"Once again, my success seems to surprise you," she chided. "You're not one of those who believe business acumen is the sole province of the white Anglo-Saxon male, are you?"

"I didn't mean it that way," I said quickly.

"One of your father's many attributes was that he never underestimated anyone. A habit, which as I am sure you understand, while not necessarily more accurate than its counterpart, is necessarily more successful."

I made a mental note not to make that mistake with Judy Chen and then shifted gears again.

"I seem to have made your son Gordon rather nervous."

She didn't flinch.

"Why do you say that?" she asked.

"I just stopped in to ask him a few questions. He threatens me with the cops, throws me out of his office and then he makes a beeline over here to talk to you."

"And thus, quite obviously, underestimated you," she said, with a wan smile.

"That remains to be seen," I said.

"Gordon is very protective of me."

"Are you sure that's all he's protecting?"

She motioned me over toward an ornately carved stone bench along the west edge of the roof. The pinwheel roof of the Kingdome lounged among a sea of cranes. To the south, a dozen yellow construction cranes encircled the hole in the ground that was to be the new retractable-roofed baseball park. To the north, a forest of bright orange loading cranes stood ready to pluck at the container ships.

"I'll tell you a little story," she said. "Then perhaps you will understand why Gordon is at times a bit overzealous in his attempts to protect me from the world."

She motioned for me to sit, pulled the cap from her head and shook her thick hair out. She used both hands to pull the hair back away from her face and then settled the cap back onto her head to keep it there. She pointed toward the south. Toward Pier Eighteen. "I came here on a boat from British Hong Kong in nineteen fifty. I was twenty years old. Unlike many others, I was not indigent. I was sent to work in my Uncle's import business. My father had smuggled a great deal of money to my uncle. My father believed that I was to be taught the business as a partner." She shrugged. "My parents were . . ."

I let her go through her life story, marveling at how different cultures, ten thousand miles removed, could so completely share the same set of hopes and dreams. It took her another ten minutes to get back to where she'd started.

"But my uncle was an old-fashioned man. Women were to him little more than animals. He treated me like a dog and when I objected, he put me out into the street without a penny."

Her eyes searched inward and then she continued. "By then, I was twenty-five. My parents had been murdered by the Communists. I was alone. I did what I had to do." She seemed to wait for me to say something, so I did.

"What did you do?"

"What else? I found a rich young man and married him."

"Just like that?"

She gave me a wink. "What else was I to do? Go to work in a laundry?" Her mouth took on a bitter cast. "He was only twenty . . . so eager. His name was Jimmy Chen. His parents owned frozen fish warehouses. He had a big trust fund. I seduced him."

She turned her gaze my way and looked at me as if she

had new eyes. She waved a hand. "To make a long story short, Jimmy Chen was a drunkard and a wife beater. I divorced him and used my half of the settlement to go into business for myself. I knew my uncle's customers. They knew me." Her eyes twinkled. "Before long, my uncle sorely wished he had made me his partner."

"And that's when you met my father?"

She nodded. "I needed better port facilities. The jobbers were squeezing me out. My goods would sit around for months sometimes. I couldn't do business that way. They said your father was a man who could arrange such things." She averted her gaze. "Your father was a very impressive man," she said.

As usual, other people's stories about my old man gave me the urge to be on another planet.

"If you don't mind me asking, what's all this got to do with your son Gordon being overprotective?"

"I knew your father then . . . I mean . . . we were involved. Gordon and I lived above the warehouse on Pier Eighteen." My face must have told her something, because she stopped her story. "I can see you're surprised. It's true. Gordon and I lived above the warehouse until he was eighteen. Money was very tight in those days. Everything I had was invested in that building. Nothing was left over for housing." She sounded almost nostalgic.

She took a deep breath. "In the beginning . . . before the divorce Jimmy Chen used to get drunk and beat me bloody. On two occasions, I had to be hospitalized." She looked up to make sure she had my attention. "Gordon was there in the room on those occasions. Once when he tried to help me, he was beaten unconscious." She paused for effect. "It was an experience which neither of us has forgotten. So I hope you forgive him for wishing to protect his mother."

If there was a snappy rejoinder for a moment such as this, it was lost on me, so I waited until she went on.

"I'm sure you must be every bit as sick to death of hearing about your father as Gordon is about hearing about his," she said. "So I am sure then that you, above all others, will appreciate the fact that I have no intention of betraying any of your father's confidences to you or to anyone else." She folded all of her fingers except one into her palm. "I will tell you the following, however. Your father did not kill Peerless Price."

"How do you know that?" I said quickly. "Did you kill him?"

"No," she said. "I did not. I know it because I know your father. Shooting a man in the head was not at all his style. That would be much too direct for your father. Your father was a master at insulating himself."

Once again, despite my best efforts, she read my face.

"You doubt me?"

"I'm keeping an open mind," I said.

She brought another finger out from her hand.

"Secondly, I will assure you that your father was not involved with the tragic incident in which that family perished."

"Because you knew my father?"

"No," she said quickly.

"How . . ." I began.

Her face closed like a leg trap. She shook her head.

"You came for answers and now you have them," she said.

Before I could ask another question, she got to her feet and walked over to the elevator. I followed along. She pushed the button and then turned back my way.

"Your father will weather this storm like he weathered so many others. He doesn't require your assistance."

"I think maybe I'm the one who requires assistance," I said.

"Then I wish you luck."

The door slid open. The maid was standing in the car, once again drying her hands on her white apron.

"Consuelo will show you to the door," Judy Chen said, before turning and walking briskly back toward her basket of bulbs.

I stepped into the narrow elevator car and turned back

toward Judy Chen. She'd stopped walking and stood on the flagstones, facing me again, her hands at her sides. "Leo," she said.

Consuelo leaned forward and pushed the down button.

"Yes," I answered.

She spoke quickly as if reciting. "Just because someone gave you a dead mouse doesn't mean you have to carry it around in your pocket for the rest of your life."

As I opened my mouth, the door slid shut.

16

REBECCA REACHED ACROSS THE TABLE AND SPEARED THREE OF MY French fries. Her theory on fried foods was that they weren't fattening as long as she ate them from my plate.

"And she admitted it?" she said, before stuffing her mouth.

"Not exactly."

She washed the fries down with some iced tea.

"Tell me exactly what she said."

We were sitting in a red padded booth in the front window of the Coastal Kitchen, a trendy little restaurant on Fifteenth Avenue East, just about at the center of Capitol Hill. She'd ordered a Cobb salad. When I'd asked Jennine for a burger and fries, Duvall had immediately gone into her Food Police routine, enumerating, in great detail, the suicidal caloric and fat content of such unclean foodstuffs. Since then, in addition to inhaling her salad, she'd eaten half my burger and damn near all the fries. Arrrgh.

"Okay," I began. "First she told me that my old man hadn't killed Peerless Price. So I asked her how she knew that, and I asked if she'd killed old Peerless herself."

"And she said?"

"She said . . . no . . . she hadn't offed Price and she knew my father hadn't killed him either because it wasn't his style."

"Do you believe her?"

"I don't know. I'd like to, but, you know . . . testimonials and a buck will get you on the bus."

Anytime I hear that So-and-so just couldn't have done such-and-such because that just wasn't his style, I recall how the neighbors of serial murderers like David Berkowitz and Jeffrey Dahmer always claim they were nice, quiet boys who kept to themselves and were always polite.

She gigged another golden fry and waved it at me.

"What reason would she have to lie?"

"None that I can think of."

"You told me the other day that only an idiot lies unless he has a reason."

She had a point, but I wasn't sure it mattered. Despite Judy Chen's testimonial, things looked worse now than they had when I started. Now I had a source who said it was common knowledge that Judy Chen's company was running illegals into the country back in sixty-nine. And, given a chance to flatly deny the allegation, Judy Chen had demurred. Color me with a cynical crayon, but I was taking that as a confirmation. Worse yet, lo and behold if this wasn't the same Judy Chen who turned out to be my old man's longtime business associate—and oh, by the way—mistress of thirty years or so. Not only that, but the whole matter of illegal aliens just happened to be one of the very issues upon which Peerless Price was regaling the city at the time of his death. I didn't like the sound of this at all.

Rebecca liberated a couple of more fries and read my mind.

"You think Price was onto it, don't you?" she said.

"That's pretty much the worst-case scenario."

No doubt about it. If Price was onto my old man's mistress and the dealings on the docks, no telling what might have happened. That scenario backed my old man into the kind of corner where all bets were off, and ending up in a bed of loam with a bullet in your brain was the rule rather than the exception. Judy Chen's stylistic assurances notwithstanding, people like my old man do not go gentle into that good night. And even if he didn't have the stomach to pop Price himself, he sure as hell was acquainted with the kind of people who did.

She reached across the table and patted the back of my hand. "You okay with all this?"

"It's frustrating," I said. "I was hoping that I could finally put a face on my father. Maybe squash all the feelings I have and all the stories I've heard into something recognizable. But the deeper I get into his life, the more he's got a quicksilver quality to him. It's like digging in sand. Every time I turn a corner, I find out something about him that points in a whole new direction, and none of it's anywhere I want to go."

She wiped her mouth and then reached for her purse.

"I know you don't want to hear this, sweetie, but maybe you ought to stop turning corners and digging holes."

Before I could respond, she gave me a devilish grin, slid out of the booth and said, "Not to mention mixing metaphors."

"Don't be a language maven. It's unbecoming."

I got to my feet and helped her on with her coat.

"You headed home?" she asked.

"I've still gotta see this Bruce Dickinson character this afternoon." I checked my watch. One fifty-five.

"The guy who wrote the book about the Garden of Eden?"

"Yeah."

Something in my tone turned her face serious.

"You know, Leo, every time you mention this lead you've got to the bar, you sound like you're a whole lot more upset about the possibility of your father hanging around in a gay bar than you are about the prospect of his being involved in a tragedy."

"What if he was doing more than just hanging around?"

"You just found his mistress, for crimeny sake."

"What if he . . ." I waffled a hand. ". . . you know."

"Swung from both sides of the plate?"

"Bite your tongue."

She pointed a long finger my way.

"See, I told you."

She may have been right, but there was no way I was

coming clean. In that moment, a conversation I'd had with Norman a couple of years back flashed across my mind. I'd come around the corner of First and Yesler one afternoon to find him standing on a fire hydrant speaking in tongues to a pack of German tourists. Later I'd asked him why he'd acted that way. He'd glowered down at me and said, "They treat you like you're retarded. I'd rather they thought I was crazy than stupid. There's more respect that way." Dude.

In this case, however, the truth was that both possibilities were disasters, both career enders and both more than enough motive to put Peerless Price in the ground. I hedged.

"I'm not fond of either of them," I said. "The only good news is that there's no way the cops are going to get onto either scenario."

"Why's that? They've got all your dad's stuff."

"That crap leads nowhere without Bermuda and Judy Chen, and there's no way either of them is going to tell the cops a damn thing."

"All the more reason to just let the whole thing die."

I hate it when she's right, so I ignored her. She slipped her purse over her left shoulder.

"I'll be home about seven," she said.

As she headed for the door, I threw a twenty on the table and reached for my coat.

BRUCE DICKINSON was exactly where his wife said he'd be, in the writers' room on the second floor of the downtown library.

I'll admit it. When I called his home and got a woman who said she was his wife, I was a bit put off. I guess I'd subconsciously assumed that anyone who would research and write a book about Seattle's gay community must necessarily be gay. Just shows to go ya.

As if to make my assumptions even more asinine, Bruce Dickinson was no more than a biscuit short of three hundred pounds. A ponytailed monster with military tattoos and forearms the size of my legs. He could have carried me around like a purse, were he so inclined, which, to my great relief, he apparently was not.

"Nixon changed all that," he said. "Before Nixon, everything operated on what might be called a gentleman's agreement. You slip the gentleman an agreed-upon amount of cash, and the gentleman agrees to look the other way."

"Which is what the authorities did for the Garden of Eden?"

"Right. The club paid the cops to leave them alone. Nobody thought anything about it. It was like the cops' four-oh-one K plan. It was how they sent their kids to college or paid off that retirement lot over at Lake Chelan. Once it became part of what might be called standard operating procedure, it became part of the status quo, and as such, worth defending."

"So," I began. "Not only did the cops not bust places like the Garden of Eden, they didn't allow anybody else to mess around with them either."

"Exactly."

"And Nixon changed all that?"

"In a heartbeat. Government was suddenly suspect. The old depression-era 'the government is my friend' illusion was dead. All gentleman's agreements were off. If the cops were watching the criminals, people started to want to know who was watching the cops. Accountability became all the rage in the public sector." He waved a big hand in my face. "Don't get me wrong. They were still allowed to be incompetent, they just weren't allowed to be corrupt."

I must have looked confused.

"It's hard for you to imagine the climate of the nineteen fifties concerning gays and lesbians. Words like 'repressive' don't cut it. It was worse than that. The suicide rate within the community was astronomical. The Garden was like a beacon in the night. All the big national impersonation acts came through every year. People could let their hair down."

"Literally," I added.

He nodded. "And figuratively as well. The movement was particularly giddy back then." He stopped talking, as if he suddenly wasn't sure he believed what he was saying. "I know it sounds corny, but there was a great deal of hope back in the late sixties. For a while it seemed the yoke had been lifted. Back before it became apparent how long the haul was actually going to be, a place like the Garden of Eden was like an oasis."

"Hence the name," I said.

"Exactly. Places like the Garden were where the first sense of a community was formed. It all started in places like the Garden and the Green Parrot and the Palomar up on Third. By the mid-seventies politicians were listening to the leaders of the gay community. By the mid-eighties, openly gay men and women were being elected. Nowadays, the mayor and the chief of police march at the head of the Pride Parade every year. And yet, down at the bottom of it all, not as much has changed as you might think."

He caught himself lecturing and stopped.

I figured . . . what the hell . . . we were having a little break in the action, maybe I'd assuage my curiosity, so I asked, "You know . . . when I started to look you up, I figured . . . you know . . . that anybody who'd write a book about . . . something like this . . . would be . . . I mean, not necessarily, but probably would be . . ."

He helped me out. "Gay," he said.

"Yeah."

"I used to be," he said.

Before I could close my mouth, he asked, "What time frame were you interested in again?"

"July nineteen sixty-nine," I said.

"The Garden was closed by July sixty-nine."

I admit it; I felt like a weight had been lifted from my shoulders.

"Actually," I amended. "It was two specific dates. May eighteenth and June first, nineteen sixty-nine."

He pursed his lips and leaned back in the chair.

"Why did you say you were researching this?"

"I didn't."

He mulled it over. "This have anything to do with your father?"

"I didn't say that."

"You didn't have to."

"Why would it have anything to do with him?"

He gave me a shy smile. "Well . . . you're too young and Wild Bill Waterman and old Peerless Price have been looking back at me from the front page every morning for a week." He leaned across the table at me. "Besides that, your father being involved would explain a lot of things."

The weight which had a scant moment ago been lifted, now settled heavily back upon my shoulders. "Why's that?"

"You happen to know what night of the week May eighteenth, nineteen sixty-nine was?"

"A Friday."

He nodded. "You notice I didn't ask you about June one." When I didn't say anything he asked, "You know why that is?"

"I'm betting you already know."

"June one was the last night the club was ever open."

I tried to sound calm. "Really."

"That was the night of the raid, man. The famous disappearing raid." He eyed me closely. "You do know what I'm talking about here, don't you?"

"Remind me," I wheedled.

He pointed a huge finger at my chest. "No way," he said. "I was born on a weekend, Waterman, but it wasn't last weekend." I tried to look shocked and offended, but he wasn't going for it. "You know damn well what I'm talking about here. If we can't manage an open exchange of information, maybe you ought to get up the road."

Much as it pained me, I allowed how I did know what he was talking about.

"Tell me what you know for sure."

I told him the story about my old man taking the car on those specific nights. "That's all I know," I said when I finished.

"If it was anybody but your father, I'd say it was damn little."

"Why's that?"

"Because, man, what this whole mystery has always been lacking was anybody with enough clout to quash the arrest and subsequent booking of nearly a hundred and fifty people. Especially when it was orchestrated by a public figure like Peerless Price. That took real balls. There couldn't have been more than four or five men in the state who had the clout to pull that off."

He was kind enough not to add that my old man was definitely one of them, but I'm a quick lad and figured it out.

"That's all I know," I said.

"That's about all anybody knows. I spent a month trying to dig up something on it and came up dry."

"What did the cops say?" I asked. "You mean to tell me departmental heads didn't roll over that one? I thought you told me police corruption was a thing of the past by then."

"For the most part, it was. The cops were clean. Before they ever even got the whole lot of them booked, an Order of Provision was issued and delivered to the precinct."

"What's that?"

"An order from a district court judge for all documents to be sealed and sent to his office. It's used sometimes in cases where the veracity of an accuser is in question, so that a person won't be tainted by the mere fact of an accusation. A judge reviews the material before it has a chance to become public. The cops just did what they were ordered to do. They packed up every bit of paperwork and sent it off to the judge."

"And?"

"The judge never got it. Or at least, that's what he says."

He was smiling. I didn't like it one bit. The hair on the back of my neck was standing on end, but I asked the question anyway.

"What judge was that?"

The grin got bigger. *"Your* old buddy Douglas Brennan."

17

BERMUDA WAS EXACTLY WHERE I LEFT HIM ON MONDAY, SITTING in that white leather chair by the window with the pictures of his past framed on the wall behind him and his glasses and canes close at hand. When I poked my head in the door, he reached over and slipped on his glasses.

He got me into focus and said, "I taught you to swim, kid. What, you forgot how?"

"You left out the part about being strapped in the car."

"That was in a later lesson."

When I was eight or nine, Bermuda would take me to the Y on cold winter afternoons. When we first started going, I couldn't swim yet. As a matter of fact, I was scared to death of the water. My parents had paid for two years of private lessons. The experience had only multiplied my fear, leaving me clinging to the wall at the shallow end while the other kids my age were roughhousing in the deep water. It drove my old man crazy. He used to leave the pool area at the country club so he wouldn't have to be party to my terror.

Bermuda had a better idea. After the country club debacle, he started taking me to the Y. I remember how surprised I was that he could swim. He explained that although his back and legs weren't up to the demands of gravity, the buoyancy of water allowed him an ease of movement which he never experienced on dry land. His motion was odd; he kicked with both legs at the same time and sort of doggie paddled with his hands, but he could swim forever, slowly, doggedly, moving back and forth along the wall of the pool, seemingly oblivious to everything going on around him.

He never pressed me about swimming either. Never said a word. He just left me alone to play with the other children. He knew that's all it would take, because he knew me.

I can still remember the day I began to swim. I remember because, for me, in order to swim, I had to be willing to die. I remember standing on the diving board, holding my nose, telling myself that a watery grave was better than spending the rest of my life on the concrete, listening to that fat Rocco De Grazia busting my chops. I remember jumping off the end and thinking that my death would, once and for all, teach my parents a lesson, and being vaguely disappointed when I found myself alive and clinging to the pool ladder.

Bermuda gestured toward the ladder-backed chair across from him. I crossed the room and took a seat.

"To what do I owe the honor of a repeat visit?" he asked.

"Confusion."

"Confusion is a high state, kid," he said. "Being confused means you're open and ready for an answer. Beats the heck out of being sure. People who are sure don't learn a damn thing. They already got the answers."

"I spent some time with Judy Chen this morning."

The rest of his face never moved; he just wrinkled his brow. "Who?"

"Judy Chen. A short little Chinese lady. Owns most of the International District these days. The one who was sleeping with my father for about thirty years. That one."

"Oh, that Judy Chen," he said. "Yeah."

He looked older than when I'd seen him the other day. In the deep shadows of the receding light, he appeared to be loose and disconnected, almost at large within his own skin.

"Don't be pokin' in there, Leo. It's none of your business. Even dead, a man's got a right to a private life."

"I thought my mother and I were his private life."

He lifted his gnarled hands from the chair.

"You live and learn."

"Maybe we were just his public life."

He let the hands fall with a slap.

"Or maybe you were both," he offered.

"Is that supposed to make me feel better?" I asked.

"I'm just trying to tell you who you are. That *is* what you came for, isn't it?"

I shifted gears.

"You ever hear of a club called the Garden of Eden?"

"Fag joint down on Western. Under the hotel. Why?"

"You ever hear about the raid on that place?"

"Old Peerless' raid? The one that they say disappeared?" I nodded.

His eyes lacked their usual bemused animation. "Everybody heard about that," he said.

"You think my father could have engineered that?"

"Could have?"

"Yeah."

"Sure he could have. Nobody had more juice than your dad. He could arrange for Mt. McKinley to disappear."

"Did he make that raid disappear?"

He hesitated, stuck out his lower lip and grimaced as he spoke, "Why would he do that? I mean . . . what was in it for him?"

He pushed his glasses back up his nose and looked me over.

"You're not thinkin' . . ." he began.

"No, of course not."

"Good, 'cause not only was Bill straight as the day is long, but he didn't waste his time on things unless there was an angle. You got any idea how much juice it would take to pull that off?"

When I reckoned how I wasn't sure, he went on.

"Just for starters, you'd have to own a district judge and a precinct captain. That's no small shit, kid. And they'd have to owe you big favors. Big enough to call in markers of their own. All the way down the line. You gotta ask yourself why would your dad call in that many markers over a raid on a fag bar. Don't make any sense." He waffled a hand in the air. "To save his own ass . . . sure." He gave me a look I didn't like at all. "Or maybe *your* ass . . . somethin' that would reflect on him like that, somethin' some yahoo like Peerless Price could use, but . . . short of that . . . it don't make sense."

He stopped talking and looked at me like I'd made a mess on the carpet. I made like I didn't notice, and pressed on.

"You remember back in sixty-nine, that whole family of Chinese they found dead in that container down on Pier Eighteen?"

"Yeah, I remember. Why?"

"Because I met a guy used to work down on the docks tells me it was pretty much common knowledge that Judy Chen's import company was the one smuggling aliens. And guess what? I gave Judy Chen a chance to deny it and she didn't."

Now even his brow was smooth. His face was as featureless and bland as a cabbage.

"Wadda you want to go there for, kid?"

"I'm just along for the ride."

He craned his neck toward the wall behind him.

"You see the picture of me up there with the big fish?"

I scanned the wall and found it. The back of a boat. Bermuda sitting in a deck chair with three other guys standing around him. The one on the right was former city councilman Richard Barre, rhymes with Larry. The other two I didn't recognize. Bermuda held in his hands what appeared to be about a thirty-five-pound king salmon. Both he and the salmon were showing their teeth. The other three guys looked like they'd rather be having a prostate exam.

"Yeah, I see it," I said.

"I let myself get talked into that. Barre owed your dad a favor. Insisted on going fishing. Your old man talked me into going in his place. Worst day of my life. You know what you've got to do to catch a fish like that?"

I had a good idea where this was leading, but I decided to be polite.

"What?"

"Well . . . let's say you want to go fishing on Saturday. Then Friday afternoon you've got to pack up and drive down to Westport. What's that—two, three hours?"

"Two and a half."

"So you get there and you get a crappo motel and you take all your shit outta the car and then go out to dinner and get shitfaced. You know how it goes, right?"

"I know."

"Then . . . five friggin' o'clock the next A.M., you've got to drag your ass out of bed, hungover as a son of a bitch, get dressed and go out on this boat with about thirty other ass-holes whose breath is even worse than yours. Then, as if everybody wasn't already about to puke, you all get a ride over to the Westport Bar, one of the ugliest mother-humpin' pieces of water on the west coast. You spend six hours bobbing around out there. They feed you the sandwiches the last group didn't eat and all the flat beer you can swallow and then take you back in over that same humpin' bar and dump you on the dock, where, for a mere thirty bucks, some other asshole takes your picture."

"I've been there," I said.

"Then you know what I'm talking about."

"What?"

"That's the question, kid. For what? All that friggin' trouble just to catch some fish who's minding his own business down there on the bottom of the ocean." He spread his hands. "It's not worth that much trouble and aggravation just to catch one little bitty fish. That's a ride I don't go on no more. You hear what I'm saying?"

"I told you. I'm not driving. I'm just going where the bus takes me," I said.

"Well, maybe you ought to get off. 'Cause when you start

sticking your nose into things you don't understand, I personally have to wonder about your motives, kid. It's beginning to sound like you're one of those sad cases who has to denigrate his father. One of those Oedipal types who secretly yearns for his mama's bed."

He read the color of my face and the tightness of my hands.

"What? You gonna hit me?" He stuck out his chin. "I been hit before. Go on. Hit me with your best shot, kid."

"Stop it," I said. "I just want to . . ."

He cut me off. "You just want to tear your old man down so's you can feel better about being Wild Bill Junior."

"I just want to find out who did what to who . . ."

He spread his hands. "Why? So you can draw a line in the sand and tell yourself the good guys are on one side and the bad guys are on the other? I thought I taught you better than that. It's not that simple, kid. People aren't one way or the other. They got a little bit of both in there. People look for simple answers . . . Usually turns out the only thing simple about the situation was them."

"If you say so," I said.

He leaned forward and looked at me sadly.

"I guess I didn't do as good a job with you as I thought. Go on . . . get out of here. I got nothin' to say to you. You get some respect, you come back and see me. Otherwise, I figure I can probably go another twenty years without seeing you."

He set his jaw like a bass and turned toward the window.

"I didn't mean for this to come between us, Bermuda."

He kept his face turned to the darkness. His lips were set in a thin line. I got to my feet, zipped up my jacket and crossed to the door.

I had one hand on the doorknob when I spoke. "I'm going to find out what's going on here, Bermuda," I said.

His head snapped around. "Don't call me that," he spat. "You hear me? I never liked that dumb-ass name, anyway. My name is Ed. You ever talk to me again, you call me Ed. You hear me?"

I said I did and stepped out into the night.

Overhead, a sky the color of dirty wool hovered inches above the treetops like an oily shroud. Along the narrow street, the yellow lights of the houses dropped tentative pools among the gathering darkness. I pulled open the car door, got in and turned the key. Nothing. Stone dead. Tried it again. Same thing. Shit.

By now, I knew the drill. If I waited for a while, it would start right up and take me wherever I wanted to go. I folded my arms across my chest and settled back in the seat. I counted my breath and contemplated my options. As much as I hated the idea, maybe, just this once, everybody was right and I was wrong. Maybe I had the worst seat in the house for watching my own movie. For the first time all day, my head was beginning to throb. I closed my eyes.

When I opened them again, the car windows were completely fogged. I guess it was the familiar sound that jiggled me awake. The flat clacking of his canes. I rolled the side window halfway down. Bermuda was wearing a light brown wool jacket and matching beret. He leaned heavily on one cane while he pushed open the double wooden gates that separated his house from the house next door. When he'd swung the gates out of the way, he reached over and retrieved his other cane from where it leaned against the side of the house and went clacking around the back in his unmistakable crab-like gait.

I rolled the window up. I was still marinating the question of what had driven Bermuda out into his yard at this time of the evening when the lights smeared themselves over the car window. The single headlights came bouncing around from the backyard, turned the corner, coming right at me now, rolled across the narrow side yard, bounced across the curb and out into the street. It was an old Buick from the mid-fifties with wide whitewall tires and little round hubcaps. A classic. Immaculate, gleaming two-tone brown with a grille like a chrome shark and three portholes in the side.

I scraped the windshield clean with my sleeve just in time

to see Bermuda's beret peeping up over the steering wheel as he tooled up the street with both hands locked to the wheel. I turned the key. Nothing. I cursed and turned it again. Dead as a herring. I pounded the steering wheel in frustration and hopped from the car. My instincts wanted to run toward the Buick's receding taillights, but my middle-aged body knew better. I jumped back into the car and tried it again. Silence. Shit.

I got out and slammed the door for all I was worth, rocking the little car on its springs. I walked up to the front of the car and kicked the tire hard, leaving a black smudge on the front of my sneaker and a dull ache in my big toe. Shit. I kicked it again. Shit.

I jammed my hands deep into my pants pockets and took three laps of the car, pausing occasionally to curse and kick some particularly delinquent spot. Sure, it was stupid, but it made me feel better.

When I deemed the car had been sufficiently punished, I crossed the street to the side yard. A single set of wide, treadless tire marks had matted muddy tracks into the otherwise perfect grass. I followed the oozing tracks around to the back of the house to a postage-stamp backyard, bordered by a weathered board fence. Maybe fifty by a hundred, half of which was a concrete slab. Big abstract oil stain adorning the middle of the slab. No garage. At the far end of the paved surface, a gray canvas car cover lay hunched in the shadows like a seal carcass.

In the meager back-porch light, I squatted and ran my hands over the ground where the Buick had first rolled down onto the lawn. The lawn was smooth and unmarked, except for the wet, new tracks. I was betting he hadn't had the car out in months, maybe years. Why now? Shit. My legs cracked and complained as I straightened up.

I retraced my steps around to the front and checked out the neighborhood. Darkness had sent a white cotton fog sliding like smoke along the street, reducing visibility to about two houses in either direction. I crossed the front lawn and stepped up onto the porch next to the gourds and the ceramic squirrel. I turned back toward the street. Still empty. To my left, the muffled sound of voices, the closing of a car door and then silence.

I pulled open the screen door, wincing at the strangled whine of the spring and checked the street again. As usual, the front door was ajar. With my elbow, I pushed it open, stepped into the room and then silently eased both doors closed behind me.

I crossed the room to his chair and looked around. A black portable phone rested comfortably in Bermuda's preferred spot. I picked it up, pushed redial and put it to my ear. The phone rang a half dozen times, clicked twice in transfer and then began to ring anew.

An electronic voice said, "You have reached six-two-four, seven-seven-six-five. Please leave a message at the beep." Beep.

I dropped the receiver back into the chair, pulled out my new notebook and made the number the first entry. Had it been anybody else's house, I would have gone through everything, hoping to get a hint as to what had been sufficiently urgent to send Bermuda driving out into the night. But it wasn't anybody else. It was Bermuda, and I couldn't bring myself to go through his stuff. Maybe it was all those pictures of my old man staring down at me from the wall. I was probably just imagining the disapproving cast in his eyes. Or maybe it was the feeling that tossing the place would somehow make every disparaging comment ever made about me true. Either way, I slipped the little notebook back in my pocket and let myself out.

18

THEY WERE CHASING ME ON THICK THIGHS THAT NEVER SEEMED TO TIRE. No matter how fast or far I ran, no matter how many new corridors I plunged down, they pounded along behind, gasping, with their wet mouths so near my neck I couldn't risk making a run for the single secret passage. Unable to escape, I raced among the narrow winding stairs to the next level and the doors to nowhere, where, like the last time, I saw the small tracks on the black-and-white checkerboard floor.

"Leo. Leo."

I opened my eyes. Rebecca stood by my side, her hand on my arm, gently shaking me awake. "Wake up. Leo. Wake up."

My breathing was fast and shallow. When I reached up and touched my forehead, I found myself hot and clammy to the touch.

"I'm awake," I said automatically.

"Sit up," she said. "You were shouting in your sleep."

I swung my feet from the bed and rested them on the cold oak floor. "I was dreaming," I said.

She was dressed for work.

"You might want to hold that thought," she said.

"I was having a nightmare."

"Not like this one." She tossed the morning paper in my lap.

I kept my eyes locked on hers. "What?" I said.

Her eyes said if I was looking for sympathy, I better find myself a dictionary. "Read it," she said.

Reluctantly, I stuck my thumb into the fold and brought the paper up in front of my face. Princess Di typeface. Pictures again. Peerless and the old man. At the bottom of the page, a picture of a small silver automatic laid out next to a wooden ruler.

SON OF A GUN

The strange saga of Peerless Price took another unexpected turn this morning when the Seattle Police Department announced that SPD officers now had in their possession a nickel-plated thirty-two-caliber automatic handgun which they believe to be the murder weapon in the Peerless Price case. Spokesperson Rhonda Peters declined further comment until ballistics tests can be completed later this afternoon.

The sudden appearance of a weapon is but another bizarre twist in this nearly thirty-year-old case of—

"Jesus," I said.

"At least," she agreed.

"How did they . . . where did the . . . ?"

"I called Tommy. He called Harvey Wendenhall down in Olympia . . . at the crime lab."

"Yeah?"

"Wendenhall says some stoner kid brought it into the East Precinct last night about eleven-thirty. In a shoe box. Says some guy gave him twenty bucks to hand the box to the desk sergeant. A note inside the box said the gun was the murder weapon in the Peerless Price case." She shrugged. "That's all Harvey knew."

I jumped to my feet a bit too quickly, sending my head swimming.

"Good," I said, as my vision cleared.

"Good? How can this be good?"

"It's good because I was about to give it up. Believe it or

not, I finally came to the conclusion that everybody else was right and I was wrong. That I *was* poking my nose in where it didn't belong. I'd made up my mind to forget about Peerless Price and get my ass back to work."

"Yeah . . . sure."

"Really, I was."

"And now?"

"And now . . . it's pretty obvious. I've managed to do what I do best. I've made somebody uncomfortable. Uncomfortable enough to do something stupid. That's good. That's very good."

"What if it turns out to be the murder weapon?"

"Then sending it to the cops was even dumber. All I've got to do now is figure exactly whose day I ruined and why."

"Any ideas?"

"Absolutely none," I confessed. "I pride myself on being an equal opportunity annoyer. I'd like to think I piss everyone off equally, without consideration of race, creed or sexual orientation. With me, it's kind of like a point of honor."

"How I admire a man with standards," she drawled.

"I'm gonna jump in the shower," I announced.

She leaned over and gave me a peck on the cheek.

"How come you're all dressed up?" I asked.

"I'm off to work. See you later."

"On a Saturday?"

She sighed and headed for the bedroom door. "I'm still behind on my work. I'd rather work today than have to stay late all next week."

BY THE TIME I made it down to the kitchen about twenty-five minutes later, I was feeling better than I had in days. The feeling that my head was stuffed with cotton was gone, supplanted by the sense of cranial airiness one has after recovering from a head cold. Not only that, but for the first time since I'd started on this Peerless Price thing, I had the feeling that somehow I was making progress, even if I didn't exactly understand how. I settled in with a pot of coffee and the sports section to see if maybe I couldn't have a spasm of lucidity about what to do next.

The Sonics had won seven in a row, but George Karl was still ranting about their lack of defense. The Seahawks were done for the season and looking to hire a new general manager. Rumor had it that the GM from Pittsburgh had been talking to new owner Paul Allen.

Halfway through my second cup of coffee, I noticed my slippers still adorning the heat registers along the south wall of the kitchen and remembered the stuff I'd left to dry. The wallet itself was still damp around the edges, while the paperwork was wrinkled but dry.

I reassembled my wallet and its contents and stuck it in my back pocket. The notebook, alas, was a goner. No loss. That's why I carry thirty-nine–cent notebooks. Over the years, I've tried every sort of scratch pad known to man. Everything from hand-tooled leather journals to miniature hand-bound books. What I'd discovered was that, regardless of the cost, with me, notebooks all seemed to have a similar life span and that it was exponentially less annoying to ruin or lose a thirty-nine–cent notepad than a thirty-nine–dollar journal.

I flipped to the last couple of pages, intending to transfer anything still readable. That's when I saw it. The emergency number from Triad Trading's office window on Pier eighteen. Six-two-four, seven-seven-six-five. I walked over to the counter and picked up the new notebook I'd started yesterday. I flipped it open to the first page: six-two-four, seven-seven-six-five. The number Bermuda had dialed before leaving last night. Curiouser and curiouser.

I wedged the receiver between my cheek and shoulder and dialed the number. Same deal. Several clicks and transfers and then: "You have reached six-two-four, seven-seven-six-five. Please leave a message at the beep." Beep. I hung up. Immediately, the phone rang. I grabbed it. A woman's voice. Tentative.

"I'd like to speak to . . ." Pause. ". . . Mr. Leo Waterman, please." She sounded like she was reading.

"Speaking."

"Um . . . you don't know me but . . . I mean we met the other day at Ed's . . . when you were there."

"Amy?" I tried.

"Yeah . . . you remember." She sounded pleased.

"I remember," I assured her.

"I found your card on the windowsill . . . I was worried . . . I thought maybe you would know . . ."

"Worried about what? What's the problem?"

"Ed's not here. His bed hasn't been slept in."

"Well, maybe he's . . ." I began. I did what people do in moments like that. I invented reasons why the situation wasn't as worrisome as it seemed. "Ed's a grown man . . ." I babbled.

She cut me off. "I've been making Ed's meals for five years, Mr. Waterman. In all that time, he's never not been here before."

"Never?" I repeated.

"And his old car is gone out of the backyard. I thought maybe you knew . . ."

"No idea," I said.

Technically, this was true. I didn't actually know a damn thing. I had a few suspicions but nothing else.

"Have you called the cops?" I asked.

"No. I don't know . . . what if Ed's just . . ." She began to sniffle.

"I'll be right over," I said quickly. "Don't do anything until I get there, okay?"

"Okay."

Everything was precisely as I'd left it the night before. For some odd reason, I felt a need to go in and check the bed for myself. The black-and-gold comforter was unwrinkled. The pillows pushed neatly against the headboard. On the table by the bed, two framed photographs of the same thin little woman with serious eyes. From the yellowed look of the photos, and the turn-of-the-century garb, I figured she was probably his mother.

Across from the bed, to the right of the door, a collection of newspaper articles and news photos had been professionally framed and matted into a single large display. From where I stood, I figured it was probably more of the life and times of Bermuda Schwartz. If it hadn't been for Amy, I probably would have missed it.

"You seen that?" She pointed.

I walked over until I was close enough to read the captions and headlines. They weren't about Bermuda or my old man either. They were about me. Sports mostly. Football stat sheets. Baseball box scores. The picture of me when I hit the jumper at the buzzer to win the semifinals of the state 3A basketball tournament and the one of me with my helmet in my hand and the blood running down the front of my face after getting our asses kicked by Cascade in the football playoffs when I was a high school junior. He'd documented my every triumph and tragedy. Standing in that quiet room reading what amounted to a shrine to myself, my body felt like an electric current was running through it. I turned back to Amy who stood stiffly in the doorway.

"Look around the house," I said. "See if there's anything obviously missing or out of place."

Her face was blank. "Like what?"

"Just anything missing or out of place," I said.

"All right," she said weakly.

I waited for her to get lost and then quickly shook down the room. Pawing through the drawers in the nightstand, checking the shelves in the closet and running my hands beneath the clothes in the dresser and as far as they would reach all around the mattress. I got down on my knees and looked under the bed. Nothing.

I was still picking dust bunnies from the knees of my pants when Amy appeared in the doorway.

"Only things I see gone is his brown coat and hat."

"Where does he keep his phone book?"

"You mean like the Yellow Pages?"

She was a nice girl, but I'd hate like hell to have to explain Noam Chomsky to her.

"No, his personal phone book. A Rolodex, that kind of thing."

"Oh," she said, and turned and started into the living room. I followed along. She walked directly to the small built-in cabinet to the left of the white leather chair and pulled it open.

"He always keeps it here," she said, rummaging around in the interior.

"How often does Ed go out on his own?" I asked.

"Never," she said quickly. "Up until a couple of years ago, he used to go away during the holidays, but I think whoever he visited with died or something, 'cause he hasn't gone for a few years."

I didn't like it. I didn't like an old shut-in being gone all night. I didn't like it that the last number he called was a place I'd very nearly gotten killed. And I especially didn't like the fact that it probably was something I said that sent him on his way.

"Here it is," she said.

She handed me a small black plastic book about three inches by five, with a gold telephone icon on the cover.

The doorbell rang. A smile split her wide face, nearly closing her eyes. She ran for the door. "Ed," she yelled.

She was still squealing as she jerked open the white door and then, as suddenly as she'd been filled with joy, she stood stock-still. I heard a male voice. Then another. Deeper this time. Every hair on my body began to rise. I started for the door. Stopped. Amy backed into the corner, leaving the door agape. Her eyes were wide. She looked my way.

Trujillo and Wessels stepped into the room.

19

"WELL, LOOKY, LOOKY," SAID WESSELS, RUBBING HIS HANDS TO-gether with glee. The three of us stood there, looking from one to another, trying like hell not to appear surprised. Wessels was still wearing that ratty gray suit and didn't look like he'd combed his hair since I last saw him. Trujillo, on the other hand, was resplendent in a blue silk pinstriped suit and a purple tie. Trujillo stepped around his partner, walked up to me and pulled Bermuda's phone book from my fingers.

"What are you doing here?" he demanded.

"Me? I came to see an old friend. What about you?"

Wessels jumped in. "We're looking for Edward Schwartz."

Trujillo shot him a sharp look. "What we're doing here is none of your business, Waterman."

"Ed's not here," Amy piped in.

Trujillo turned toward the girl. "And who might you be, miss?"

"I'm Amy Sorenson." She said it like it was the first day of school.

"What's your connection to Mr. Schwartz?" Trujillo asked.

She told him. At length. It took her a full five minutes to get back to the present. "And when Ed . . . Mr. Schwartz wasn't here this morning, I called Mr. Waterman."

Trujillo turned his attention to me. "Where's Schwartz?"

"No idea," I said. "Maybe you guys will get lucky again

and somebody'll deliver him to the precinct house in a shoe box."

"Turn around," Trujillo snapped.

"Why?"

He raised his voice. "I said, turn around."

I stayed put. "What for?"

"I'm arresting you for interfering with a police investigation."

"Oh, gimme a break, Trujillo. How bogus."

He looked back over his shoulder at Wessels, who reached to the back of his belt and produced a pair of handcuffs.

"Turn around," Trujillo said again.

I heaved a sigh and did as I was told. Wessels stepped forward and clamped the cuffs on me hard enough to stop circulation, grabbed me by the back of the neck and marched me out onto the porch, across the street and stuffed me in the back of their silver unmarked Ford.

IF YOU GO to the King County Jail, you stay for at least six hours. The county doesn't get reimbursed by the state for inmate stays of less than six hours, so it doesn't matter a whit what your infraction was, or how many of your friends are waiting with bail money clenched in their sweaty palms. You do six hours.

The drunk held his arms in front of his face in the Muhammad Ali peekaboo defense, bobbing and weaving in his sleep, warding off dream blows. He'd been that way all night. He had the back end of the cell all to himself. Projectile vomiting will generally increase the size of one's personal bubble. For the past hour or so, he'd been making his peace with Mary, whoever Mary was. Or at least he was trying to. Even in his hallucinations, Mary wasn't going for it.

"Swear to God I'll change," he blubbered. "I can do it. I know I can. You'll see, Mary. This time . . ."

He tried to stand, slipped on his own purple puddle and fell heavily onto his right side. He rolled in it.

"No, don't say that, Mary. Don't say that. Swear to God,

I'll change. This time . . ." His words trailed off. Small snores started. I hoped he was doing better in his dreams, but I somehow doubted it.

Quincy the Rasta man and I shared the small cot nearest the cell door. He'd been stretched out on the cot when they'd pushed me into the cell. About the time the drunk first started spewing, Quincy sat up and invited me over for tea and sympathy. I accepted. Since then, we'd alternately made conversation and watched the drunk like a TV. We'd decided we weren't renewing his option for another season.

Quincy was holding forth. It was my own fault. I'd been curious, so I'd asked. I'd seen these guys in the streets for years, and although the politics bored the shit out of me, I'd had a few questions I'd been dying to ask. This was the best chance I was going to get.

"My dreadlocks are an antennae, mahn. Dey give me perspective on the moral bankruptcy of de West, of Babylon. Dey de visible rejection of the assimilation process. The black man have no say in it. He just supposed to find a way to fit in."

He waited for me to argue.

"How do you get them to stay that way?" I asked.

"You rub dem with coconut oil and palm oil and den beeswax, and den you start curling dem. You do it right, dey stay dat way."

"What's the word 'Rastafarian' mean?"

"It's two words, mahn. Ras mean 'prince.' Tafari, now dat was da name given to Haile Selassie before he crowned emperor of Ethiopia. Prince Tafari."

"Why Ethiopia?" I asked. "It's a long way from Jamaica."

"It's in de Bible, mahn. It say, 'Ethiopia shall soon stretch out her hands unto God.' Psalms sixty-eight thirty-one."

"And Haile Selassie is the living God?"

"Yes."

I was confused again.

"But he's dead."

"Don't matta, mahn. De spirit lives. Some things are universal." He took out a battered pack of Luckies. "You got a light mahn?" I shook my head and pointed to the four-foot-by-four-foot sign painted on the green block wall. NO SMOKING was first among the don'ts.

He shrugged. "What dey gonna do, mahn, put us in jail?"

He had a point.

"Maybe he's got one," I said. He looked over at the drunk.

"Doan wanna smoke that bad." He put the cigarettes back in the pocket of his green Army jacket.

Thousands of anxious fingers had worn the green paint off the bottoms of all the chain links in the screen. I kept my hands in my pockets. A metal door banged somewhere in the building. A distant conversation slowly receded. The drunk stirred, mumbled something unintelligible, broke wind and went back to snoring. The door at the end of the hall hissed open. Footsteps.

The jailer stopped in front of the mesh. "Waterman?"

"That's me."

"You're outta here. You . . ." He pointed his baton at the Rasta man. ". . . to the back of the cell."

"No fucking way, mahn. I'm gettin' nowhere near that smelly fucker."

"You want me to get some help in here? That what you looking for, Bob Marley? Huh? You're gonna be with us for a while. I get Waterman here straightened away, I'll be back down to fix you up with a haircut. That shit on your head looks unsanitary to me. Rules say we got to maintain sanitary conditions."

He grinned and patted his palm with the baton.

"You best be bringin' some help, mahn."

"What's your last name?" I asked.

"Why you want to know, mahn? You writin' a book?"

"Somebody coming for you?"

He shook his head.

"Gonna have to sit this one out," he said.

"What you in for?"

"Drunk and disorderly," he said sadly. "It's dat demon rum, mahn. Dat demon rum."

"Give me your name, and I'll see what I can do about getting you out of here."

He twisted his hair while he thought about it.

"Reeves. Quincy Reeves."

He spelled it for me.

"Give Bluto here a break, and I'll see what I can do."

Quincy shrugged, picked his multicolored hat off the cot and moved to the center of the room. The jailer opened the door wide enough for me to slip out and then slammed it behind me.

Rebecca and Stubby Watts were waiting for me in the visitor area. Stubby owned Evergreen Bail Bonds. Back in the good old days, I used to do a lot of skip trace work for him. That was back when us primitive types used to look for folks by hand. Nowadays, he's got a staff of electronic bounty hunters who sit in front of computer terminals. If you want to hide from Stubby, you better pull a Ted Kaczynski. You better find a cabin out in the middle of Bumfuck somewhere, and you better adopt a lifestyle where you don't generate a single piece of official paperwork. Not a pay stub, not a parking ticket, not an overdue charge at the library, not a nothing. Because the first time your name or any of your known aliases gets entered into somebody's computer, anywhere in the world, Stubby's boys are going to be all over you like a cheap suit.

I hugged Rebecca and then shook his hand.

"Stubby," I said. "There's a guy in there named Quincy Reeves. See what you can do about getting him out."

"What's he in for?"

"Drunk and disorderly."

"Buck and a half," Stubby said.

"Spring him. Send me the bill."

Duvall watched as Stubby pulled open the door and disappeared inside. "You made a friend?" she inquired.

"Yeah. Quincy's a Rastafarian. Nice guy."

She cocked an eyebrow. "Jailhouse romance?"

"Not funny," I snarled. "Get me out of here."

We pushed open the double doors and stepped out into the street.

"Where are you parked?" I asked.

"Second and Madison."

I took her elbow and turned north. We stayed close to the buildings, out of the wind and out of the way of the hoards of scurrying commuters who filled the sidewalks. The swirling air carried the faint odor of diesel fuel and the promise of rain.

"By the way. Thanks. I'm sure getting me out of the slammer put a hell of a hole in your day."

"Don't mention it," she said. "At this point, I'm so far behind, it doesn't matter anymore."

We crossed Fourth Avenue and headed down the steep slope of Madison, the wind scourging our faces, our hair a half a block back.

I paid the fourteen-dollar parking charge. Under the circumstances, it seemed like the least I could do.

Rebecca pushed her seat-belt harness beneath the collar of her coat, turned the key and looked over my way.

"Where to?"

"Ballard. I need to get my car."

She shook her head. "They impounded it."

"Shit."

"You can get it back from Southside Towing between eight and five tomorrow."

"For a mere ninety-five bucks."

"Plus tax," she added, dropping it in reverse.

"Son of a bitch."

I fastened my seat belt. The CD player sent Frank Sinatra's resonant baritone rolling through the car. I settled back in the seat as she backed out of the parking stall. *"A brand new love affair . . ."*

"How about dinner?" she said. "The Asia Grill maybe?"

I checked my watch. Six-fifteen.

"A bit early for dinner," I groused.

"I just thought it might cheer you up."

She slipped the Explorer into drive and eased out onto Madison. The Metro bus in front of us had a sign on the back offering a fifty-dollar reward for the arrest and conviction of vandals. The sign had been tagged with bright blue paint. TOLO it read.

"I can't for the life of me figure out how Trujillo and Wessels got to Bermuda's place," I said, as much to myself as to Duvall.

"The gun belonged to Mr. Schwartz," she said.

"The gun in the box?"

"Yeah."

"How do you know?"

"While I was waiting for you, I called Harvey Wendenhall to see if the ballistics results were in yet."

"And?"

"They got a fourteen-point match. It's the murder weapon."

"And it was registered to Bermuda?"

"He bought it in May of sixty-nine. Warshal's Sporting Goods on First Avenue."

A shiver ran down my spine. She read my face.

"You're worried about Mr. Schwartz, aren't you?"

"Yeah," I said. "Big-time. Turn left as soon as you can."

"Why?"

"Just do it."

Instead, she pulled the wheel hard to the right, slid to a stop along the curb and jammed it into park.

Several angry horns bleated above the din of the traffic.

"As you'll probably recall, Leo, I'm not particularly good with phrases such as 'just do it.' "

She had that look she used to get in grammar school. At this point, you either put up your hands or you apologize.

"Sorry," I said. "I didn't mean it the way it sounded."

"If I thought you meant it the way it sounded, you'd be on the sidewalk by now," she said.

Whatever fool said love never means having to say you're

sorry must never have been in a serious, committed, nineties relationship. Once per infraction, however, was definitely my limit.

We sat in silence for a moment.

"What's going on?" she said.

"I've got a bad feeling Bermuda went down to Pier Eighteen."

"Why in God's name would he do that?"

"Because . . . I think he knows what happened to Peerless Price."

"So?"

"So . . . I think my last visit scared him. I think he wanted to talk to Judy Chen."

I told her about the last number Bermuda had called.

"When he didn't get an answer, I think he went to the only place he knew to go. Back in his time, that's where she lived. She and her son had a couple of rooms up over the warehouse."

"Where you were attacked."

"Yeah," I said.

"Why Judy Chen?"

"Because she knows too. She practically told me so. Somehow or other, they both know what happened to Peerless Price."

"What did you say that scared Mr. Schwartz so?"

"It wasn't anything I said. He just knows me is all. He knows what a hardheaded bastard I am."

While she thought it over, I had another idea.

"Why don't you let me drive you home, and then I can run down to Eighteen and satisfy myself."

She pulled the lever back into drive. Another chorus of angry horns greeted our sudden reappearance in the street.

"Not a chance," she said.

20

THE GUARD STEPPED OUT OF THE SHACK, DIRECTLY INTO THE PATH of the Explorer. Rebecca slid the car to a stop about a foot from his shins. He stood in the glare of the headlights and wrote the Explorer's license number on a clipboard. He was a short guy, with skin about the color of coffee with too much cream, sporting the world's last full-blown, Julius Erving Afro. As he walked, the brown guard cap wobbled about on the wiry mound of hair. He strolled over to the driver's side, slipped the clipboard under his scrawny arm and rocked back on his heels.

"Hep you folks?"

I leaned over and thrust my trusty "piece of the rock" insurance adjuster card out the window. "We need to have a look at the place where the guy and the car went in the water."

He took the card. "Prudential," he said. "Good company."

"Solid as a rock."

"Heh, heh, heh," he chuckled. "Like a rock," he sang.

I thought it best not to correct his commercial confusion.

"Like a rock," I agreed.

He handed the card back to Rebecca.

"They some problem?"

"Just a formality," she assured him.

He nodded knowingly. "Hep yourself, then. You axe me,

he din have no binuss down there inna first place," he said. "Way down on Eighteen. Far left as you can go."

I directed her down the long central aisle.

"Go slow," I said. "Check the aisles on your side. I'll check them on mine."

"What am I supposed to be looking for?"

I swept my hand across the windshield.

"Anything but orange containers."

We were creeping along at about three miles an hour. The mercury vapor lights lining the yard cast their odd light only on the tops of the corrugated canyon, leaving us to squint through ghastly green gloom.

"Take a left here."

She wheeled the car around the corner. We drove for a quarter mile and then turned right toward the river. Two hundred yards ahead, our headlights were reflected back into our faces by the front window of Triad Trading's little office. We crept along until we pulled to a stop in front of the building.

"Nothing," she said.

I pushed open the door and stepped out.

"Be right back."

I checked the door on the office. Locked. I tried to slide all the windows. Same thing. Then I walked across the lot and worked my way around the warehouse, one door at a time, stepping carefully so as not to break an ankle on the rubble. Everything was locked up tight. I'd worked my way over to the door I'd entered the other night and was admiring the shiny new padlock and chain, when I heard her voice.

"Leo," she called.

I raced back around the building toward the car. I slowed to a walk when I saw her. Rebecca squatted in the grass by the corner of the nearest container. She'd liberated the flashlight from the glove box and was shining it down on the ground between her feet. She raised her eyes at the sound of my feet on the gravel. The soft ticking of the engine was the only sound. Across the river, the dry-docked ferry floated dark and lifeless like a flood-ravaged hotel.

"Look," she said.

I closed the distance and peered down over her shoulder. The top third of an aluminum cane. White handle. Sheared off to a jagged end, just above the height adjustment holes.

She brought the light down close to the jagged end. A smear of what in this light looked like black grease adorned the broken end. We both knew better.

"Blood," I whispered.

She shook her head. "Too thick," she said. She bent nearly to the ground and sniffed the broken end of the cane.

She straightened up and looked me in the eye.

"Well?" I prodded.

"Brain matter."

I groaned and walked in a small circle.

"You sure?"

She nodded. "I'm sure," she said. "The smell is unmistakable."

My stomach rolled once and then settled tenuously back in place. Instinctively, I reached for the cane, but she grabbed my wrist.

"Don't touch," she said. "Or Mr. Watts will have to get us both out of the cooler."

She was right. Despite my inclination to work around the cops, there was no taking a powder on this one. The old anonymous phone call wasn't going to cut it. They'd talk to the guard and make us in the proverbial New York minute. No. We were going to have to call the cops and wait around until they showed up. Oh, joy unbounded.

We both stood up. She reached in the pocket of her coat and pulled out her cellular phone. She flipped it open and waved it in front of my face. "Do you want to do the honors or should I?" she asked.

I showed her a palm. "Let's get our stories straight first."

I could tell from the expression on her face that she was

going to do her Goody Two-shoes number on me. She didn't disappoint.

"What stories? I'm not going to tell them any stories."

"Don't start that Little Miss Perfect in the front-row crap with me, okay? If I tell 'em I came down here because I had information that suggested Bermuda might be down here, I'm going to the can for the second time in one day, and I'm telling you, I'm not going quietly, and you're not going to get me back out for a measly five hundred bucks."

I could tell she believed me. She didn't like it, but she asked, "What do you have in mind?"

"Let's keep it simple. Let's just tell 'em that we were dissatisfied with their progress at investigating the assault on me, so we decided to come down here and see if maybe we couldn't turn up something on our own."

"Like public-spirited, self-actualized citizens."

"Exactly."

"You really think they're going to buy that offal?"

"It makes more sense than the truth."

She thought it over. "Okay," she said finally. "You're right. It does make more sense than the truth."

"You make the call. It'll look good for you in case anybody gives you any crap about being in here with me under false pretenses."

She pushed the POWER button and began to dial. I wandered over to the muddy incline between the office and the warehouse, staying off to the side, keeping my feet out of the muck. I could hear Rebecca speaking into the phone. Below me the river belched up a sudden low ripple and then went silent again.

In the murky artificial light, I could make out the narrow tracks of the Fiat running from where I'd parked it, down the muddy incline toward the river. Despite the temperature, the memory of the dark water sent a bead of sweat running down my spine. I shuddered so hard my cheeks flapped. Suddenly freezing, I pulled my jacket tighter about me. What caught my eye, though, was another set of tire tracks, much wider and flatter than those of the Fiat, running parallel, the right wheel inside the Fiat's tracks, the left veering out to the left, as if a much larger vehicle had been parked in the same spot since I'd left the Fiat there on Tuesday. I shivered violently again.

Worst of all, as nearly as I could tell in the low half-light, the other set of tracks also led off into oblivion. My stomach rolled again at the thought of Bermuda and the cold, rank water below.

Rebecca spoke behind me. "They're on the way."

"Move the car, will you?"

She snapped the phone closed and stowed it in her pocket.

"Move it where? We want to make sure we don't contaminate the scene."

"Just turn it so the headlights point down here."

She walked my way. "What's down there?"

I pointed. "See the other set of tire tracks?"

"Oh . . . yeah."

I tried to keep the anxiety out of my voice.

"Would you please move the car?"

She fixed me with a baleful stare and then began to move. As she turned toward the car, I clearly recalled why it is I work alone.

The power steering belt screamed as she first cut the wheel to the right, looping out toward the front of the warehouse, and then all the way back to the left, to get the lights pointing directly at the river.

I shielded my eyes with one hand and waved at her with the other. She stuck her head out the side window.

"What?"

"Turn your high beams off," I yelled above the engine.

When she snapped down onto low beams, I could see it clearly for the first time. Somewhere in the back of my mind, the part of me that always tries to stay optimistic had been hoping that maybe there'd been a delivery. That maybe some light trunk had pulled in here to leave a load. Bad news. If it had, this was its last delivery of the day. The muddy tracks led all the way to the edge. Anything that was still rolling at that point in the incline had ended up in the river.

I was busy enacting and then rejecting scenarios wherein there was some other explanation for the tracks. Anything other than the possibility that some no-eared maniac had sent Bermuda and his Buick careening down into the waterway. Duvall was suddenly at my elbow.

"Couldn't those be the tracks from the tow truck that rescued your car?"

I shook my head. "No way." I pointed to the warehouse on our right. "It floated way over past the building there. They pulled me and the car out about fifty yards downstream."

She took my arm. "We'd better wait in the car. They won't like it if we've been stomping all over a potential crime scene."

As we turned back toward the lights and the surging of the engine, I caught a glimpse of something out of place over by the corner of the office porch. I knew right away. Nothing in a place like this was that gentle shade of brown. Dry-rot brown, creosote brown, rust brown, but never beige, baby, never beige. My heart sank toward my shoes.

I pulled Rebecca along with me. "You still have the flashlight?"

She rummaged around in one pocket, then the other, and handed over a small black rubberized flashlight. I flicked the button and pointed the weak yellow light. A brown wool beret rested on its edge, held perpendicular to the ground by the side of the porch.

"It's his," I said.

"You're sure?"

I told her about watching Bermuda leave his house last night.

"We'll have to let them identify the hat on their own," I said.

She was a quick lass. Ornery, but quick. "Or they'll know you've been withholding information."

"Exactly."

Over the top of the Explorer I could plainly see the pulsing red and blue lights as they reflected off the sea of containers and, in the distance, I could hear the rushing of tires on gravel.

TRUJILLO AND WESSELS must have had the night off. Trujillo arrived an hour or so after the first cruiser, wearing a brown ski jacket and a pair of stonewashed jeans. Wessels never put in a guest appearance at all. I figured a boozer like Wessels was well into the shank of his drinking night by now and couldn't risk showing up half in the bag. Couldn't say I missed him.

By the time Trujillo showed up, the forensics team had collected the piece of cane we'd found, along with several other shards we'd missed, and discovered the beret on their own. The two police divers had been down to the bottom of the river twice, the first time to confirm that, yes, there was indeed a car down there, the second to attach the cable lines for the pair of heavy-duty tow trucks which had showed up a half an hour ago.

About that same time, Gordon Chen had brought a gleaming blue Lexus SC400 skidding to a halt among the drab pack of official vehicles.

He hit the gravel running, trotting up to Trujillo.

He jerked a thumb in my direction.

"I want this man arrested," he shouted.

Trujillo stayed calm. "Take it easy, Mr. Chen," he said. "We have the situation in hand."

Gordon Chen came at me hard. "You son of a bitch."

As I wasn't in the mood to be attacked by amateurs, I bumped myself off the fender of the Explorer, timed his imminent arrival and stiff-armed him hard in the solar plexus. He staggered backward two steps and began gasping for breath.

I wagged a finger in his face.

"Not tonight, Gordo. I've had a hard day."

Trujillo took him by the shoulder and turned him back toward the Lexus, but Gordon Chen wasn't through. Still gasping, he flung Trujillo aside and came stiff-legging it back my way.

"You stay away from my mother," he wheezed.

Trujillo had recovered his balance and grabbed Chen by the elbow.

"Take it easy," he was saying. "Take it easy."

"My mother is very frail," he whined to Trujillo. "This man is killing her. She's not strong."

Trujillo did a good job. Slowly, in stages, he managed to stuff the young Chen back into his sixty-thousand-dollar chariot and get him on his way. He even had presence of mind enough to get far off to one side so he wasn't pelted by the rooster tail of dirt and gravel that Gordon Chen left in his wake. Trujillo fanned the air in front of his face.

He looked over at me and shook his head.

"Don't know how anybody that out of control can run a company," he commented.

"He certainly is an excitable boy," I agreed.

From the whoops and shouts emanating from the far side of the warehouse, I guessed that the car had breached the water and was in the process of being dragged up the bank. I couldn't tell for sure, because I'd been relegated to sitting in the Explorer, while Duvall had immediately been made part of the forensics investigation team.

Trujillo sauntered over and began asking me the same questions he'd been asking me for the past hour and a half.

"So let's go back over this supposed guy with no ears . . ." Trujillo asked. "I mean, what is he? Norman Bates or something? What . . . he just kills anybody who shows up down here? Is that what you're trying to tell me?"

"I don't know," I said truthfully. "All I know is that he took one look at me and decided he wanted to punch my ticket. Why? I don't have the foggiest."

Trujillo stroked his chin.

"And then of course it follows that whatever problem this

mythical no-eared man had with you, he also must have had
with Edward Schwartz."

I shrugged again. "I don't see how that could be. Before
this week, I hadn't seen Ed Schwartz in nearly twenty years."

He touched his temple with his index finger. "Maybe it's
just a coincidence."

"Maybe if you guys had put more effort into finding the
guy in the first place, we wouldn't be here doing this
tonight."

I watched as the color ran up his neck and darkened his
face. Before he could open his mouth to respond, however,
one of the police divers, his black wet suit gleaming in the
lights, came around the corner of the building and called out,
"Detective."

Reluctantly, Trujillo switched his focus to the sound of
the voice.

"Yeah?"

"Car's about up."

"Thanks."

He poked me in the chest with a finger.

"You stay right here. I'm not through with you yet."

With that, he went crunching off across the gravel and disappeared around the rusted corner of the warehouse.

Although I was making it a point not to show it, that same
question was bothering the hell out of me. Either this guy
was a serial killer of some sort or something about both Bermuda and me had immediately set him off. Problem was, I
couldn't imagine anything Bermuda and me had in
common . . . except of course Wild Bill Waterman.

I was still massaging this idea about ten minutes later when
Rebecca and Trujillo came back around the warehouse. Whatever flush Trujillo had in his face when he left me had disappeared. He was fish-belly white, walking stiffly along beside
Duvall, mindlessly wiping the corners of his mouth with his
thumb and index finger.

And that wasn't the bad news. Rebecca was the bad news.
Here was a woman who spent her days up to her elbows in

bloated cadavers, and much like Detective Trujillo, she had the look of someone who'd seen something they were unlikely to forget. My stomach shrunk in toward itself like a dying star.

Trujillo walked right past me without a word, let himself into the unmarked Ford and began to talk into the radio mike. Rebecca hooked her arm in mine. "An old Buick," she said.

"Was he . . . ?"

"Uh-huh."

I took several deep breaths before I spoke.

"Could you tell . . . you know . . . how . . ."

"Someone crushed his skull," she said evenly. "Then whoever it was drove pieces of his canes through his eyes and ears."

A groan slipped from my chest.

"Not by hand, either. With something like a hammer."

I wanted to speak but wasn't sure I was able.

"He was killed in a frenzy, Leo. The kind of frenzy I've only seen from angel dust cases. Just howling mad rage."

Over her left shoulder, an orange coroner's van backed out of sight behind the Triad warehouse, its yellow light flashing, its backup safety device beeping in four-four time.

Trujillo was still ashen as came trudging over from his car.

"I want you at the Downtown Precinct at eight o'clock sharp tomorrow morning. I'll have a departmental artist on hand. We're gonna need a composite."

"Better make it about nine-thirty," I said.

"Don't screw with me, Waterman, or I'll send you down there in a cruiser right now. That way, you'll be there when I need you."

"I need to pick up my car at eight," I said. "Somebody impounded the damn thing."

He pointed a stubby finger at me. "All right, nine-thirty."

He started to leave but changed his mind.

"Waterman. For the record, I'm going to tell you one more time. You stay out of this. I don't want to see your face again. You understand what I'm telling you here?"

I said I did, but he wasn't finished. "I don't know how, but I've got a feeling that you poking your nose in where it doesn't belong is responsible for poor Mr. Schwartz here." He wiped his mouth again. "I ought to drag your butt over there and make you look at what some sick son of a bitch did to that poor old guy. Maybe then you'd have sense enough to let professionals do their jobs."

"Professionals like your partner Wessels?" I asked.

He turned his attention to Rebecca. "Do us both a favor, Miss Duvall. Get him out of here."

We stood and watched as he tromped off around the corner of the building. "Let's go home," she said.

21

IT TOOK THE BETTER PART OF THREE HOURS TO CREATE A REASON-
able likeness of the Man With No Ears, and even then, it was
unsatisfactory. While each of the individual features was
more or less correct, and we'd duplicated the general shape
of the face and fall of the hair, something remained amiss.
All in all, what with the racial difference, I figured the average person, shown this drawing, should be able to distinguish
between the suspect and, say . . . Karl Malden.

"Can I have a copy?" I asked.

The police artist was a woman whose name tag read SGT.
TASKER. She said to call her Fran. A redhead with so many
freckles it nearly constituted a tan. She was a pleasant
woman, who seemed to be at ease with pushing forty and
straining at the seams of her blue uniform.

"Sure," she said. "Hang on, I'll make you one."

I rested one of my cheeks on the desk as she left the room.
This morning's headline had read WATERMAN DRIVER MURDERED.
POLICE PROBE LINK TO PRICE CASE. Same MAN ON THE MOON typeface. Pat had left me four, progressively snottier messages since
seven-thirty this morning. If he was pacing around waiting for
a callback, he was going to get a lot of exercise. *Cur this!*

Tasker sauntered back into the room with one of our Identi-
Kit pictures in each hand. "It just can't recreate the anima,"
she said.

"The what?"

"The anima. The soul of a person. The person that's always in there looking back at himself."

I looked at our final product. She was right. We'd selected the right pieces, but the pieces had failed to yield a person.

"You know what's funny about these Identi-Kit pictures?"

"What?"

"They work great for some people and not at all for others."

"How so?"

She wobbled the picture in her hand.

"It's the amina thing. Some people can look at one of these things and make the jump to a real living face. They see the perp in the street, they're all over him. Other people . . . you could make one of these that was dead bang on of their mother, and they wouldn't have a clue. They just can't make the jump from paper to flesh. Can't be trained to do it either. Department's gone nuts trying to train them. Doesn't work. Either they got it or they don't. It's weird."

She held the other picture out. "Here, take this one too."

I folded both pictures twice and slipped them in my pocket.

"How do painters manage it?" I asked.

"Manage what?"

"To create real people when they paint."

"Talent," she said. "They put the amina back in. They take it from inside themselves and put it into their work."

She caught me taking stock of her and said, "I went to Cornish. Way back when. I wanted to be a fashion illustrator." She put her hand on her hip and took a couple of fancy steps across the room. She let go a hearty laugh and slid behind her desk.

"Pretty glamorous, huh?"

I reckoned how it was indeed *très haute* and then asked, "You'll tell Trujillo I did my duty as a citizen?"

"I'll E-mail him instantly," she assured me.

I put my hand on my hip and flounced from the room in

a grossly exaggerated sashay. I could hear her laughter booming behind me as I stepped out into the hall.

Gaylord LaFontaine answered the door himself. He was wearing rubber gloves. Carrying a toilet brush in his right hand.

"Oh—I was—" he stammered.

"Brushing your teeth?" I queried.

He brandished the brush. "Maybe yours if you're not careful."

I held up my hands in surrender. "I'll be good," I vowed.

"Come on in," he said.

I waited while he trotted down the hall to the bathroom and divested himself of his armor and lance. He came back drying his hands on a paper towel and reading my mind.

"My sister takes the kids on Sundays. Takes 'em to lunch and then a movie. Gives me a little break in the action."

"Nice to see you're using your leisure time so wisely," I said.

He scoffed. "Leisure. What's that?"

I followed him into the family room. The floor was a minefield of brightly colored plastic toys. "Davey got E-mail privileges," he said as we picked our way across the floor. "Jason and Megan have been sending him messages every night before they go to bed. They're real excited about it." He began picking up toys from the floor. "Kind of gives the kids a way to be connected to their dad, even while he's away."

"E-mail's great, isn't it?" I said.

"I'm just now getting into it."

He stood in the center of the room with his hands on his hips. He went into his grammar-school teacher voice. "Toys gotta stay in this room. That's the rule. It's rough in here, but at least a body can walk around the rest of the place without breakin' a leg."

We spent the next ten minutes picking up toys and lobbing them into the big cardboard box in the corner. We got most of the big stuff.

"So how you doing on your investigation?" he asked as we ambled over to the couch and sat down.

"I'd like to think I'm making some progress," I hedged. "What I know for sure is that, somehow or other, it all stems from that container full of bodies."

"I wouldn't be surprised," he said. "Tragedies like that have a way of takin' a divot outta people."

I pulled one of the Identi-Kit pictures from the pocket of my jacket, smoothed it on the edge of the coffee table and handed it to him.

"You ever seen this guy before?"

He looked it over carefully.

"Can't say as I have," he said.

"How about without the long hair?"

He shook his head. "Guy his age oughtn't have hair like that. Makes him look like a horse's ass," he said.

"Since I was here last, have you thought of anything else? Something you didn't remember the other day."

He bowed his head. "Just the smell," he said. "The smell inside that metal box." He looked up at me. "Ever since you come the last time, I been cleaning like a madman, tryin' to get that smell to go away."

Not exactly what I had in mind. I got to my feet.

"Sorry," was all I could think to say.

"You don't forget something like that," he said. "Changes your whole life." He looked up at me. "I was never quite as gung ho again. Knowin' . . . you know . . . that something like that could happen and then the whole thing could get swept under the rug 'cause it was political."

He got to his feet and, together, we started for the door. Halfway across the room Gaylord LaFontaine spied a red fire truck hiding in the magazine rack and sent it spiraling back toward the box.

The way I figure it, investigations come in four styles and two of them are easy to spot. When you're asking the right people the right questions, everything goes like clockwork and everybody's happy. Case closed. Another satisfied customer.

The opposite extreme is equally as easy to spot. When you're asking the wrong people the wrong questions, nothing at all useful happens, and the case likewise tends to be over in a big hurry. Except that, in that scenario, nobody's happy. It's the other two possibilities that are hard.

It takes years of experience to differentiate between those situations where you're asking the right questions of the wrong people and those situations when you're asking the wrong questions of the right people. Today, I had the overwhelming feeling that I just wasn't asking the right questions. That's probably why I was wracking my brain, trying to think of something else to ask Gaylord LaFontaine as we walked to the front door. And then . . . it was out of my mouth before I thought about it.

"The port guy," I said. "The one who told you it was political and that you should keep your nose out of it."

"Yeah?"'

"You remember his name?"

"Sure," he said. " 'Cause it was like that runt who used to run Cuba before Castro. Bastista was his name. Ralph Batista."

22

I'D KNOWN RALPH BATISTA FOR AS LONG AS I COULD RECALL AND, for some odd reason, I'd never once entertained the possibility that somebody like Ralph might have been thrust straight from grace to the gutter by a single catastrophic event. I'd always figured he'd eased into sleaze. You know, the standard hard luck story. Laid off. The wife starts banging her Akito instructor. Our hero screws up one thing after another, starts drowning his bridges. Of all people, I should have known better.

One of the things twenty years of working as a PI will teach you is that pain and sorrow are equal opportunity employers. It's not a question of whether they'll come knocking on your door; it's only a question of when, and of how you're going to handle it when the wheel stops and suddenly it's your turn to answer the Double Jeopardy question about who in hell you are and what it is you're doing here. Answer in the form of a question, please.

You gonna let it stop you cold? Gonna be a victim like Ralph? Gonna let the sight of a dozen or so moldering corpses make such an impression on your psyche that your life comes to a screeching halt? I mean . . . you could hardly blame a guy . . . could you? I mean hell . . . after all . . . fourteen dead bodies.

Or are you going to be a tough guy? One of those crew-cut souls who strangles hankies, sheds his dry tears and then marches resolutely onward with his life. You know . . . stiff upper lip and all of that.

Or maybe you join the masses somewhere in the middle. You shed your tears and stumble onward . . . cringing . . . from that moment on destined to spend a lifetime peeping back over your shoulder, flinching at loud noises and waiting for the other shoe to drop.

Sometimes I think it doesn't much matter which path you choose. Nobody dodges all the slings and arrows, and nobody gets out alive. Hell . . . maybe guys like Ralph have it easy. In the long run, maybe the express route from the penthouse to the outhouse turns out to be less painful than the route with all the stops. Kind of like getting hit by a falling safe would surely be preferable to being picked to pieces by birds.

The tough guys . . . the ones who seem to roll their cuffs and step over adversity . . . they're fucked too. They get to spend the rest of their days wondering whether the reason they were so effectively able to go on with their lives was not because they were strong, but was because they never gave a damn to begin with. Wondering if maybe their mothers and ex-wives hadn't been right about what shallow, one-gutted pieces of shit they really were.

For the masses, it's the happiness industry. They go to therapy. They sit around little rooms, singularly and in groups, trying to find their inner child so they can convince the poor little bastard that this disaster of a life isn't their fault. Using whatever happened to them in the past as a blanket excuse for their hollow, half-assed existences, they try like hell to drag everybody else down into the hole they're in. They tell guys like Ralph that they're sick and need professional counseling. They tell the tough guys that they have unresolved issues and will never be whole unless they too spread their inner lives upon the floor for public inspection. Catharsis, you know. Makes them feel sensitive instead of weak. If that doesn't work, they take Prozac.

* * *

The Zoo was hopping. First of the month. Checks were in. George, Harold and Normal were holding down their deeded stools at the far end of the bar. Behind them, at the snooker table, Red Lopez leaned back against the wall holding a cue, his eyes narrowed to slits. Flounder stalked about the table, up one side and down the other, chalking the tip of his cue as he walked. Earlene and Heavy Duty Judy shared a table and a couple of pitchers with Big Frank's jacket. I scanned the bar, but Frank was nowhere in sight. Ralph was over in the corner with his arm thrown around Billy Bob Fung's neck, slobbering in the poor guy's ear as he talked. Billy Bob kept pulling back and picking at his nose.

I checked my watch, One-twenty. Hopefully, they weren't too far into their drinking day to work. Up in the front of the room, with the last of the lunch crowd, the jukebox blared out country western. Jimmie Dale Gilmore, singing through his nose, wanting to know if I'd ever seen Dallas from a DC-9 at night.

I could tell right away that nobody had read the paper. The only thing this crowd liked better than a reason to party was a reason to cry. If they'd known Bermuda was dead, they'd have been holding their own version of an Irish wake.

I made it all the way to Harold's elbow before anybody noticed.

"Hi ho," said George. "It's the swimming detective."

"Howdy, fellas," I said.

Harold threw an arm around my shoulder.

"You gotta be more careful with your driving."

They yukked it up. I signaled Terry to bring the fellas a round.

"Any of you guys want to make a little cash?"

"No yard work," George said quickly.

"Detective work," I said, pulling the Identi-Kit picture from my pocket and laying it on the bar. "I need for you to find this guy."

They huddled together over the picture.

"Ugly bastard," George said.

"Bad hair day," Normal added.

George pulled a frayed notebook from his pocket.

"Wadda ya got in mind?"

I told of my encounter with the Man With No Ears and of my little ride in the river. "Guy looks like this," I said. "Only places he can get lost are the square of the International District. Get together as many people as you can muster. Make copies of the picture. Canvass the whole district if you have to, but . . ." I paused for dramatic effect. ". . . be careful. This guy is dangerous. He damn near punched my ticket for me, and unless I'm mistaken he killed Ed Schwartz on Friday night."

"Ed Schwartz," George gasped. "Bermuda?"

"Yeah," I said. "It's in all the papers."

Harold jabbed the picture with his finger.

"What this guy have against Bermuda?"

"I don't know. That's what makes it scary."

I gave them the Reader's Digest version of the story and then threw a hundred bucks' worth of fives onto the bar. "Here's some cash to keep your whistles wet and I've got another fifty for the guy who turns him."

They began to scuffle over the money. "And George . . ." I said.

He clutched an unruly assemblage of cash against his chest with both hands. "Yeah?"

"Leave Ralphie out of it."

"Sure," he said. "He still got that bug up his chimney about you, anyway."

I crossed behind the snooker table to the men's room. The minute I jerked open the men's room door, I solved the puzzle of the missing Frank. Big Frank stood at the urinal, leaning against the toilet partition, dead drunk asleep with his dick in his hand.

"Frank," I said once. Nothing. "Frank," I bellowed.

He blinked several times and stood up straight. He looked

over my way and then ran both hands through his greasy brown hair.

"Leo," he said. "Yeah . . ." He grunted several times. "I think I better have me a bracer," he said and started my way.

I held up a hand. He stopped. I pointed down at his fly.

"You probably better put that away," I said.

He looked down at himself and grinned.

"Oh, yeah."

He stuffed himself back into his pants and lurched back out into the bar. I checked the toilet stall. Empty. And then followed Frank.

With the exception of Ralph and Billy Bob Fung, the entire crew was gathered around George over at the bar. I walked over and put a hand on Normal's shoulder. He followed me to the far side of the room.

"I'm gonna have a little talk with Ralph," I said. "I want you to keep anybody from coming into the men's room while we chat."

He eyed me closely.

"You ain't gonna hurt him, are you?" he asked.

"No," I said. "I'm just going to talk to him."

"I don't think he's gonna want to talk to ya, Leo. Lately, he don't like you at all."

"That's why I need you to keep people out."

He nodded. "Okay. But don't hurt him."

I walked over to Ralph and Billy Bob and threw an arm around Ralph. "Hey, Ralphie, how you doin'?"

He was bleary-eyed and smelled of cheap scotch. Beneath a worn gray suit jacket, his yellowed long underwear top was wet.

"Get the hell away from me," he said.

I spoke directly to Billy Bob. "You don't mind if I borrow Ralphie for a minute, do you?"

Through a series of head moves and facial tics, Billy Bob indicated that he would, as a matter of fact, be downright joyful were I able to get Ralph to stop drooling in his ear.

"I ain't goin' nowhere . . ." Ralph started.

I grabbed him by the back of the collar, spun him around and marched him straight through the men's room door. When we got inside, I kept him moving, all the way to the back and the toilet stall, where I plopped him down on the seat with a thud and closed the door behind us.

"We're going to have a little talk," I said.

He half-rose and started a roundhouse right toward my head. His elbow hit the side of the stall, reducing the movement to more of a push than a punch. I caught the fist in my left hand and pushed him down onto the toilet with my left.

"Stop it," I said. "I'm not in the mood to be hit. You smack me, and I'll knock you on your ass."

"Oh, yeah, big man?" he sneered.

"Fourth of July weekend, nineteen sixty-nine. That date mean anything to you, Ralph?"

He turned his face to the wall.

"I thought you might recall that Chinese family. You remember them? The ones they found in the container. The parents, the grandparents. Or maybe you just remember the kids. I hear the smell was really something."

His eyes bulged in his head. He hiccuped once and then, using the graffiti-covered walls for leverage, scrambled to his feet. I thought he was coming at me, so I spread my feet for balance and put my hands up. Instead he turned his back to me, dropped to one knee and began vomiting into the filthy toilet.

I pushed open the stall door and stepped out into the room. He was full of beer, so it took a while. When the beer and everything else in his innards was gone, he kept on heaving until it sounded as if his muscles simply would no longer contract.

Normal popped open the door. "Leo," he yelled. "Got some people out here need to go real bad."

"Tell 'em to go piss off the back porch," I said.

When I stepped back into the stall, his eyes were full of water and a thin line of spittle connected his lower lip to his shirtfront.

"Who was supposed to let them out?"

"I don't know what—"

"Hey," I shouted. "Save it. You want to go up on Queen Anne with me and talk to a guy named Gaylord LaFontaine?"

His eyes flicked up at me. He remembered the name. I could tell.

"He used to work for U.S. Customs. Remember? You told him to keep his nose out of what was going down on Eighteen. Told him it was political and that he should keep clear. Remember now?"

He gave a nearly imperceptible bob of the head.

"Who was supposed to let the people out of the container?"

He said it so softly, I didn't hear it the first time.

"Who?"

"Jimmy Chen."

He had me going. "What Jimmy Chen?"

"Judy's ex-husband," he said, without looking up.

"I thought he'd been gone for years."

"He was. Showed up again that summer. She give him a job workin' down in the yard." He wiped his mouth with the back of his hand. "If I'da known, Leo. I'da . . ."

Suddenly his eyes overflowed and tears began running down his face. "He was supposta let 'em out that Thursday." He looked at me. "Never showed up. Those people . . . If I'da known . . ."

"What happened? How come he didn't do his job?"

Ralph shrugged. "Disappeared," he said. "Ain't never seen him since," he said. He stared up at the ceiling. "I ever see that son of a bitch again . . ."

He moved his gaze to me. "I always figured it was your old man," he said.

"Why's that?"

"He wanted that son of a bitch gone, but Judy didn't want to hear about it. Made him promise to leave Jimmy alone."

"But you figure he did it anyway."

He hunched his shoulders.

"Two roosters and one hen."

I'd have felt better if he'd said nearly anything else.

"But you don't know for sure."

He shook his head.

Normal pushed the door open. "Terry's up my ass, Leo."

"Be right out," I said.

23

THE STREET WAS INDEPENDENT OF TIME. BENEATH THE TOWERING oaks and maples, the huge old houses frowned down at the street like dowager aunts. Tim Flood's house, like most of its neighbors, was better than twenty rooms. Three stories of tapered columns, gabled windows and gingerbread flourishes covered in brown shingles. A three-foot brick wall, into which an ornate wrought-iron gate had been set, separated the sidewalk from the front yard. I opened the gate and walked up the broad front steps to the double doors. I knocked, waited for about two minutes and then knocked again, harder this time.

A bell somewhere on the door tinkled as Frankie Ortiz pulled it open. He wore a pair of khaki trousers, a navy blue V-neck sweater and a pale blue button-down shirt. It was the first time in my life I'd ever seen him without a tie and jacket.

"Hi, Frankie." I said. "Sorry to intrude."

He stuck his head out the door and checked the street in both directions. "Ya shoulda called ahead," he said.

"You'd have told me no."

He stepped out onto the porch and closed the door behind him.

"I seen where you popped those two Vegas cowboys."

"Thanks to you."

He gave me a look of mock surprise. "That what you come here for? To thank us? How thoughtful."

"No," I said. "I need to talk to you."

"To me?"

"To both of you."

His eyes ran over me like ants.

"Tim don't see nobody but Caroline."

"I'd really appreciate it if you'd ask him."

Frankie shrugged. "Way I see it, our accounts are even, Leo. You give us a hand with the girl; we slip you a warning that somebody wants to waste your ass. Nobody owes nobody nothing."

"I'm asking a favor," I said.

"A favor, huh?"

"You've seen what they're saying about my father?"

"Be kinda tough to miss there, Junior."

"How about it?" I asked.

He smoothed his pencil-thin mustache with the side of his finger.

"You been talkin' to Eddie Schwartz lately?"

"Yeah."

He checked his manicure and then the street again.

"Not much incentive for talkin' to you then, is it?"

"No. I guess not."

He gave it some thought.

"You wait here," he said finally. "I'll go ask Tim."

Five minutes later, he reappeared at the door.

"You caught him in a good mood," Frankie said.

He opened the door all the way, and I stepped into the vestibule.

"Come on," he said, "you probably want to take that coat off before you get in there."

I took his word for it and pulled the coat off as we ambled to the end of the hallway, and then on through the double French doors at the end of the passage, which left us in a small foyer between the main house and the giant solarium at the back. Frankie stepped to one side and ushered me into the stifling sunroom. Like my last visit, it was at least eighty-five degrees inside the glass room. The humidity was like the Texas Gulf Coast in August.

A dazzling array of orchids, exotic plants and shrubs, many pushing the thirty-foot glass roof, dripped in the moist air. The place was a greenhouse with furniture. It felt like a sauna.

The remains of Tim Flood were masquerading as a pile of bones, dry, white and nearly lost amid the cushions of an ancient wicker settee that fanned out behind his head like a halo.

"Sit," he said, motioning toward a green wicker chair. Sweat was beginning to roll down my backbone. I sat.

Frankie pushed an old-fashioned bar cart over next to me and asked me what I wanted. I took a bottled water and downed about half of it. Frankie poured something disturbingly yellow into Tim's glass, added two ice cubes and then took a seat on Tim's right, with his hands folded in his lap.

Tim looked pretty good. Smaller than I remembered. His hawklike nose had become more prominent with age; his bony liver-spotted hands gripped the padded arms of the lounger like bird's feet, but the hard little eyes showed no concession to time.

Tim generally liked to shoot the breeze a bit before getting down to business. He was big on tales of the good old days. Of ghost fleets on Lake Union, of breadlines and Hooverville and union elections that were settled by sawed-off baseball bats up the sleeve. Today, however, he wasn't in the mood for small talk.

"Tell me about Eddie Schwartz," he said.

I gave him the whole story, omitting nothing except what Ralph had said about Jimmy Chen.

When I finished, Frankie jumped in.

"What the hell was he doing down on the docks?"

"I think he wanted to talk to Judy Chen."

"Why would he want to do that?"

"I don't know."

Tim sat up straighter in the chair. "What do you want from me?"

"Somebody told me Judy Chen had her ex-husband working for her down on Pier Eighteen. Said it was the ex-husband who was supposed to let those people out of that container."

"Somebody, huh?" Frankie repeated. He looked over at Tim. "Now what little somebody might that be?"

"Eddie Schwartz tells nobody nothing," offered Tim.

"Judy neither," added Frankie.

Frankie and Tim passed a quick look between them.

"Ralphie," Frankie said. "The lush."

Tim turned his predator eyes on me.

"Ralphie still alive, huh? I'da thought he'da swallowed himself to death by now."

"He's working on it," I assured him.

"That thing ate him up."

"What thing?"

"The container thing. He ain't never been the same since that. Before that, he was a pretty good man. After that . . ." He made a drinking motion with his thumb.

Moisture was beginning to seep out through my scalp. I took another big sip of my bottled water. "Is it true?" I asked.

"What? That Ralphie likes a drink?" Frankie said with a smile. "Yeah. I think that's safe to say."

I kept my cool and kept plodding forward.

"That Judy Chen had her ex-husband Jimmy working for her down on Eighteen and that he was the one supposed to let those people out of that container."

We sat in silence for a moment. I listened to the sound of my own thick breathing and imagined that I could hear the constant movement of water throughout the room.

Tim's voice suddenly sounded hoarse. "You know, Leo, you outlive your friends; you outlive your secrets, too. It just happens. You wake up one day and none of the reasons why you was keeping secrets matter a rat's ass anymore, cause nobody who's still breathing gives a flying shit."

I had no idea what to say. He took a deep breath, fixed me with a stony stare and continued.

"I don't like what happened to Eddie Schwartz."

I nodded and stared at the tops of my shoes.

"Eddie was a good man. Better than a lot of guys with legs."

"You and him was tight," Frankie said.

"Yeah," I said, without looking up. "When I was a kid."

Tim rustled around in the chair.

"Old man like Eddie . . . a good man . . . shouldn't go like that."

"No," I agreed. "He deserved better."

Tim leaned way back into the shadows of the chair, nearly becoming lost again among the cushions, with only the sharp tip of his nose poking like an arrow out into the light.

"Frankie says you want a favor."

Suddenly, we were at the last bus stop in the free ride zone. This was my chance to drink my water, pay my respects and get on up the road. After this, nothing was free.

I looked at where I thought his eyes should be.

"Yeah, I do."

"Then you'll owe me," he said.

This was the "Last Train to Clarksville" section of the program. Owing Tim a favor was no small matter. Tim's favors were not multiple choice. If he wants a package delivered to Detroit, you go to Detroit. If what he needs is somebody to shoot the mayor, then you shoot the mayor. No questions asked.

I took a deep breath. "I know," I said.

Frankie shifted in his chair. "You know, Leo, if it was just any schmoozer sittin' there in your chair, I'd think maybe the guy didn't know what in hell he was letting himself in for. But you know, it being you and all, I gotta ask you how come this is all so damn important to you. I mean . . . what the fuck do you care?"

I kept my voice flat. "How could I not care? In my whole life, my old man's the only standard anybody's ever judged me by. Everything I've ever done has been held up to his light for inspection. Like it wasn't important on its own. Like the only thing important about it was how it compared to somebody's image of my old man, and what he might have done." I spread my hands. "How could I not care?"

Frankie sat back in his chair and looked over at Tim. I saw the tip of Tim's nose move up and down. Frankie rested his chin in his hand.

"You don't quote us," he said.

"Naturally."

"What do you wanna know?"

"Who killed Peerless Price?"

"Not a clue."

I must have looked dumbfounded.

"I thought maybe . . ." I began.

From the recesses of the chair, Tim laughed.

"You thought if your old man needed somebody hit, he'd come to me, is what you thought, right?"

"Something like that," I admitted.

"He would," said Tim, "usually."

"But not a reporter," Frankie said quickly. "You're lookin' for more trouble than it's worth. You don't waste reporters."

"Not even for Bill," Tim said.

" 'Sides that," Frankie said, "Bill . . . your old man . . . he pretty much had Price under control. Price had been busting his ball for years. Your old man had his ass covered."

I tried something else.

"What did my old man have on Douglas Brennan?"

They passed another look. I waited.

"Who says he had anything?" Tim asked.

"He had enough to get Douglas to issue an Order of Provision over that raid on the Garden of Eden."

Frankie raised an eyebrow. "Kid's been doing his homework, Tim."

"He's a detective," Tim said, and they both had a good laugh.

"What do you need to know about Brennan for?"

"I need to squeeze him a little."

They both broke out laughing again.

"Jesus, Leo," Frankie chortled. "Ain't you squeezed that poor old bastard enough yet?"

"Guy on death row's hard to squeeze," Tim added.

"The papers say he's gonna get a new trial. They say the judge made some procedural mistake. I figure Brennan can't afford anything coming to light that could potentially screw that up."

They silently talked it over again. Tim spoke first.

"Some say that little Mexican he offed down in Tacoma might not have been the first."

"Or even the second," added Frankie.

For reasons I don't understand, I had a terrific urge to point out that Felicia Mendoza was Guatemalan, not Mexican, but I resisted.

"Do tell."

Frankie leaned out across Tim, putting his face close to mine.

"You ask him about the fifteenth floor of the Carlisle Hotel in nineteen fifty-seven."

"What about it."

Frankie shook his head. "I can't say no more. Some of the people involved are still around."

I was tempted to ask if any of said "still around" people were, by chance, in the room at this time, but decided against it.

"The Carlisle Hotel, fifteenth floor, fifty-seven."

"You just ask him. You'll shrivel his dick up like a roll of dimes."

"What if he—" I started.

Tim cut me dead. "Come on, Leo. Show me something. Smart private dick like you ought to be able to run a little bluff. Give your old man that much info, he'd come out of there owning the guy's house."

I'd gotten everything I was going to get there, so I pressed on.

"What about all those people who died in that container?"

The atmosphere in the room seemed to grow thicker. Neither man spoke or, for that matter, even looked at the other.

"The container thing was a mess," Tim said suddenly.

Frankie looked at his boss with mild surprise.

Tim lifted both claws. "Leo's family," he croaked.

If Tim's pronouncement was supposed to make me feel warm and fuzzy, I'll have to admit that it had much the opposite effect. For the first time since entering the room, I was no longer sweltering.

"Yeah," Frankie said, "what Ralphie said was true. Judy gave her ex-husband a job out in the yard."

As much as I hated to interrupt, I just had to know.

"Why? Why would she give some guy . . . some drunk who used to beat the shit out of her a job?"

Frankie touched his forehead with his fingers. "Who knows why broads do the things they do. Specially Chinese broads. You ever find out for sure, you write a book. You'll make a million."

Tim leaned out into the light. "She told your old man she felt sorry for him. She was hoping maybe the guy could get his act together, maybe the kid could have a father. You know, that kind of thing."

"What happened?"

"Your old man wanted him gone."

I made it a statement. "He was jealous."

Tim snorted. "You think your old man would waste his time on shit like that?" He waved a bony hand at me. "Jealous," he said derisively. "Over some skirt."

Frankie made a noise in his throat. "What that Jimmy Chen fucker did to piss off your dad was to try to queer the whole operation."

"How?"

"He went to Peerless Price. Spilled his guts."

"Why would he do that?"

"Fucker was crazy. A juicehead," Frankie said with feeling. "He hated Judy. He really hated your old man 'cause . . .

you know . . . he and Judy were . . ." He let it hang. "Fucker was crazy," he said again.

"What happened then?"

Frankie was rolling. "From the moment that fucker took the job, heat started coming from everywhere." Frankie painted the air with his hands. "Price was all over it in the papers. Customs and INS was fallin' all over each other. I mean, it didn't take no genius to know who the rat was, but Judy didn't want to hear about it. Nope. No sir. She made your old man promise he'd leave him alone."

"Did he?"

Frankie wagged his head. "Technically speaking," he said. "I mean, you know, that fucker had to go. Not like there was any doubt of it at all. Question was just how and when. Bill . . . your old man . . . asked us if maybe we couldn't . . ." He searched for a word. ". . . persuade this Jimmy Chen asshole that his health would stay better if he was to get the hell out of town and stay that way."

Tim's voice sounded tired as he spoke from the shadows.

"Leo," he began, "you gotta understand. None of us knew the details of Judy's business." He waved a hand around. "Not me or Frankie and not your old man." He held the hand still now, stiff palm facing me. "Honest to God. None of us knew one goddamn thing about that family in the box."

"Swear to God," Frankie repeated.

"Things got out of hand," Tim said.

"Fucker was crazy," Frankie said for the third time. "We were gonna bust him up a bit. Make him go tell Judy he quit on his own, so's it wouldn't look like Bill had a hand in it. You know, put the fear of God in him."

"And?"

"Things got out of hand. The guy was a handful and a whole lot bigger than we figured. Never seen a guy fight so crazy before. Hadda have Eddie Schwartz sit on his chest."

"Bermuda was there?"

Frankie made a disgusted face. "We didn't know this Chinaman from Charlie Chan. Fuck, they all look alike to me.

Bill sent Eddie to finger him for us. Eddie was supposed to wait in the car, but, you know, Eddie was a good man. When things started to go sideways, he hustled his ass out and gave us a hand."

"Sideways how?"

"I told you, the Chinaman fought like crazy." Frankie looked over at Tim. "Busted Tim's nose. Stuck a finger in one of my eyes. I hadda wear a patch for a month and a half, for Chrissakes."

"So?"

"So . . . you know what they say . . . it was like feelings were running high. Tim was bleeding all over his suit. Eddie's riding the guy's chest like a buckin' bronco. I'm down to one eye." He hesitated. "I kinda lost my temper."

"Yeah?"

"I guess I sorta lost it entirely."

"Never seen him like that," Tim offered.

"I thought the fucker had blinded me," Frankie complained. "It was so lame we never even told your old man. When we was done, we stuffed him in a boxcar headed to Florida."

"What did you do?"

Frankie actually looked embarrassed.

"I cut off his ears," he said.

24

EXCEPT FOR RALPH AND A PAIR OF SECRETARIES IN THE FRONT booth, the Zoo was deserted. The rest of the afternoon regulars were out looking for Jimmy Chen. Terry wiped his hands on a red towel and started down the bar. When I waved him off, he went back to washing glasses.

"Whatever it is you got everybody up to, Leo, it sure knocked the crap out of business," he said above the running water.

I shrugged and then leaned over and spoke directly into Ralph's ear. I'd already run the whole thing down for him twice, but it didn't seem to have any effect.

"Lea me alone."

He gargled it out through a mouthful of beer and then used his sleeve to polish the dribbles off the bar.

"No can do," I said. "Much as it pains me, my old friend, on this one, all roads lead to Ralphie."

He began to rise from the stool, but I clamped a hand on his shoulder and pushed him back down.

"You din tell me Eddie was dead," he said.

"That's why I've got to know what happened, Ralph. Somebody's got to pay for Ed Schwartz."

"Lea me alone," he said again.

"It wasn't your fault, Ralph," I said.

He shot me a red-rimmed glance and then went back to studying the foam on his glass.

"It was just one of those things," I went on. "There wasn't anything you or anybody else could have done."

"Your dad . . ." he started, and then shook his head sadly and swallowed the rest of his beer.

"Trust me, Ralph. There's plenty of blame to go around on this one. Judy Chen should never have given that scumbag Jimmy a job. It was dumb. My father wanted Jimmy Chen gone. That's what started the real shit. He asked Tim and Frankie to fuck Jimmy Chen up and get him out of Dodge. None of them had any idea Jimmy was the one who was supposed to let that family out. Things went haywire. Frankie and Tim lost control of the situation. Jimmy Chen got a lot more fucked up than anybody intended. It didn't have anything to do with you."

"I coulda . . ."

"You coulda nothing. If you'd known, you'd have let them out. You're not the kind of guy to let a family die out there in the sun. Everybody knows that."

I don't know why I felt the need to lighten Ralph's load. I knew it wouldn't do any good. He'd been feeding off of his own guilt for so long that it had become part of his life cycle. Taking it away from him now would be tantamount to removing the feeding tube from a coma victim.

When I looked up, one of the secretaries was slipping quarters into the jukebox. The jazzy little bass run told me what was coming. Van Morrison's voice whispered out from the front of the room.

"Tim didn't kill Peerless Price."

Ralph looked up from his beer and opened his mouth.

"I asked him," I said. "This very afternoon."

He leaned down, resting his forehead on the rim of the glass.

"He's got no reason to lie to me," I added. "And with Ed Schwartz dead, neither do you."

Ralph didn't move. His cheeks puffed in and out.

"You knew Price was buried in my backyard, didn't you?

That's why you ran off from the house that day. You were afraid we were going to find the body, so you ran off."

When he lifted his head, the rim of the glass had imprinted his skin, leaving him with a big circle etched in the center of his forehead, like a huge blank eye. "No . . . I . . ." he began.

I shook my head. "That's the only way it shakes out, Ralph. The problem has always revolved around the question of how you bury a body in somebody's yard without them knowing about it. I've spent the last week or so kicking that one around, and finally, just this morning, it came to me." I tapped my temple. "You don't. Can't be done. You'd have to know how long the people who lived in the house were going to be away from home. You'd have to know that there was someplace in the yard with fresh dirt. Someplace you could bury it that nobody would notice. You'd have to know that a structure was about to be built over the spot where you buried the body so you wouldn't have to worry about animals or the weather. You'd have to know how the house was situated. That the neighbors couldn't see into the backyard."

I clapped him on the shoulder.

"It doesn't scan any other way, man."

He put his head back down on the empty glass. I raised two fingers toward Terry. He pulled a couple of fresh glasses from the dishwasher and began to pour beer.

"She came to the rally," he said softly.

"The night before the Fourth of July?"

"Uh-huh."

"Judy Chen?"

"Yeah."

"She showed up at the big rally up at Volunteer Park the night Price disappeared?"

"Carrying the kid," he said. "A hell of a mess," he said. "Hell of a scene. Your mom being there and all . . ."

Terry arrived with two fresh beers. Ralph raised his head and slid his empty glass across the bar. He now had two interlocking rings imprinted on his head. Three more rings and he'd be an Olympic sponsor.

He downed half the beer and wiped his mouth with the back of his hand. "Wasn't nothin' Bill could do. What with the big rally and all. You and your mom sittin' up there on the stage with him." He looked at me with pleading eyes. "What was he gonna do at a time like that?"

"He sent you and Ed Schwartz," I said.

He nodded and finished the beer. I signaled Terry for another.

The secretary had also played the flip side. A younger, brasher Van was begging her to stay.

A bead of sweat ran through the stubble on Ralph's cheek and dropped onto the bar. "She said Peerless Price showed up where she was living, down on the docks. Wanted to know where Jimmy Chen was. Pushed her around. Threatened her and the kid. Said he was gonna bring all of them down, if she didn't roll over on Bill."

It made sense. Peerless Price must have been desperate. He'd been counting on Jimmy Chen to finally give him what he needed to bring Wild Bill Waterman to his knees. He'd publicly announced his intention. And then, just like that, Jimmy Chen was nowhere to be found.

Terry waddled down the length of the bar and exchanged glasses with Ralph. I waited for him to get out of earshot.

"And?"

He looked me full in the face for the first time.

"She shot him. Said it was self-defense. Said she was protecting the boy."

He chased the words with another half a glass of beer.

"The cops say the gun belonged to Ed Schwartz," I said.

"When she gave Jimmy Chen the job, your dad insisted she have a gun, you know, in case . . ."

So he did what he always did with errands, he palmed it off on Bermuda, who ended up with his name on the registration certificate. No problem there. Like Tim said, Eddie Schwartz tells nobody nothing.

"Bill said me and Eddie should pick him up and put him

in the greenhouse floor. Said we'd figure out what to do with him later."

"Why'd he leave the body in the greenhouse? Why not wait for the dust to settle and then dump it somewhere else?"

Ralph finished the beer. "Asked him one time. He said he'd thought it over and decided he had more control of it where it was. Thought maybe he'd just leave it there. That way him and old Peerless could keep an eye on one another."

I had to admit, it was slick. Most folks wouldn't have been able to go on with their lives with a body buried out in the yard. The old man, though, was smart enough to realize that what he needed was control of the corpse, and the best way to maintain control was to keep it where it was. Long-range planning. Dude.

I threw a twenty on the bar and motioned for Terry to come on down.

"Give this gentleman whatever he wants," I said.

I found Normal first. Standing on the corner of Second and Cherry palming a guy by the head. The guy's feet were still moving, but it wasn't doing him any good. Normal had the little guy a foot off the sidewalk and was holding the picture of Jimmy Chen about three inches in front of his nose. I jogged across Second Avenue against the light. I was afraid the big fella might crush his skull like an egg.

"I asked ya if ya seen this guy," Normal said.

The guy stammered out something. Norman waved him around.

"Normal," I yelled.

He turned his head in my direction and then slowly set the guy down. The guy went scurrying up the sidewalk at light speed, checking back over his shoulder and rubbing his temples.

"He knew more than he was letting on," Normal said.

"Where's George?" I asked.

"Over in Chinatown."

"Go find Harold and George and meet me in Hing Hay Park," I said. "I've got a different job for the three of you."

25

THE SURVEILLANCE CAMERA ABOVE THE DOOR WHIRRED MY WAY and clicked to a stop, its electronic eye trained on my forehead. The speaker emitted a series of cracks and pops and what I thought might be the sound of two garbled voices and then snapped silent. I stepped back out into the street and waited. It didn't take long.

The door slid back. Gordon Chen stood in the narrow elevator car. He looked bad, like he'd been up all night with a toothache. His high-style hair hung down over one eye. He needed a shave.

"Go away," he hissed. "Don't you ever come here again."

When I smiled and started across the sidewalk, he stepped out of the elevator. "I'll kill you," he said. "If you continue to harass my mother, I'll kill you. Don't think I won't."

He started a big right-handed haymaker at my head. I moved my head a foot to the left and let the fist sail by, grabbed him by the forearm with two hands and swung him hard in a wide arc, as one would throw a sledgehammer. I used his own momentum to bash him, back first, into the side of a red Toyota Camry parked at the curb. The air shot from his lungs with a wet cough. His face turned the color of oatmeal.

He began to slide down the side of the car.

"Ooooooh . . . uuuuuuug," he groaned as he reached the

sitting position, gasping for breath, his arms now wrapped around his body.

I'd had about enough of old Gordo. I had a terrific urge to kick him in the head, but restrained myself.

"Uuuuuuugh," he wheezed, clutching his chest.

I walked over to the elevator, and pushed the UP button. The door slid shut. Up I went.

She was standing right in front of me when the door slid back, wearing a purple Husky T-shirt and a pair of jeans. Her hair was kept back from her face by a white plastic band and she held a pair of black-rimmed eyeglasses in one hand.

"Where is my son?"

"He's downstairs. He'll be up in a while."

"You hurt him." She made it an accusation.

"Nothing serious," I said. "Just knocked the wind out of him. He'll get over it."

It was all one room. The center was a sunken living room. Several green-and-white-flowered sofas facing a rosewood entertainment center. The central area was surrounded on all sides by what amounted to a mezzanine. On each of the four sides four steps led down into the center of the room. On this side, a hall ran the entire width of the building. On my left, a kitchen and dining area. Directly across the way a bank of black-tinted windows looked out over the Port of Seattle.

When I stepped out into the room, we were only about a foot apart.

"I don't remember inviting you into my home," she said.

"I know about Jimmy Chen and the people in the container."

She stood silent for a moment and then, without a word, turned and walked down into the living room. I followed her. She walked to the far end and stood staring at me, tugging on her lower lip.

"I know about Peerless Price and the gun my father had Ed Schwartz buy for you. About the night of the big rally up in Volunteer Park, how Ed and Ralph Batista came and took the body and buried it."

She opened her mouth to deny it, but I beat her to the punch.

"It's your own fault. You shouldn't have sent the cops the gun," I said. "It just encouraged me."

"My son's idea," she said quickly. "He hoped it could be traced directly back to your father. That if they had the gun that would be the end of it." She clapped her hands. "Open and shut. You'd go away, he said."

"The gun told me I had somebody's attention."

"Hindsight," she muttered. "I kept it for all these years, just in case. A little insurance policy." She shrugged.

"What I don't understand is how you could give Jimmy Chen a job in the yard."

She looked me over carefully. "I've had thirty years to ask myself that question. You'd think I'd know the answer by now."

"Do you?"

"It depends on what day you ask me," she said. "On my good days, I tell myself that I was being charitable. That he had nothing. No one. No nothing." She sighed. "On darker days, I convince myself I did it because of the guilt. The way I felt . . . because . . . perhaps I had used him. Perhaps I had taken advantage of his youth and lack of character for my own ends." She paused. "I had, after all, ended up with that which was once his."

She stepped over and sat on the nearest couch. "When I'm really feeling sorry for myself, I tell myself it was for Gordon. I tell myself that Jimmy was Gordon's father. I hoped that with my help he might be able to salvage his life. That perhaps my son could have a relationship with his father." She pointed a finger in my direction. "You of all people should understand what it is to live under the shadow of a father. Think of what Gordon has had to deal with. You chafe under your father's legend. Imagine what it must be like to wear Jimmy Chen's ignominy."

She caught herself and wagged her head again. "Every day, for nearly thirty years, I've cursed Jimmy Chen and said a prayer for those people who perished because of me. Because I put my personal pipe dreams before their safety. I don't need the likes of you to remind me."

I pulled the folded Identi-Kit picture from my pocket and dropped it on the table in front of her. Behind me, the elevator door slid shut and the car began to move. "What's this?" she asked.

"Open it up and see."

She flattened the picture on the table, pushing out toward the edges with her palms. In the soft light, I could see the maze of fine lines and the looseness of the skin on the backs of her hands.

The sound of the elevator door brought my head around. Gordon Chen stepped to the top of the stairs. He still looked a little green around the gills. Judy looked from the picture, to Gordon, to me and then back to the picture.

"I don't understand," she said. "This is . . ."

I looked up at Gordon.

"You want to tell her, Junior, or should I?"

"I swear to God, I'll kill you," he wheezed.

"He's back, you know," I said to Judy. "Jimmy Chen. Your son's been taking care of him. Giving him money. Letting him live in the old apartment in the warehouse."

She looked to her son for a denial, but he stood at the top of the stairs shaking his head with his eyes closed, his hair swishing the air. I went on. "Did he tell you that Ed Schwartz was killed down on Eighteen, night before last. Did he?"

Her mouth dropped partially open. "Gordon," she said.

His eyes were open now. He began to scream at his mother. "All these years, you told me he was dead!"

"I thought it best," she said quietly. "How could you . . ."

Gordon wasn't in the mood to listen.

"He's my father . . . Do you hear me? My father . . . How could I not take care of him?" He cut the air with his hand. "After you robbed him of his dignity . . . took away his manhood . . . made him into a circus freak. He's my father," he said again. He pushed his hair back from his narrow face.

"He came to me in the street. I thought he was a tramp. He disgusted me. I wouldn't let him touch me. I tried to give him a dollar to go away."

He looked down at his mother. "He had a picture. Of us. The three of us on the beach at Alki. He was my father." He pointed at me. "This monster that you and *his* father made was my father."

I spoke to Gordon. "Your mother didn't know what happened to him, Gordon. It wasn't supposed to turn out the way it did. They were just going to bust him up a bit and scare him out of town. Things got out of hand."

"Out of hand?" he bellowed. "You call cutting off a man's ears out of hand? You call making a man into an animal out of hand?"

The picture slipped from Judy Chen's fingers. She got to her feet and started up the stairs toward her son.

"I don't understand," she said. "Ears?"

Gordon backed away. "Get away from me. Don't you touch me."

"Gordon," she said softly.

"Jimmy Chen won't be a problem for much longer," I said. "By now, there's about a hundred cops showing that picture all over the district. They'll have him in custody before very long."

Gordon Chen's eyes rolled in his head like a spooked horse. His lower lip trembled. His hands opened and closed. For a long moment, he stood completely still, staring down at his mother, making up his mind, and then, without another word, he threw himself into the elevator car and pushed the button. The door slid shut and he was gone.

She read the expression on my face.

"Don't judge my son too harshly, Leo. His life has been difficult. It wasn't easy having Judy Chen for a mother."

"A lot of people would say a guy who drives a sixty-thousand-dollar car and runs a whole corporation has it pretty good."

She made a face. "The business runs itself. If the figures

get out of line the accountants call me. We fix it. Gordon calls people on the phone and sleeps with the receptionist." Her eyes twinkled. "In many ways Gordon has the same problem with being the son of Judy Chen as you have with being the son of Bill Waterman."

I massaged the idea for long enough to know I didn't like it.

"What was this about ears?" she said.

I laid it out for her. Everything I knew. About halfway through, she started to cry. By the time I'd finished, she had herself back together. "My God," was her only comment.

She walked over to the stairs, went up into the kitchen and got herself a paper towel for her nose. "What now?"

"Peerless Price. The people in the container," I said. "As far as I'm concerned, that's all ancient history."

I could see how relieved she was, so I felt bad about what came next. "Ed Schwartz isn't ancient history, though. It's only a matter of time before the cops find Jimmy Chen. God only knows what he's going to say. If I were you, I'd call my attorney."

"And you?"

"What I know stays with me. Jimmy Chen is your problem, not me."

A buzzer began going off. Two buzzes. A pause. Three buzzes.

Judy stepped back down into the living room, picked up a remote control and pointed it at the small monitor over the elevator. A black-and-white picture blinked to life. George milling around the downstairs doorway. "Leo. Leo . . . you up there?"

Judy pushed another button and nodded at me.

"Yeah, I'm here, George."

"Norman and Harry are on him. You was right. He's headed down by the Dome."

"Thanks," I said. "I'll be right down."

She hit the remote and the screen went blank.

"It seems my son has underestimated you again."

I stepped over and pushed the DOWN button.

"He's an excitable boy," I said, stepping into the elevator. "He ought to learn to control himself. He'll live longer."

She reached in and put a small hand on my arm.

"Don't let anything happen to him, Leo. He's all I have."

26

THE BUILDING RAN RAMSHACKLE FOR AN ENTIRE BLOCK, FROM South Atlantic all the way down to South Massachusetts. A single-story snake of a building, with a dozen ancient loading ramps lapping out toward First Avenue like filthy tongues. Above a thick collar of litter, the peeling wooden facade stared out at the street through a dozen roll-up doors, spaced evenly along the block.

Harold pointed to a white steel door a third of the way down the building. "Went in the white door. Ain't come back out."

We were on lower First Avenue, two blocks south of the Kingdome, diagonally across the street from the mess that was scheduled to become the new baseball stadium in the year two thousand.

I checked my watch. Five fifty-five. Dark had arrived in a hurry. Whatever final flames the sun might have offered had been doused by a thick band of storm clouds hanging low along the western horizon. The street was empty on a Sunday night. Quiet enough to hear the roar of traffic on the Interstate, four blocks to the east.

"What're we gonna do?" asked George.

"I don't know," I said.

Truth be told, I was in a quandary. On one hand, I definitely wasn't up for any more dancing in the dark with

Jimmy Chen. That much was for sure. All I had to do to avoid that little scenario was to call the cops. Cowardly, but effective.

On the other hand, I felt some unexplainable need to see if maybe I couldn't get Gordon Chen out of there before the shit hit the fan. I couldn't imagine why, either. Hell, I didn't like him a bit. I couldn't think of a single thing about him I liked, other than his car. He was a snot-nosed little mama's boy who couldn't fight his way out of a paper bag. I had a million reasons why I shouldn't care a whit about what happened to his scrawny ass and none of them mattered.

I pointed to George. "You go across the street and flop in that doorway like you're out of it."

"Typecasting," Norman suggested.

I looked up at Normal. "Go around the back. See if there are any people doors in the back. If there are, find a place where you can see them and get comfortable. Harold, you go with Normal."

"What're you gonna do?" he asked.

"I'm going to work my way down the front of the building, see if maybe I can't find some way in other than that white door."

It was a decent plan. The Chens were on foot. George and I would be within line of sight of one another, so we shouldn't have any problem there. If they came out the back, Normal and Harold knew what to do. One of them would follow while the other came running back for us. Not a bad plan. Too bad we never got a chance to see if it would work.

"Let's go," I said. "Everybody be careful. The old guy is dangerous."

George started across the deserted street toward his doorway, Harold and Normal linked arms and disappeared around the corner to the right. I got about three steps across Royal Brougham Avenue when Harold and Normal came sprinting back around the end of the building, with a blue-and-white police cruiser in hot pursuit.

To my left George stopped in the middle of the street, his

eyes wide. The squeal of tires told me what the problem was. A second cruiser slid to a stop about ten feet from the old guy. Both uniforms burst from the car with their guns drawn. I checked over my shoulder. Same thing from the first police car. I folded my hands behind my head. The Boys followed suit. Before anybody said a word, a third car wheeled out from behind the building. A silver Ford. Oh, shit.

Before the Ford squealed completely to a halt, Trujillo came barreling out the passenger door on the run.

"What the hell are you doing here?"

I moved my head toward the building.

"He's in there," I said.

Wessels leaned out over the Ford's roof, grinning like a possum.

"I know goddamn well he's in there. We did a house-to-house on the neighborhood this morning. That's what the people of the city of Seattle pay me to do."

He spoke to the nearest guy in uniform. "You and Roberts take these guys downtown. Book 'em for interference."

"Book 'em, Danno," Norman intoned.

The cop pulled his handcuffs from the back of his belt and started for me. Trujillo stomped around in the dust. "I warned you. Goddamnit, Waterman. If you and these . . . these . . ." He seemed at a loss for a noun. ". . . screwed up this stakeout, I swear to God . . ."

"Book 'em, Danno."

As the cop pulled my right hand behind my back, a dark figure bolted from the white door. I used my left hand to point.

"There he goes," I said.

Jimmy Chen ran with all the grace of an arthritic scarecrow, but his legs were long and he covered more ground than his awkward stride at first glance suggested. Before anyone could move, he was across the street, running south toward the new Mariners ballpark.

"Book 'em, Danno."

The minute Jimmy Chen started up the chain-link fence

surrounding the stadium excavation, Trujillo began barking orders. He pointed to the cop who was about to cuff me. "You and Roberts get down to the gate on the east side. Call for backup on the way."

The kid dangled the handcuffs. "Should I . . ." he stammered.

"Go," Trujillo shouted.

He pointed at the other two uniforms. "You two, come with us."

The SPD cruiser roared to life and went screaming up First Avenue.

Trujillo saved the best for us. "You stay right here. All of you. You hear me? You're under arrest. Your asses damn well better be right here when this is over. If you're not here when I get back, I'll charge you with attempted escape. A felony, you hear me?"

We must have looked terrified, because, without getting an answer, he turned and began running across the street, his gun pumping now in his right hand.

Trujillo and the two uniforms threw themselves into the fence feet first, levering themselves up and over in a few powerful lunges. Wessels was out of breath before he ever got to the fence, his knees wobbly, his running line crooked. It took him three tries to get over and even then, he ripped the hell out of his suit jacket on the way down. I smiled.

I took my hands off my head and looked over at the Boys. "Gone" was the operant word. They were a hundred and fifty yards up the street heeling and toeing it for all they were worth back toward Pioneer Square. Apparently, they had been somewhat less than intimidated by Trujillo's dire threats. I was still pondering what I was going to do next when a movement in my peripheral vision pulled my head to the right.

Gordon Chen was struggling over the fence about ten yards north of where the others had crossed. Instead of jumping down from the top, like the others, he climbed down. Probably didn't want to mess his hair.

Instead of following the others up the concrete ramp, Gordon began running along the fence line, heading east toward the freeway.

Without willing it so, I found myself crossing the street.

"Oh, Christ," I muttered, beginning to jog. Timing my steps like a high jumper, I sprang upward, stuck the toe of my right sneaker about halfway up the fence and pushed myself to the stiff-armed position on the top rail. I steadied myself for a moment, brought my left foot up even with my hands and then launched myself up and over.

I squatted on the packed dirt and checked things out. The site looked like a medieval castle under siege. A maze of wooden concrete forms rose like battlements for as far as I could see in either direction. The tops of the walls bristled with black steel reinforcing rods. Everywhere scaffolds and ladders leaned against the walls like remnants of a long-ago battle.

Overhead, four giant yellow cranes loomed ten or twelve stories into the night sky, defining the corners of the stadium, their yellow superstructures lighted as a precaution against low-flying planes.

I went after Gordon Chen, looping off to the right, following the fence, jogging past a dozen Porta Potties, moving carefully in the dim light until I came to a broad concrete road leading down into the bowels of the stadium. I figured this must be where they brought in the heavy equipment. I took a chance and followed the pavement inside.

In the near darkness, my eyes had trouble sorting out the jumble. I stood for a minute, allowing my nervous system time to adjust.

It was like a giant dirt bowl. Around the perimeter, dim halogen banks lighted the tops of the walkways, pushing long shadows down along what would someday be the seats, their timid luminance utterly lost among the dark clutter spread out over the future field of dreams.

The field itself was a morass of banded lumber and wet piles of dirt and gravel. Out in the center a steam shovel sat idle, its great steel jaws open and at the ready. A scattered herd of pachydermatous cement trucks grazed contentedly among the rubble.

I moved fifty feet to my left and started up the dirt embankment toward the top of the stadium. The ground was firm and packed from thousands of footfalls. I stopped about two-thirds of the way up and took stock. I could see the cops. Wessels was two hundred feet in front of me, his gun in his right hand, creeping along beside a row of banded four-by-fours. One uniform was skirting the left edge of the field and one the right. Trujillo had climbed to the peak of a mountain of dirt out in the middle of the field by the steam shovel. He spread his arms and then moved them quickly inward, signaling the uniforms to move quicker.

No Jimmy. No Gordon. I waited.

It didn't take long. Below me, I could hear Wessels' labored wheezing. The noise was probably why my eyes picked up the movement before he heard it. Both of us were too late.

Jimmy Chen stepped out of a gap in the piles of lumber with his arms raised above his head. Frank Wessels got about half turned when Jimmy brought whatever it was he held aloft straight down like an ax. The sound reminded me of the time I dropped a cantaloupe while screwing around in the supermarket. Sort of a wet thunk. Wessels went down in a pile. Jimmy Chen stepped back into the darkness and disappeared.

I began to shout. "Trujillo. Over here."

He looked around. I yelled again and waved my arms. "Here."

When his head snapped my way, I pointed. "Down here. He got Wessels. Call for an ambulance."

I didn't wait for an answer. I began moving down the embankment as fast as I dared. Ahead of me, the wall separating the box seats from the field bristled with steel whiskers. If I got out of control, I could end up skewering myself like a kabob.

When I got back to the edge of the pavement, I hopped

down and began running. I missed Wessels the first time. He was one row of lumber further out than I'd estimated, lying in the fetal position on his left side, his service revolver nearly touching his nose.

Even in the deep shadow, I could see it wasn't good. A seeping furrow ran straight down his forehead toward his nose. His breathing was ragged and rattled in his chest; his lips were covered in blood.

I knelt by his side and placed my fingers on his neck artery. His pulse was irregular and unstable. I still had my hand on his throat when he coughed up a mouthful of blood and stopped breathing.

"Here," I shouted. "Here."

As much as it pained me, I pinched his nose, pulled his mouth open, cleared the airway with my fingers, just like in the book, and commenced CPR. Two breaths into his mouth. Fifteen compressions of his chest. "Over here." Two breaths into his mouth. Fifteen compressions of his chest. "Over here." I got into a rhythm. Breathe, push, scream. Breathe, push, scream. Breathe, push, scream.

By the time the first uniform found us, I was gasping for breath and could hear a siren in the distance. He took one look at my red face, holstered his revolver and took over.

He lasted until the siren was screaming in our ears, and then I took over again. Two breaths into his mouth. Fifteen compressions of his chest. I was still at it when Trujillo arrived with the cavalry.

A burly EMT in a whiter-than-white uniform shirt shouldered me aside and began working on Wessels. I stood up and leaned back on the pile of lumber. I was so winded, I had imaginary snowflakes swirling around me in the air. It was all I could do not to try to reach out and capture one in my hand. Trujillo stepped up into my face, opened his mouth to speak and then closed it again. Instead, he reached into his pants pocket and pulled out a neatly folded handkerchief.

"Here," he said. "Wipe your mouth."

Even down here, forty feet below street level, the pulsing red and blue lights swirled through the air.

Behind me I heard a voice say, "He's breathing on his own."

It sounded as if sirens were approaching from all directions.

We stood and watched as they got Wessels started on oxygen and an IV and then rolled him onto a gurney. It took the two EMTs and both cops to lift the big fella and carry him out to where they could use the wheels. When they were gone, I stepped around Trujillo and started for the center of the field.

"Where the hell do you think you're going?"

"Shoot me," I said and kept walking.

He came running up from the rear and spun me around by the shoulder. "Don't be an idiot," he said. "I've got backup coming."

That's when I saw Jimmy, out in what I thought was going to be left field, down on all fours clawing his way up the steepest part of the embankment toward an assemblage of gray steel beams which rose five stories into the sky. I pointed. Trujillo followed my finger.

Trujillo immediately started after him. I started after Trujillo.

We zigzagged through the infield until we reached a spot directly below where I'd seen Jimmy Chen. He was still there. A gaunt scarecrow of a figure, about three-quarters of the way up, down on his haunches, apparently winded and too tired to continue climbing.

I reached up, grabbed the steel handrail above my head and hoisted myself up to the level of the box seats. Trujillo was too short to grab the rail, so I had to lean over, grab his wrist and drag him up to the next level with me. He straightened his jacket and then started up after Jimmy Chen.

Unfortunately, his tasseled loafers with their leather soles were not up to the task. For every two steps he made it up, he slid back three. I grabbed him by the arm and dragged him upward. Pulling both of us, I had to stop twice for breath. Jimmy Chen never moved until we stopped for the second time, maybe three hundred feet below him.

Trujillo was wasting his breath screaming orders to stop and threatening to shoot. It was too dark to see Jimmy Chen's face, but I somehow suspected Jimmy would be about as impressed as the Boys had been. Trujillo was shouting again.

"This is the Seattle Police Department . . ."

I couldn't stand it any more. "Will you shut the fuck up?" I said. "I'll swear you warned him. I'll swear you Mirandized him. Just stop the screaming." Trujillo looked insulted and then started upward.

I didn't have much choice. If I stayed below him, he was going to lose his footing and come rolling downhill like a bowling ball, probably wiping me out on the way. I got to my feet and started up.

I pulled him the rest of the way to the top. We sat with our backs on the cold concrete, our chests heaving, our limbs unwilling to move. Three hundred feet to my right, Jimmy Chen dragged himself the last few yards and collapsed. I nudged Trujillo. He shook his head.

I got to one knee. Below us, down at field level, at least a dozen cops were headed our way. I figured I'd wait until they got here. Jimmy Chen hadn't moved and I'd had all the excitement I could stand. Trujillo would have been better off if he'd been similarly inclined. Unfortunately, he wasn't. Wanted the collar, I guess.

Whatever the reason, when I looked up again, Trujillo was moving along the top rim of the stadium toward Jimmy Chen. He was behind the lights, moving slowly in the near darkness, about thirty feet to my right, when he suddenly disappeared from view. I figured he was out of gas and resting again. That's when I heard the groaning and started after him.

He'd fallen in a concrete hole. Maybe five feet square and three feet deep. He lay twisted in the bottom, trying to push himself up on one elbow. I jumped down with him and helped him gingerly to his feet. His left shoulder hung way below his right. His eyes were glazed with pain.

"Get me out of here," he said through his teeth.

"Maybe we ought to wait for—"

He said it again, so I got him to his feet, laced my fingers together down at knee level and invited him to step in. He put his right foot in my hand and his good hand on my shoulder. I boosted him up and out and then crawled up beside him. From where we stood, two enormous concrete pillars blocked our view of Jimmy.

We started moving again. Slowly this time. Concrete holes appeared out of the gloom at thirty-foot intervals. We skirted them and kept moving until we finally moved behind the last grandstand pillar and out into the right-field bleachers.

Seventy-five feet away, Jimmy Chen leaned heavily against the gray steel superstructure, his mouth open and gasping for breath. It was an odd moment for a revelation, but fatigue does funny things. It was there and then that I realized what all the gray steel was for. It and its twin on the far side of the park were what the roof slid back upon when it was opened.

I was still marveling at the wonders of modern engineering when Trujillo stepped around me and brought his gun to bear on Jimmy Chen. It took him two tries. The first time, his training took over, and he tried to lift both hands into the classic combat stance. No go. The pain in his shoulder turned him white. He leaned back against the concrete, took several deep breaths and aimed one-handed.

"Halt," he shouted, sidestepping toward Jimmy, his weapon thrust out before him.

Jimmy looked up briefly and then turned his back on Trujillo. He put his right foot up on the first rung of the welder's scaffolding and started to climb.

I was watching Trujillo as he dropped to one knee, rested his wavering elbow on the other and took aim, so I don't know where Gordon came from. The next thing I knew Trujillo had squeezed off a round.

When I looked up, Gordon Chen stood between the little

cop and his father, his hands held high over his head, his mouth forming a silent scream as the red flower bloomed in his chest.

"God," Trujillo said in a rough voice.

Gordon went down in sections, first to one knee, then both, and finally flopping over on his side. Before either Trujillo or I could move Jimmy Chen stepped from the scaffolding over onto the uppermost rim of the stadium, pulled the oversized stocking cap from his head and then, without the slightest hesitation, stepped off into oblivion.

27

EVEN FRANK WESSELS LOOKED SAD WITH TUBES COMING OUT OF HIS nose. Trujillo sat by the bedside, with his right arm in a sling. He looked up when he heard my feet on the floor.

"How's Wessels?" I asked.

"They say he's gonna make it."

"Good."

"Thanks to you."

"Just don't tell anybody I put my mouth on his, okay?"

Trujillo grinned. "They say he might have brain damage."

"How will we tell?"

He began to laugh, then frowned and cradled his damaged arm.

"How's the arm?"

"Broke my shoulder. Got a couple of months at a desk."

"Give you a chance to catch up on your paperwork," I said.

He winced as he got up out of the chair and followed me out into the hall. "The Price family's all over the brass," he said. "Want to know what in hell is going on."

I made eye contact. "Curiouser and curiouser," I said.

"The computer ID'd the stiff in about five minutes. Guy named Jimmy Chen. Got him six feet of priors and a psychological profile that would make Ted Bundy nervous. Spent the last fourteen years in a Florida psycho ward. They just let him out a month and a half ago." He kept checking me for reactions. "Now here's the interesting part, Waterman. This Jimmy Chen used to be married to a well-known local lady named Judy Chen." He hesitated and then asked, "Name mean anything to you?"

I looked at the ceiling. Nice tiles.

"There's a lot of Chens," I offered.

Trujillo leaned against the wall with his good arm. "Now *this* Judy Chen is sitting down on a bench on the seventh floor, where they've got her son Gordon Chen on life support because he purposely stepped out in front of a bullet of mine intended for this Jimmy Chen."

He inclined his head. "You do remember our young friend . . . the excitable Mr. Chen, don't you?"

I allowed how I might recall.

He gave me a one-handed shrug. "You want to help me out here?"

"No," I said. "I don't."

He licked his lips and then looked down at his tasseled shoes.

"I never shot anybody before, Waterman. Twelve years and I never had it out of the holster. I never wanted to shoot anybody. I just wanted to do some good. Shooting people wasn't what I had in mind. Especially not somebody who stepped into a bullet on purpose. Gimme some help here, will ya?"

"Wish I *could* help," I said honestly.

"There's still the matter of interfering with a police investigation."

"Was saving your partner's ass part of the interference?"

He looked over at Wessels.

"Depends on how you look at it."

"You've got your murderer, Trujillo. Let it go. There's nobody else left to protect and serve. Anything you do from here will just be jerking off in public."

We had one of those Maalox eye-contact moments before he sucked it up and played his hole card, as I knew he would.

"Well then." He stroked his chin. "Then . . . what with the murder weapon belonging to your father's driver, and Peerless Price's body being dug up in your backyard, I don't see as how we've got much choice but to publicly conclude that your father was somehow or other involved in the murder of Peerless Price."

I was ready. "No matter what I say, you guys are going to cover your own asses," I said. My turn to shrug. "You know it, and I know it. Why bother with the bullshit?"

He opened his eyes wide in mock astonishment. "What?" he said. "All of a sudden, after a whole week of making a major pain in the ass of yourself all over town, all of a sudden you don't give a shit?" He snapped his fingers. "Just like that."

"Just like that," I repeated.

He eyed me closely and then ran his hand through his thick hair.

"I don't get it."

I wasn't sure I understood it, either. It wasn't like I'd made a decision or anything. I'd been standing at the rim of the stadium. In front of me, the day's last red rays tinted the once white shirts of the crew working on Gordon Chen. Over my right shoulder, ten stories down in the construction site, ants in yellow windbreakers struggled to lift Jimmy Chen's broken body from the pin-cushion of black rebar onto which it had fallen.

As I'd stood there, it had felt as if a thin sheet of metal had slid from my body, moving slowly down from my chest to my legs and finally slipping out onto the ground, where it lay beneath my feet like a long silver shadow. In that instant, I knew what I'd always known. That there wasn't anything I could do about my father. Or my mother, or Peerless Price, or Ralph, or any other long-buried remnant of my upbringing. I'd imagined myself a knight on a noble quest; turned out I was more like a scavenger nosing about a carcass. Guys who can't account for their own motives probably better not be inventing motives for anybody else. Especially not the dead.

I guess that's why I felt so bad about all the moralizing I'd been doing with Ralph. Turned out, we weren't all that different. We'd both been carrying that mouse for most of our lives. Different pockets maybe, but the same damn mouse. Go figure.

I met Trujillo's gaze. "You do whatever you have to do," I said.

He wasn't ready to give it up. He hugged his bad arm with his good and leaned back against the wall.

"Gonna be a public relations nightmare," he prodded.

He winced when I put my hand on his shoulder.

"It's old news, is what it is," I said. "Time to get over it."

Judy Chen sat on the padded bench staring down into her lap. I got down on one knee in front of her. Tonight, she looked her age. Dark circles surrounded her eyes. The lines at the corners of her mouth were so deep she could have been made of wood.

"How's Gordon?"

"He's going to live. That's all they'll say."

I reckoned how it could be worse, and she agreed.

"The cops have ID'd Jimmy," I said.

She moved her head slightly. "I know."

"All you've got to do is handle your end. There's nothing coming from anywhere else."

She looked at me for the first time. "'Thank you," she said.

I told her she was welcome and then held up a finger.

"One thing, though."

"What?"

"Just between you and me and the lamppost, Judy. I don't for one minute think you made Peerless Price lay down on the floor so's you could shoot him in the back of the head, Mafia style." I shook my head. "No way," I said. "You didn't shoot Peerless Price."

She opened her mouth to speak, but I put a finger on her lips.

"Gordon did, didn't he? He heard Peerless rampaging around and threatening you. He remembered the beatings from years before. He went and got the gun. Walked right up behind him."

She was shaking her head, but I pressed on.

"And to make matters worse, I think maybe the poor kid thought he was shooting Jimmy Chen. For nearly his whole life, he's been walking around with the knowledge that he tried to kill his old man."

"That's why I told him Jimmy was dead. He doesn't remember anything about that night," she said. "Never has."

I got to my feet. "I don't know much about psychology, Judy. But I think things might be a lot better for both of you if he did."

She dropped her eyes to the floor.

"Good luck," I said and started up the hall.

"Leo," she called.

I stopped and turned around.

"Your father would be proud of you," she said.

I couldn't help myself. I laughed out loud.

"Yeah," I said. "I get that all the time."

28

THEY'D BUZZED HIS HEAD, REDUCING THE ONCE LEONINE MANE TO a field of irregular white stubble, not unlike the last scruffy remains of fall corn. Orange wasn't at all his color, but fashion was a fairly low priority item, as far as King County was concerned. It was like Henry Ford and the Model T. You could have the jail coveralls in any color you wanted, as long as it was orange.

I took a chance that he'd see me. I figured it was possible, because I've been in jail. Nothing serious, you know. Contempt of court, that sort of thing. Two weeks at a time, here and there. But I estimated that Judge Brennan had been in the county lockup for the better part of nine weeks now, and when you've spent nine weeks locked up with people whose basic problem is that they have great difficulty controlling themselves, you get real flexible as to what you will or won't do for a change of pace.

Jail has a way of humbling the most hardened criminals. Not so Douglas Brennan. He came out the jail door into the visitors' room every bit as arrogant as he'd gone in, with that snide smile bending his lips and that patrician air swirling about him. The jailer left his handcuffs on, so Judge Douglas J. Brennan was forced to hold the stinking telephone receiver with both hands, sort of in the "now I lay me down to sleep" position.

"What do you want?" he sneered.

"Just dropped by to say hi," I said, keeping the filthy mouthpiece as far from my lips as possible. "Papers say Dan Hennessey is going to get you a new trial."

He smirked. "It's a done deal. With a competent jurist, I'll be back on the street in ninety days."

"So . . . you're probably looking to keep a pretty low profile between now and then."

"What do you want?" he said again.

"It's not so much what I want as what it is I've got to trade."

He was wary now, sensing the hook.

"Such as?"

"A little peace and quiet."

"What's that supposed to mean?"

"Just what I said. A little peace and quiet while your new trial is going on. A chance for the judicial system to work its magic."

He got to his feet. "I don't have time for this foolish . . ." He began to pull the receiver from his ear.

"The Carlisle Hotel, nineteen fifty-seven," I said quickly.

He was good. Other than flicking his eyes toward the back of the room to make sure we were alone, he kept whatever he was feeling bottled up inside. "Is that supposed to mean something to me?"

"Only if you happened to be one of the people on the fifteenth floor that night."

"What people would that be?"

"In your case, Brennan, the one who walked out alive."

He craned his neck, taking in the bare room.

"I don't know what you're talking about."

I smiled. "Sure you do, Doug. That's why my old man had you in his pocket. And that's why you're going to tell me what I want to know."

"You've got nothing."

"I've got exactly what he had, Brennan. You know how he was about keeping records."

His nasty smile told me what I needed to know. I decided to take a chance. "I've got copies of everything he gave to you."

He gave me the kind of pitying look one gives an injured animal.

"Gave to me? Gave what to me?"

"You know, Doug, the documentation my old man traded you for the Garden of Eden material back in sixty-nine."

I'd hit a nerve. For the first time since he'd walked in the door, he wasn't amused. He checked the room again. We still had the place to ourselves.

"You wearing a wire?" he asked.

"Nope."

"Let me see."

I stood up, removed my coat, laid it on the stainless steel counter and turned the pockets inside out. I yarded my T-shirt up around my neck and turned in a complete circle.

I read his lips through the glass.

"The pants," he mouthed.

I patted the shirt back into place, dropped my drawers to my ankles and repeated the graceful pirouette.

I put myself back together and picked up the receiver.

"What do you want?' he asked me again.

"I want you to listen to me," I said. "And then I want you to tell me what I want to know." I tapped a finger on the smudged plastic between us. "But first, I want you to understand . . . if you bullshit me, I'm taking what I've got to the DA. Today."

"And if I don't?"

"Then what I've got will never see the light of day. They may get it from some other source, but they won't get it from me."

"And I'm supposed to take your word for this?"

"I don't see as you've got much choice."

It took him a minute, but, in the end, he didn't either.

"Deal," was all he said.

My turn to check the room.

"It's simple, Brennan. All I want to know is what it was about the raid on the Garden of Eden that made my old man go to the considerable trouble of making it disappear."

He was sneering again. Rubbing his cheek against the phone.

"That's all?" he asked incredulously.

"That's all."

He let out a great whoop of laughter.

"And what if you don't like what I tell you?"

"As long as it's the truth, we've still got a deal."

He rocked the chair back onto four legs, pressed his forehead against the Plexiglas, gave me a great big grin and told me exactly what I didn't want to hear.

29

I SAT IN A RED CANVAS DIRECTOR'S CHAIR, SIPPING A DESIGNER root beer, while he threw himself around the room in pursuit of the little ball. The big guy with the iron hair wasn't bad, but he lacked Pat's desperate desire to run down every shot. In the end, Pat just plain outhustled him.

Although the wall between us was clear plastic, Pat didn't notice me until the two of them opened the door and stepped out. His blue pullover was plastered to his body with sweat. Water beaded his scalp.

As usual, he was cool. If I hadn't known better, I'd have sworn he was expecting me. He turned to his partner.

"Monsignor McCarty. Have you ever met my nephew, Leo Waterman?"

He was thick, with a red pockmarked face. His bulk looked better suited to football than handball. He wiped his hand on his shorts and stuck it out. "I don't believe we have," he said.

His hand swallowed mine whole, but his grip was gentle. "Bill's boy," Pat said.

The Monsignor now began to massage my hand in earnest.

"Knew your father well, Leo," he said. His blue eyes twinkled. "If you don't mind the expression . . . a hell of a man."

He and Pat shared a small chuckle; I rescued my hand.

Pat and the monsignor exchanged good-byes. Pat peeled the sodden black gloves from his hands as we watched

McCarty walk down the hall toward the showers. Pat waited until he was out of sight.

"You haven't been returning my calls."

"I've been busy."

"I take it you've read the paper."

In this morning's edition, the SPD had announced its intention to hold a news conference at noon. PRICE TAGS AT NOON. A little more than three hours from now, wherein they would announce their findings as to the untimely disappearance and subsequent discovery of Peerless Price. Oh, joy unbounded.

"I've seen it."

He walked a dozen steps down the hall to a Dutch door. The girl inside handed him a forest-green towel. He wiped his head as he walked back my way.

"Any idea what they're going to say?"

"I'd guess they were going to say that, what with the body being found where it was, and the murder weapon belonging to Ed Schwartz, they'll say it seems likely that his death stemmed from his relationship with my father."

"*Seems likely?*"

"Unless they've got something real solid, they won't go any further than that for fear we'll sue them."

"But they've got to say something to satisfy the Price family."

"That's how I see it," I said.

He heaved a sigh. "And I suppose you'll feel compelled to prove them wrong."

"No," I said. "I've had enough. Let 'em say what they want."

He stopped mopping his face.

"Really?"

"Really."

He wiped his hands on the towel.

"And to what do we owe this sudden spasm of lucidity?"

I did good. I let the jibe go. I like to tell myself that if he'd shut the fuck up and not acted like an asshole, I'd have gotten

on my merry way. But, then again, I like to tell myself a lot
of things.

"I've decided you were right," I said. "The past ought to
be buried along with the people who lived it."

" 'Tis a pity you didn't come to that realization before you
prolonged our family's public embarrassment." *You cur.*

I got to my feet. "You know, Pat, you of all people should
be glad I pushed the envelope a bit."

He smirked. "And why would that be, Leo?"

I could feel the blood rising to my head.

"Because my poking around put the Garden of Eden raid
to rest, once and for all."

He was good. He looked bored. "The what?"

"The Garden of Eden. Remember? Little place down under
the Chase Hotel on Western. Bunch of guys sitting around
waving their meat at one another." His shoulders stiffened.
"They arrested the whole lot of you. Your brother Bill had to
squeeze Doug Brennan to keep the whole thing under wraps.
That's what you've been shitting bricks about ever since this
whole thing started, isn't it?"

He opened his mouth to speak, but I beat him to it.

"Don't bother with a denial. You don't need it for me. I
could give a shit. Just take my word for it that Brennan and
I have reached a point of . . . what did they call it back during
the Cold War . . . mutual deterrence. Nothing about that night
is ever going to see the light of day."

He reached over and patted me on the shoulder.

"Must have been that blow to the head."

On his way past the towel girl, he slung the towel in
through the door without stopping.

"Pat," I called to his back.

With a show of great reluctance, he stopped and turned
back my way. "I thought you were quite through," he said
wearily.

"You still run every morning?"

"Why?"

"Well . . . lately . . . with all that crap going on with the udge, I've been running Greenlake in the mornings. I thought maybe some morning you'd like to . . . you know . . . take a lap."

He thought it over at length.

"I'll bury you," he said finally.

"I know."

"What time?"

"Six?"

"Five-thirty." *You cur.*

"Tomorrow?"

"Where?"

"By the Shell House."

"I'll be there."

Before he turned the corner, he looked back over his shoulder.

"Don't be late," he said. *You cur.*

"No fuckin' way."

30

THE MOVEMENT OF MY SNEAKERS RIPPLED THE NEWLY FALLEN WIL low leaves, sending dry yellow waves puffing out from m feet in all directions as I walked. About halfway down th path, I moved off the pavement, pushing my way throug the web of weeping tendrils, over toward the rear of the sag ging boathouse.

As I emerged into the sunlight, I found myself brushing a my arms and shoulders, trying to stem the tide of hitchhikin leaves now attached to my blue windbreaker. At least on soldier had found his way down my collar and rested col and crisp against my neck. I reached back to get it out bu squeezed too hard and sent the shattered pieces skitterin down my spine like a colony of ants. I silently cursed an pulled the jacket tighter about me.

I cursed again, this time out loud, when I saw the twiste wooden walkway which wound around the front of the abar doned shack. At least a third of the treads were missing. Anoth third were cracked or broken. This early in the morning, this tim of year, a dip in Lake Union was pretty much gonna ruin my da

I heaved a sigh so big I noticed it, spread my feet wide and began stepping lightly, moving from intact section to in tact section, stopping after each movement, peering dow into the dark water, waiting for the quivering structure t come to a momentary rest before moving on.

I kept at it until I reached the front of the shed. What had once been a gentle ramp down to the water was now nothing more than a half dozen decaying pylons poking up from the shallows like bad teeth. The rolling door which had once spanned the building lay broken and piled upon itself, leaving the little shack agape, yawning out at the lake through a narrow tunnel of trees.

He was sitting in the doorway with his feet dangling over the water . . . checkin' his eyelids for holes . . . an Old English forty ouncer clutched tightly in his mitt.

He didn't look up. He left his chin on his chest.

"That you Georgie?" he gargled.

"It's me, Ralph," I said.

Without looking up, he waved the bottle in my direction.

"Gwaaan. . . ." he mumbled. ". . . getouttahere."

I stepped over into the doorway and sat down beside him. A mile away, over on the far side of the lake, across Westlake Avenue, nearly at the top of the hill, the brick gables of my family manse stood dark and sentinel among the trees. Although I'd always been able to pick out my own house from across the lake, today it seemed more exposed to the eye than I could ever recall. Must have been all that trash we'd cleaned up. Ralph pretended to snore.

When I pulled the fifth of schnapps from my sagging jacket pocket, his eyelids fluttered. I took my time removing the bottle from the bag and then, with even greater deliberation, wadded the sack into a tight ball. When he still didn't move, I picked the bottle back up, unscrewed the top and took a long pull.

"Ahhhh," I enthused.

Ralph licked his lips and shot me a look from the corner of his eye.

"Here's what happened," I said.

And I told him damn near the whole story. The only things I left out were Tim and Frankie, 'cause I didn't want to end up in a crate, and Pat, 'cause I didn't figure it was any of his business.

Forty minutes later, the sun had slipped behind a cloud and the breeze carried the season's first hint of blue northern ice. By then, Ralph was sitting up, clutching the remaining schnapps between his thighs like a fireman's pole. His empty beer bottle had rolled over the edge and now bobbed about on the surface of the black water.

"Jesus," he said when I stopped talking. He took a long pull on the bottle and then wiped his mouth with his sleeve. "We're born naked and hungry," he slurred. ". . . and then things go bad."

I reached for the bottle.

2787 3

CONCORD FREE
CONCORD
MA
PUBLIC LIBRARY